❀ ❀ ❀

ONCE AND ALWAYS

❀ ❀

GRACE BRANNIGAN

P.O. Box 100
East Jewett, New York, 12424 USA

Once and Always

Women of Character Contemporary Series
Echoes From the Past
Once and Always
Heartstealer
Wishing on a Rodeo Moon

Women of Strength Time Travel Series
Once Upon a Remembrance
Soulmates Through Time
Treasure So Rare

Romantic Short Stories
Two Babies, a Cowboy and Sara
Deception

Website: www.GraceBrannigan.com

All Characters, places and events are fictitious and are not associated or inspired by any person living or dead.

Once and Always
Cover Art By: Stephanie White of Steph's Cover Design: paranormal, fantasy, horror & more
By Grace Brannigan
Print Edition Copyright 2013   Elaine Warfield

ISBN: 978-1-939061-31-7

❄ Chapter One ❄

MEMORY COULD BE GENTLE. At other times it left scars.

Anna Barlow had read those words this morning and somehow they felt like a reflection of her life. She stared out over her ranch's fields now, trying to shake off the cobwebs of old memories.

Newly warmed earth and northeast temperatures collided, creating ground vapor as the sun fought its way through heavy clouds. She shivered, brushing at the cool morning mist that settled in her hair. Her mare stood unmoving beneath her, her nostrils blowing gently from their run. Anna patted Spirit's neck, wishing she could forget she was barely hanging onto the ranch. . . her home.

Every tree, stick and grain of dirt of the Double B Ranch belonged to her. The barns and dilapidated fences . . . the makeshift corral. She couldn't walk away from her only real home. Her grandfather Martin Barlow had brought her here at the age of fourteen. Now, everyone she'd ever loved was gone. Martin. Tyler.

Restlessly, Anna nudged her gray mare toward a well-worn dirt path that led down to the barns and house.

She'd survived worse. Somehow, she'd get through this too. Anna touched her right cheek and curled her fingers against the scarred flesh, her fingers tracing the faint ridges almost absentmindedly. Her face had once been her biggest asset. Now it brought her only anger and at times self pity. She hated feeling sorry for herself, but God Almighty she was only human.

Giving in to a reckless edge of emotion, Anna urged her mare into a bone-jarring trot down the hillside. When they reached level ground, the spring wind tore against her as they loped across open pasture. She inhaled the clean air into her lungs, reveling in the familiar thunder of hooves beneath her. Gradually, the sting of failure lessened. Self-absorbed and prideful these last two years, she'd allowed the fire that ruined her face to take over her life.

She had to live with her mistakes, but somehow she'd find a way out of this mess.

Ω

Tyler Stanton jerked his collar up against the morning chill. The Barlow's Double B Ranch looked the same, yet subtle changes had dimmed its splendor in the six years since he'd been gone. The grounds were unkempt, the buildings in disrepair and the horse barns, once full and so proudly outlined by the Catskill mountains around them, were badly in need of work. He walked through the dusty paddock area and entered the empty barn, memories unexpectedly twisting his guts into knots. Long rides and midnight rendezvous' swam through his mind, the images like a reel of film playing in his brain.

He thought of Annie, the intensity of their love and

then the ultimate deterioration of everything in his life, taking her love with it. Her big eyes were there, filled with fierce determination before a barrel competition, softened in love play, their conversations by turn razor sharp and playfully innocent. He and Annie had been buddies, friends, and for a few intense weeks, lovers. Then it had all gone sour. She'd chosen to stay with an ill-tempered old man and had done nothing when Tyler was run out of town. He had never figured that one out; sweet, loving Annie, letting him take a fall. He looked up at the sky, deliberately easing the tension in his shoulders. How had he thought her sweet?

He wondered how Annie would feel if he told her she'd be a rich woman if she'd left with him that night long ago. Instead, the years had been tough on her and by all accounts she was losing everything.

Tyler exited the barn, his boots scuffing up bits of old hay and gravel. Hearing the sound of a fast approaching horse, he walked outside and around the side of the barn toward the open pasture. Hooves beat the ground in a flat out run. A horse and rider appeared, galloping hell-for-leather through the soft mist clinging to the grass. Recognition slammed him. He'd never forget that intensity of control, Annie's fit and trim body, hair the deep color of dark chestnut out behind her. Tyler couldn't take his eyes off Annie. He admired the pure symmetry between horse and rider as they skimmed the ground. He was reminded of the skill that had made her a champion barrel racer.

Tyler's heart hammered. How he loved the beauty of running horses. There was nothing like it, especially on a dead quiet morning. He tried to tell himself it had nothing at all to do with seeing Annie again after six long years.

He'd thought he was prepared for this meeting with

her. Instead, he resented that he felt sucker-punched. Christ, it seemed like only yesterday he'd chased her across this very field on horseback. When he'd caught her and pulled her from her horse, it was as if they couldn't get enough of each other. They'd made love under the hot sun, the grass cushioning their bodies. Six years ago time had been meaningless to them.

As he watched, Annie wheeled the wiry gray horse around a lone barrel in the pasture, then urged the animal into a ground-eating lope in his direction. Tyler stood still as a gust of wind lifted his hat from his head, tossing it like a challenge onto the grass.

Annie drew closer. Three yards away her horse's hindquarters dipped and rear hooves slid, digging up clods of grass and dirt. The gray's front legs were almost straight as she came to a stop, narrowly missing Tyler's hat. Tyler ran an expert glance over the animal's flexing muscles. Annie maintained only light contact with the horse's mouth. He almost smiled.

"Tyler!"

Dust swirled around them. Bending, Tyler retrieved his hat and slapped it against his leg, then stared at the new crease along the hat brim. "Still the same old Annie. Bouncing your horse around to get attention."

"Same old Tyler, too," she came back. "Smart remarks and all." She sat stiffly, staring away from him. Her rigid shoulders told him he wasn't the only one being poked by memory shards. "You're the last person I expected to see."

She didn't look at him, but kept her upper body half-turned in the saddle. Dark shoulder length hair swung past her cheek, hiding part of her face. The back of his legs stiffened and Tyler stifled an urge to move closer. She was thin, almost too thin.

"Nice horse. Pretty magnificent riding across the flat

like that."

"Didn't know I had an audience."

Annie's horse tossed its head, the jangle of the bit the lone sound as she brushed long elegant fingers over the animal's withers. Tyler found he could breathe again, hadn't even realized he'd been holding his breath.

"Can't you look at me, Annie?" It grated on him that it bothered him so much. He smiled grimly. He could wait, he had plenty of time.

The sun suddenly shot out from behind a cloud. Annie turned to shield her eyes from the glare. The light, bright and unforgiving, shockingly outlined the scars marring the entire right side of her face. Her skin, once flawless, was now mottled and discolored, the flesh a mix of uneven red and white patches that ran like licking flames right to the corner of her mouth.

"Annie!" Tyler knew shock laced his voice. Pain split him in half, shooting to his toes and jetting back up to his brain. His legs trembled where they'd been stiff a moment before.

She jerked her head back and if possible, her face turned even whiter except for the scars, and her eyes. . . her eyes were a deep, wounded green.

"I prefer Anna," she said tersely, now looking at him. "I didn't expect to see anyone or I'd have put on my concealing makeup and spared you seeing this. People don't usually come around unless calling first."

Tyler pressed a fist against his hip. It wasn't the first time he'd seen such terrible scarring. But it was the first time he'd seen it marring Annie's face. She'd always taken pride in her looks, her skin and makeup. She'd hated being teased about her facials and hair appointments.

"Now that we have that out of the way—" hostility cracked in Annie's voice.

"How did it happen?" His voice sounded grating,

even to himself. Inside, he was gasping for air.

She seemed to move back, even by the slightest fraction.

"Why are you here?" she asked.

Tyler shoved back the sympathy for what she must have suffered. It was obvious she didn't want it. He'd figure that part out when he was alone, the ache in his gut. "I guess you never expected to see me again."

She turned just enough to conceal the scarring, but he saw the tremble of her fingers on the reins.

"I'm sorry that Martin died," he said gruffly. "No matter what had happened between us, I know how much you cared about him." He stepped back and cleared his throat. "I saw your ad in the horse quarterly." He was used to dealing with people, but now he felt momentarily at a loss, too aware of her watchful eye. He felt a curious empathy, but he didn't want to feel even that slight connection to her.

She pulled at the frayed material of her jeans while a light breeze played at the edge of her faded shirt. "If you saw the ad then you know the ranch is up for lease."

"There's no sense in beating around the bush. I want to buy it."

Her glare was hostile. "It's not for sale."

"I've been checking around. You might not have a choice."

Her fingers twisted into the frayed holes at her knee. "You've been talking to people?"

"My lawyer made a few discreet inquiries. Sell it to me now and I'll make it a painless transaction."

"Go to hell."

"The old man tried to hand deliver me and my father there, or did you forget?"

"I remember everything." Her eyes, now greenish hazel, held a haunting sadness.

He looked away, hating that he felt off balance. He needed to retain the anger that had driven him back here where his life had so drastically changed. Seeing her pain shouldn't matter after all this time, not after what her family had done to his.

"Good," he said. "Then we're all on the same page as far as the past goes. I'll make you a fair offer on the property. You owe me first shot at it."

Her eyes widened in outrage. "I don't owe you or anyone else a thing! Everything I have I paid for a long time ago."

"Is that how you sleep at night?" He asked grimly. "We have a different recall of the past."

"All the charges against you and Grant were dropped."

"My father never got over it. Lack of evidence doesn't clear a man's name. Sometimes a man's good name is all he has. Martin was an unscrupulous bastard—you know it had to be him who falsified those breeding records. He turned on my father when he got caught. Listen to your conscience, Annie . . . I know you have one."

"You don't know anything about me."

"I can't believe you're changed that much."

Ω

Anna stared down at the man she'd loved at nineteen. At one time she had thought they'd always be together. She knew if she dwelled on what-might-have-been, she'd go insane and some days she felt damned close to it. Survival was the key, so she pushed away the hurt of whispered promises made and quickly forgotten. "How is your father?"

Tyler stared up at the clouds as they skittered across the sky. "My dad teetered between sobriety and the bottle his entire life. In the end he lost the battle."

"Grant is gone—I'm sorry Tyler. He was a good man. I admired his extensive knowledge of animals." Grant had died so young. "He'd been a hero to me." A quiet man whose life revolved around his horses and his son. She'd heard it said he was a hell-raiser in his early days, but she'd never seen any evidence of that. "I-I truly am sorry."

Tyler's expression remained closed. Blue eyes and almost black hair gave him a face women would always love. She had certainly thought herself in love with him. Now he'd shaken her by showing up out of the blue making demands and accusations. She searched his face but the years had put a hard edge in his voice and an unyielding light in his eyes. How could anyone love him the way she had loved him?

"So what about the property?" he asked.

"I'm not desperate." Maybe if she said it enough times she'd believe it.

One dark brow rose. "So you've got several offers to choose from?"

"They've been coming in fairly regularly." Her evasiveness was merely a defense. "But that's my business."

"I heard you haven't accepted any offers yet." He placed his hat on his head and adjusted it just so, and the familiar gesture formed a tight knot in her throat. "And yet here I am ready to make an offer and I get the idea you want to get rid of me."

"It sounds like your lawyer made more than a few discreet inquiries." She felt incredibly vulnerable, as if everyone knew she'd failed to keep the ranch afloat.

She'd managed to keep the memories locked away. Tyler acted as if he despised her and that hurt. The past was done, but if not for her, he'd have gone to jail six years ago. They had never found out who was responsible for the fraud, but lives had been ruined because of someone's apparent greed.

Anna touched her cheek and just as quickly dropped her hand, pressing her fist into her thigh. With the bright sun in her face, she knew he had a clear view of the skin that even the most skilled surgeon hadn't been able to correct; her once smooth right cheek now a myriad twist of coarse, discolored flesh, the corner of her mouth puckering slightly. Ugly. She was under no illusions as to what she looked like. The edge of the leather reins bit into her fingers. She wanted to be left alone, but that was no longer an option. At some point she might have to face people and their curiosity. The question of where she would go was never far from her mind.

Abruptly, she said, "I've gotta go. I have to take care of my mare and some other business." She nudged the horse forward, but Tyler stepped in front of her and grabbed the bridle's cheek strap, keeping her horse still. His glance seemed to soften as it rested on her face. She wanted nothing from him, especially the remembrance of what she used to look like, who she used to be.

"You don't compete anymore?" he asked.

"No."

"You lived and breathed barrel racing. I never thought you'd give it up."

"I had no choice . . . don't you realize that!" She shook her head. "I've moved on," she added deliberately, indicating her face.

"How did it happen?"

"A fire. Nothing you need to know about." Her neck and head ached from sitting so stiffly. "Why did you have to come back?" The cry was almost wrenched from her.

"I've got every right to return to my roots. Maybe I'll finish what I began. I want to clear my name."

Finish what he began. He hadn't come back looking

for her. She pulled in a ragged breath, a deep hurt surfacing and the words spilled out. "You left me without a backward glance. At nineteen, I barely had any self-esteem, but when I lost both you and Martin I was devastated." The part inside that had never healed bled a little more. She hadn't been worth waiting for. "You left so quickly, not even bothering to phone or write. How could you do that?"

He looked taken aback, but then narrowed his eyes. "You chose Martin. That spoke for itself."

"He's the one who came and found me when nobody else wanted me. He brought me here. I knew how much it would hurt him if I left."

"But it was okay to hurt a Stanton," he said harshly. "My father couldn't handle that he'd been blacklisted. There wasn't a ranch within a hundred miles that would hire either one of us after word got out. This tight community lives and breathes horses and we both know Martin had influential people in his pockets. With my father's previous criminal record, the talk and suspicion would have crucified him, and with my less than stellar past, we left."

"No one set out to ruin you and Grant. It was such a mess, everything happened so fast."

"The accusations against us were very well thought out."

"No! We were all hurt."

"Some hurts are pin pricks, others gaping wounds."

Tightening her fingers on the reins, Anna vowed he'd never see her gaping wounds. She took several deep breaths, determined to retain control of her emotions. "Tell me what you did do after you left. Did you go on to school for engineering?" She had regained some of her cool and tried to keep her expression passive. How many times had she wondered what happened to him? How many nights had she cried herself to sleep, alternately aching for Tyler and hating him? At nineteen it had hurt to know how easy it had been for him to leave her behind.

His jaw clenched. "No. An old friend of my dad's offered me a job in California. When we were released from custody, we headed west with the shirts on our backs."

"I—I came to see you, but you'd left." Without a word.

"Why would you come? You made it clear whose side you were on."

"There were no sides!" Anna said fiercely. "If there were, we all lost."

He laughed. "Don't delude yourself. There was only one side—the old man's side. You made your choice quick enough the night he caught us making out in the cottage. By the way, I see you got rid of the cottage. Too many memories?"

"What you're saying is unforgivable." It hadn't been making out. She'd loved him and made love with him. He'd whispered he loved her. "How gullible I must have seemed." All of it had been a lie. She pressed her lips together so they wouldn't shake.

Tyler made a sound of impatience. "I didn't come here to rehash history. If you won't sell then I'll lease the place. I'll top any offer put on the table."

"Why come back when you act like you hate it here? Why torment both of us like this?" Anna felt mortified by what she'd said. She sounded so vulnerable and it was years too late for personal questions.

He stared at her as if he could see the vulnerable part of her that used to care about him.

"It's about getting back something vital that should never have been taken away, my name, my pride. What better way than me taking over this place and making it viable for everyone to see? It sticks in my craw the way this town turned its back on us."

"So it's about revenge," she stated quietly, disappointed.

"Revenge involves emotion, and there's no emotion left in me for this place. I could care less about Marsh Plains."

Or for her. As far as he was concerned she'd turned her back on him, and therefore he'd wiped her from his heart.

"You make it sound so simple and final." Anna hadn't wept over the loss of their love in a long time, but she wanted to weep now. "As if we're strangers." Their lives could have been great together, but now the waste felt like such a tragedy.

Anna knew that no matter how much she didn't want to lease the ranch, the end was near. She had enough money to take her through two more tax rolls and that was all. This was a last ditch effort to buy herself more time.

"Think about it Annie. With the Double B heading downhill fast, how many options do you have left?"

"If you leased the ranch, what would you do with it?"

He didn't show any surprise at the abrupt turnaround. "First thing it's going to need is a major facelift."

"I know what the ranch looks like." The deterioration was a festering sore.

"I train reining and pleasure horses and I'd take in boarders for starters. Of course, if people decide to turn their noses up at a Stanton running this place, then I might have a long, lonely summer ahead." His mouth twisted. "So you see your success in keeping this ranch out of tax delinquency depends on my success, or rather the success of whomever you let have the lease. Would you rather take a chance on a stranger instead of me? I'd be willing to sign a year-long lease with all the money up front."

"What if no one will do business with you?" She could hardly credit she was considering giving him the lease, but desperation made circumstances tough.

His mouth twisted. "You'd still get your money." He pulled his hat brim down. "However, I'll come out on top, even if I have to go out of state to bring in clients."

Anna believed him. Despite his reasons for wanting the ranch and what he felt she owed him, she understood what compelled him. He wanted to retrieve his family honor. Whether he would achieve that objective to his satisfaction, she didn't know. She knew firsthand how destructive bitterness could be.

"There are other ranches in the area," she said, "places that don't need as much work as this place. I can't think you'll be happy here."

"Only the Double B will do. With that said, along with the lease, I have a proposition for you."

Uneasily, Anna waited.

"We should form a partnership—let it be known that we're working the ranch together. That way, we present a united front. At the very least, it will make people question the old scandal. Your reputation is sterling and speaks for itself. If we pool our knowledge you can take in your own training and I'll handle mine. The way I see it, we both win."

Anna's stomach churned and she feared she'd be sick.

"It's kind of ironic," she said. "I remember telling you my vision once. The two of us working to build a prosperous horse training facility." And raising a family. Was he mocking her? "How can you expect me to just fall in with what you want? It's been six years. Tyler, it's not like you can just pick up where you left off."

"We'd run this strictly as business. We both know there's no going back. You know barrel horses. You've ridden the best and you're familiar with the people in that arena. Think about it, it's your call, Annie. It's a great opportunity if you're willing to take the chance."

Fear and confusion yawned before her. The old Anna had had the face and confidence to mingle with top horse professionals. As she was now, she wanted to stay hidden. She'd lost the edge. Admitting that was like pushing barbs into her skin. "I—I have to think about it. . . working again with horses, being in the center of the hubbub. . .."

It whet Anna's appetite for what she loved best, but she shoved back the excitement. She knew her limits. She had created them. She bit the inside of her cheek, wanting the chance so bad she could taste it. "I've battled to keep my head above water, and putting myself in the public eye is stressful," she admitted with some difficulty. "Being around you . . . I don't know if I could do that either."

"If you think long and hard about your financial situation, you'll have to handle it."

Only three days ago the hot water heater had died and she'd just spent her extra cash to have a new one installed. She had about two hundred dollars in her savings account.

Taking a deep, fortifying breath, she looked Tyler directly in the eye. "While I'm deciding, I suggest you take a good look around at the house and the barns. As you've noticed the cottage and the hay barn are gone." The saddle horn bit into her palm. The cottage where they used to meet.

"The front pasture fence is the only one that's been maintained and the rest of the fencing is in bad shape. If we decide to go ahead with this, I'd want the guesthouse to live in. The remainder of the grounds would be yours."

She dismounted and leaned back against her mare. "Now if you'll excuse me, I'm bringing Spirit into the barn." She tugged gently on the reins and the horse followed her. Despite what she considered to be an obvious dismissal, Tyler fell into step beside her. Ignoring him, Anna walked around the barn and past the small corral.

As she neared the barn Danny Kirk hurried out to meet her. Danny's habits were like clockwork. He was always on hand to help her. His dark red hair was neatly combed and his long-sleeved work shirt was buttoned to his neck as usual, despite what promised to be a warm morning.

Anna smiled. "Good morning, Danny!" she called, almost relieved to see him. He was a good distraction from Tyler.

Danny gave her his ready smile, his pale blue eyes wide and slightly innocent looking, despite the thirty two years she knew him to be. As he turned toward her, he kept one hand behind his back. Anna didn't know what she'd do without Danny since Martin died. Even though she'd told him two years ago she couldn't afford to keep him on, he showed up for work every morning, as he'd done since she arrived at the ranch eleven years ago. She just didn't have the heart to turn him away when he so obviously wanted to be here.

"Miz Anna." Danny approached them slowly, darting glances at Tyler. "Are you done with this girl? I'll cool her down and put her out on grass." He held up the hand he'd hid behind his back and held out a small bunch of blue flowers.

"Thank you, Danny." She accepted the flowers and put them to her nose. "You're always trying to spoil me."

He shook his head immediately, his expression serious. "No, no, you're not spoiled. You're just right."

Anna laughed, touched by his sincerity. "You can take Spirit." Danny took the reins. "Thank you." She looked at Tyler, then back at the other man. "Danny, do you remember Tyler Stanton?"

Danny froze and Anna saw the recognition in his eyes, but then Danny ducked his head down and hunched his shoulders.

"I remember," he mumbled.

"How are you, Danny?" Tyler asked quietly.

"I do good work," Danny said, shifting from one foot to the other. "I show up for work. I get Ms. Anna groceries. She needs me." Danny looked at her as if for confirmation. "You need me to work for you."

"That's right, Danny," she said. "I don't know how I'd get along without you." She put her hand on his arm. "But you know I may be leasing the ranch for a year, which means you'll have a new boss." When Danny made no response, she said, "You can take Spirit inside now and we'll talk about it later."

Danny led the mare inside, but Anna could tell it was with great reluctance that he left as he kept looking at Tyler over his shoulder. She chewed her lip, wondering what thoughts went on in Danny's mind. She didn't want her leasing of the farm to interfere with Danny's work here. She turned to Tyler, "You know how Danny can be. He hasn't seen you in some time and change throws him. It might take him awhile to adjust. But he will adjust."

"I can't see that there'd be a problem. We used to get along all right. What have you told him about me?"

Anna raised a brow. "Are you implying I've tried to influence Danny? I haven't told him anything. In fact, I'd say telling Danny about you wouldn't even warrant a footnote on my to-do list. Danny may be different, but he's got eyes in his head. He probably knows as much as anyone about what happened six years ago, maybe even more. He looks out for me, especially since the fire."

"He brings you flowers—I used to think he loved you, Annie, the way he followed you around."

"Danny's caring is simple," she said sharply. "He's never let me down. He's the only one I've been able to depend on these last six years." She moved away to lean against the split rail fence, careful not to crush her flowers. Her easily stirred anger didn't make her feel good. "I don't want to revisit the old anger. Is that too much to ask?" She turned her head to look at him.

He narrowed his eyes. "It's like you're implying everyone abandoned you."

She stared at him in silence.

Impatiently, he said, "You made choices, Annie. We all did. And we have to live with them."

She looked away from him, closing her eyes as dust swirled on a sudden breeze. "If we go through with this lease one condition is that Danny continues to work here. I haven't been able to pay him much, but he comes every morning regardless and he knows what to do."

"He was always good with the horses, but if he creates problems, then all bets are off."

"You have to take into account he's special."

"I'm not a monster, Annie. Does this mean you'll let me have the lease?" he asked bluntly.

Anna swallowed hard. There was no going back. "Are you sure—I don't want to get things underway and then you change your mind?"

"There's been no doubt since I saw your ad. Once I make up my mind, it's set."

"Yes, I know." Anna nodded coolly. "Like a stone." She felt ill and her vision blurred a moment. Could she be in close contact to Tyler every day and expect to survive? "Look at the rest of the property and then we can talk." She turned and walked back the way she'd come. She needed a walk, some time to clear her thoughts and settle her emotions. No one had forced her to make the choices she'd made, but she hated the road she'd taken and the dead end she'd run down. As Tyler had said they'd all had to make choices. For her, there had only been one choice and she had paid for it ever since. That choice had lost her Tyler, and then she'd lost her grandfather.

Ω

Danny gently patted Spirit's muzzle as he kept an eye on Miz Anna and Tyler where they stood talking just outside the barn door.

"You can hear everything they say," he said to the mare. "Mama always said you wasn't supposed to listen in on other people's private talks. Maybe we shouldn't be listening. But it's not like they're whispering . . . and some of it is about me."

Danny had a tight ache across his chest, kinda like when he was eight and his dad run off. He ran the brush over Spirit's flanks carefully, knowing the horse's every muscle and contour by heart. When she moved restlessly, he smoothed his hand down her neck and hushed her. "Shh, shh, girl," he whispered, "it's okay. You're gonna go out and play real soon." Danny carefully unhooked the crosstie chains from Spirit's halter and led the mare down the aisle.

"Now Spirit, you know how I take good care of the barn and you for Miz Anna. Isn't that the truth? She doesn't have to worry about anything. If it breaks, I can fix it."

Danny thought about what Miz Anna said and it worried him. "Miz Anna is giving up the ranch. How can I believe it? Years and years Miz Anna had been alone and now she had to get help, even though I'm here every day."

Danny led Spirit down the barn aisle and out the back door. "It's just hard that she doesn't have money to fix stuff. I told her one time I'd ask at Taylor's hardware about nails and boards for work, but she got all mad. I thought she was gonna cry." He shook his head. "I didn't talk about it again." Danny frowned. It was her place but she was letting Tyler come back and tell her what to do. He used to like Tyler, but he'd made Miz Anna cry back then.

Danny sighed, not sure what to think about all this. Maybe he should ask his mama about it. She would know how to figure this stuff out. Danny heaved a sigh of relief. "Yup, Mama would know." Maybe they could fix a way to make things go back the way they were.

❈ Chapter Two ❈

TYLER WATCHED ANNIE LEAVE. He couldn't shake the questions filling him. He needed to know what had happened to her in the six years since he'd left. There was such an emptiness about her compared to the Annie he'd known, who'd always been so full of questions and life. Had it been the scarring on her face that affected her so deeply or something else? She still wore her emotions on her face. He knew she thought he was a cold bastard. Maybe she was right. He wasn't that kid anymore who believed the sweet words she used to whisper. He had nothing to lose by prying into her business. He'd find out about the real Annie.

He'd been taken back by Danny's apparent indifference to his return. They'd worked closely together six years ago. He had known Danny since he'd come to work at the Double B when they were both in their early teens. Danny had a learning disability and had dropped out of school early, but he'd always had an uncanny knack with horses. Tyler had always thought of them on good terms, if not friends. Tyler wondered if Danny did have feelings for Annie and resented that he'd returned. He'd have to talk to Danny and make sure they didn't have any problems working together.

Tyler looked across the fields at the mountains covered by a light blue haze. He thought of what she'd said, that his return to the Double B was all about revenge. He'd denied any emotion, but that wasn't entirely true. Walking around this ranch, he remembered how much he'd liked being here, but it had always revolved around her, since the first time he'd seen her when she was just fourteen and he'd been sixteen. Martin had brought her home to the ranch one day, a skinny kid, her big eyes taking everything in. Martin had uncharacteristically given everyone the day off, and Tyler wasn't supposed to be there either, but he'd run back to the small cottage he shared with his father and he'd seen them arrive.

She'd been dressed in clothes that were threadbare and sneakers that were tightly laced and clearly too big for her slender feet. It wrenched his insides when she'd told him years later how Martin had come and found her. She'd been at the last of a series of foster homes after her mother died following an emergency appendectomy. Annie was the only child of Martin's dead playboy son who'd abandoned her mother when she had gotten pregnant. Tyler had felt privileged that she'd shared her story with him and silently applauded Martin for finding her when he'd discovered her existence. Martin might have been a rotten old bastard in some ways, but he'd always taken care of Annie.

Tyler shook those thoughts from his head. He intended to look around, but he knew deep down it didn't matter what the ranch looked like, he'd already made up his mind. After seeing this place again, after seeing Annie, he could no more walk away then he could cut off his hand. Besides that, for a moment when they'd talked he'd almost felt like he'd abandoned her all those years ago. That was ridiculous. He had been run out of town and she'd chosen to stay with Martin.

Now, being here, smelling the air, filling his senses with everything the ranch had to offer, he wanted this ranch more than ever. He'd come cross-country to bring his father back for the last time and he intended to stick around, at least for now.

Tyler walked quickly away from the barn. His feet followed the narrow footpath to the house instinctively. Everything looked so familiar, yet overgrown. The hedges alongside the path hadn't been trimmed back in a long time. The footpath itself was rutted from the weather and would have to be smoothed out and filled in.

Once out in front of the house, he retrieved his camera from his rental car. Taking pictures would help him decide what areas of the ranch needed attention first. He'd developed the habit of taking before and after pictures when he took on a new project.

As Tyler walked past the split rail fence along the front of the house, his glance fell on the empty flowerbeds in front of the fence. Annie used to take pride in the abundance of flowers planted each year around the house and barns. Now, the beds lay barren, reflecting the overall neglect the house and property had fallen under.

Tyler stopped a moment as he stared at the house. The wide verandah wrapping the entire house had ivy creeping uncontrollably around one side. The white two-story looked pretty rough with the window frames peeling and badly in need of paint. The once fancy lattice under the verandah had split and in some places was nonexistent.

Tyler walked the uneven stones to the verandah and

climbed the creaking stairs. Several steps were loose. When he reached the dark wooden door he pushed it open. Entering the house, he was brought back in time as his boots echoed on the cerulean blue tile.

It felt strange to be in the house. When he'd worked here Martin had rarely invited him inside, and his father had only entered through the back of the house. The only time he'd seen the rest of the house had been when he and Annie had snuck upstairs together. There had been a definite distinction made between the stable hands and the Barlow's by Annie's grandfather.

Tyler glanced at the rich maple paneling on the walls as he walked through the short foyer. He stopped to look at the framed awards hanging there. Annie's barrel racing certificates and ribbons. He paid attention to one shelf in particular. Enclosed in glass was an ornate silver buckle with rose flower accents and a gold plated hoof pick engraved with the name Annie Barlow. The numerous awards were all dated two years or older. Not a hint of dust on any of the frames told Tyler they were meticulously looked after. This wall told its own story. He knew Annie well enough to know she had to miss competing. She used to thrive on the cheering fans and the crowd. The rodeo arena had been her stage and she had shined like a star.

Light spilled in from the narrow floor-to-ceiling windows. Tyler whistled softly, crossing the foyer to the room on the right that had been used as an office. He stopped inside the room with its familiar dark interior. Crossing the worn wooden floor, he reached up to push aside the maroon drapes. Early morning light filled the room. As he looked at the huge oak desk, he pictured Martin sitting there with small yellow envelopes in neat piles before him. Tyler remembered standing beside his father that first week waiting for his first real pay, suppressed excitement fidgeting through him while he waited his turn. Martin had seemed interested in him then, asking questions about how he liked working with the horses. He'd even promised him a raise if he stayed on and did well. Everything had changed when Martin brought Annie to the ranch. As Tyler and Annie became friends, it had seemed to drive a wall between him and Martin.

Tyler turned from the desk. There was plenty of space to set up his computer desk, collection of CD's and software. The existing furniture was heavy and old but in good condition. A leather couch sat against one wall and the remaining space in the room was taken up with a card table and chairs. The room didn't look like it had gotten much use and still looked pretty much like the way Martin had left it.

Tyler walked back out to the foyer and crossed the hallway. He entered the dining room and stopped in wonder. The dining room had been converted into a work area. He stared in fascination at the richly-hued stained glass panels hanging on the walls and carefully stacked on workbenches. He wondered if this was Annie's workshop. She'd created pictures and intricate scenes with colored glass and the talent displayed amazed him. A partially completed piece on the workbench showed a howling wolf with a background of snow and mountains, the sky only partially completed, a swirl of cloudy blue, pink and pale yellow glass. Tyler lifted the glass in wonder.

"What are you doing in here?" Annie demanded from behind him.

Tyler released the panels gently, straightened and turned on his heel. Annoyed with himself, he felt heat move up his collar as if he'd been caught doing something wrong. "I've been considering possibilities for all the rooms," he said coolly. She might as well get used to seeing him in this place. "You did mention I should look at everything."

Annie moved into the room, opened a drawer in a cabinet against the wall, pulled out some sheeting material and draped it over several panels. She turned to face him, her arms crossed in front of her. "Of course I did, but that wasn't a blanket invitation to go through my private things."

"Sorry. I was surprised to see all the glass here and I guess I forgot everything else."

She looked around the room and he saw a blank look in her eyes, as if his invasion of her private work area had totally thrown her. "Moving this stuff to the guest house might take up to a week."

"Your work is remarkable."

She shrugged but he thought he saw a slight softening around her mouth. "It's special to me. Working with glass relaxes me."

"I never knew you were so artistic."

"Maybe there were a lot of things you didn't know about me."

Tyler couldn't ignore the jab. Was she right? "It would be interesting to watch you put a piece together."

The lift of her brow told him she found his interest suspect.

"You could keep this as a work area," he said, ignoring her obvious skepticism. "Then you wouldn't have to move any of this."

"T-that's generous." She was obviously taken by surprise. "I'm sure you'll want to put your own things in here." She lifted her chin. "Besides, I think it's best if we keep our private lives separate. The house will be yours for the term of the lease."

Tyler nodded. "You're right," he said briskly. "If

you're willing, I want to sign the lease this week. Have you thought about my suggestion to work together? Maybe you'd consider reentering the show arena."

The sudden shadows in the room gave her face a vulnerable cast as she circled the room restlessly. Unexpectedly, she stepped close, showing him the scarred side of her face. "Reenter the show arena? Look at me. My face colors every decision I make. How often I go to town for groceries, how badly I want to see a movie. I can't even tell you the last time I went to have my hair cut." She turned away and gave a hollow laugh. "Hell, I've been cutting it myself. Imagine me going into the beauty center for my monthly facial. Mary Sue would cringe if I showed up now."

"Did that happen?" There was nothing he could do to ease the pain of such an experience.

She looked at him incredulously. "No, but only because I was smart enough not to test my own theory. I've seen enough startled reactions that I'd never ask someone to touch my face. Look at your reaction today. That's mild in comparison to some." She looked away.

What could he tell her? He didn't know what she'd gone through, but it bothered him that she'd been hurt by other's reactions. "I was taken by surprise to see you had been hurt and I never knew. I admit I was shaken." In some way, those feelings were connected to the way he used to feel about her.

"My point is I don't know if I'll ever have the guts to work around the public again." She clenched her jaw. "The scarring is the first thing people see. They can't help it. They stare and I'm damned sensitive about their curiosity."

"People's curiosity or rudeness doesn't make you less of a person. You're a good rider, that's what should matter. What I want you to contribute is your riding skills."

"But one goes with the other and I'm afraid my scars will override any skills I have. It's unavoidable." Annie rolled her eyes and gave him a cynical look. "Put bluntly, people may recall my barrel racing wins, but they'll be more curious about my scarring. I know. It's been two years, but those reactions still hurt. Yes, it might be self-pity, but I don't care." She took a turn around the room, her pacing reminding him of an animal in captivity.

"You mentioned you wear makeup sometimes." Tyler wanted to soothe her, but he kept his fists in his pockets, wondering where those thoughts came from. A residue of old feelings? "You can't hide the rest of your life."

Annie's face turned pasty white, her greenish-hazel eyes dark in her face. "I know that! And you can keep your opinions to yourself. You've been gone a long time, you don't know anything!"

Tyler decided to try another tact. "Can you deny that the idea of being in the thick of things once more stirs your blood? I could see it in your face when I first mentioned it. You can be instrumental in bringing the ranch back to the way it used to be."

"It's not that simple." She looked away from him, biting her lip, obviously torn. "Make no mistake, what you want to do is incredibly important and exciting to me. I'd love to be a part of it, but beyond the initial excitement—" She turned away, her voice muffled. "-- I'm not the same person."

Annie's admission laid her vulnerability bare, underlining his ignorance regarding her suffering. She'd made the omission, but he knew she'd only go so far in telling him anything right now. Tyler stifled his impatience. He wanted to know everything about her, what had occurred in the intervening years, but also knew that the telling would come at a cost to Annie, and to him.

Ω

Anna turned back to Tyler when he remained silent. He lifted one brow and the dark hair fell over his forehead, just like it always had. A dark sensuality enveloped him, and it frightened her that she still felt an attraction for a man who'd had no problem walking away from her. "It makes me angry when I look at you. I want my feelings for you to be colder than stone."

"I'm not the same person either," Tyler said evenly. "I've been hurt too, but all that matters is that we establish a business relationship. Once we sign the lease," he added, "I'll be busy with more mundane matters. The hay has to be cut and baled, the lawn needs mowing on a regular basis. I plan to bring in some of my own horses and besides the painting and staining there's a dozen other things that are going to crop up. It'd help if I could count on you through his whole process."

That tingle of excitement hit Anna again, but she cautioned herself to proceed slowly, think clearly and weigh her options. She hated change, the uncertainty it sometimes brought. "I have no choice, I have to act on this. I'll let you lease the property." She put up her hand. "Before we go further, you need to know that in addition to Danny remaining, I want a clause that says either one of us can get out of the lease if it's not working."

"I'm not going into a lease with that hanging over my head. You could get cold feet two months down the line," Tyler said impatiently.

"So could you, but that's my condition." She lifted her chin. "I don't plan to be unreasonable. I need this to work as much as you do. We can start off by going over the lease and what we both expect. If we can come to an agreement, we'll go to the lawyers and finalize everything.

Maybe we can put a six month trial period in there."

He studied her intently. "Can I trust you to hold to this?"

Anna stifled her resentment, and a small dig of hurt. "There was a time when you wouldn't have questioned my word. If we're in this together, we have to trust each other. So what will it be?"

"Let's do it."

Ω

Tyler drove down the narrow darkened streets of Marsh Plains, tired and wanting only to get to his hotel room. He felt curiously unsettled after his meeting with Annie, especially after the snide comment he'd made in parting. He'd never known her to lie or given him any reason to think she couldn't be trusted and he was angry with himself for acting like that. The problem was, she hadn't chosen him six years ago, and if he was honest, that thorn had stuck in him all these years. She'd chosen a mean old man over him and left him swinging in the breeze. He'd been striking back like he was a kid. God almighty, when would he learn from his past mistakes?

The streetlight turned red and he stopped, recalling in high school how they used to joke that if you sneezed while driving down Main Street, you'd miss the town. All his life he'd been a kid in and out of trouble, until his father brought him to live at the Double B and that had kept him out of jail. He'd discovered a love of horses and found his niche. When Martin brought Annie to the ranch, everything in his world had changed. They'd had so much in common, yet not much at all. He'd never wanted to slide back to the old ways. She'd tagged after him in those early days of her arrival because she'd been scared and had been impressed with his knowledge of horses, but he hadn't minded that she followed him around. Her beauty had always seemed slightly unreal to him, and although in the beginning she'd consciously or unconsciously used her looks to get favors from others, she never tried that with him. Annie had always been upfront with him, until that last night.

Gripping the steering wheel, Tyler stared at the buildings on either side of him. Some of the places he recognized, others were either gone or replaced with new buildings. Since he'd hit the city limits his chest had been tight, as if he had unfinished business. In reality, he did have unfinished business. He realized that part of him had been left behind six years ago. The optimistic young man. He just wasn't certain how to recover that part of himself.

The light changed. As he moved ahead, Tyler recognized Oakey's brightly lit Ice Cream Palace. A glance at his watch showed it was ten o'clock. On impulse, he cranked the wheel to the right and pulled into the parking lot.

Tyler stared at the brightly lit pink and brown ice cream cone sign out front. He turned off the truck and climbed out, stretching his legs as he stared at the place he remembered from when he'd been a kid. He pulled the wooden screen door open and moved inside, the door slamming loudly behind him. The pastel colored booths still lined the small parlor, and the ice cream counter ran the entire length of the place, stools waiting for the next kid to sit down and spin.

Tyler looked at the man behind the counter and unless he was wrong, it had to be Jake Oakey. He looked like he was well into his eighty's, and though he was stooped with age he had the same welcoming smile. He'd been bald as long as Tyler remembered. He still had an impressive arm for his age, and Tyler remembered sitting on the stool listening to Jake Oakey tell stories from his wrestling days. Tyler didn't move from the doorway, questioning instead the impulse that had brought him inside.

"What can I get for you?"

"I know it's late," Tyler said, "but I saw the lights." He reached for the door behind him. "I'll let you get on with closing down."

"You might as well have something to make it worth your while for stopping," the old man said cheerfully.

"Do you still make those root beer floats with chocolate peanut butter ice cream?"

"It's been a long while since anyone asked. Come closer. I'm almost blind, you know, and I can't see your face."

Suddenly reluctant to reveal his identity, Tyler took a step back. "Never mind. It's late, and I'm sure you want to close up." He pushed the screen door open.

The old man snapped his fingers. "Tyler!"

Tyler stopped cold and looked over his shoulder at the man.

"Tyler Stanton!" he exclaimed, grinning.

Holding himself stiffly, Tyler said, "That was a lucky guess."

The old man laughed. "Of course I recognized your voice, it just took me a minute. You'd drink root beer floats until I thought you'd be sick on them."

Tyler's heart pounded. "I did a couple times." The first time he'd run into this place he'd been nine and trying to outrun four kids who wanted to beat his face in because he wouldn't give up his lunch at school. Despite the drumming in his chest, he walked over to the counter. "But I always came back for more. I haven't been in the area in six years."

Jake nodded. "I was sorry to hear what happened." He squinted and leaned closer. "Looks like you turned out okay, though," he added with a chuckle. "I don't put much stock in gossip."

Tyler lifted a brow in surprise. "You're probably the only one."

"Sometimes tempers flare and things get heated up, and then with Martin dying like that, it was a real mess. 'Course, there's always folks that will hang onto whatever they choose to believe, no matter what the facts are."

Was he warning him he'd meet with hostility? Tyler knew memory was long in such a small community. "If you're still up for making that root beer float," Tyler said, "I'll take you up on it."

"'Course." The old man wiped the counter with his rag. "While I'm throwing that together, you can tell me what you've been up to, Tyler."

He watched Jake make his float like in the old days. Suddenly, the tightness in him eased, surprisingly replaced by a feeling of coming home.

"I've been living in California."

"My granddaughter lives out there. She had a great job until everything went bust in the tech world."

"I guess I was lucky. I got into tech after that bad downward spin."

"And now you're back here. How's your dad?"

Tyler stared at the smiling woman in the 1960's advertisement behind Jake. "My dad died two weeks ago." The tightness returned, burning his throat this time. He thought about the grave he'd stopped by this morning, the small wreath he'd placed on the new stone in honor of his father.

Jake set the root beer float on the counter in front of him. "I'm sorry to hear Grant passed on," he said, his voice low in sympathy. "That's not the best homecoming, now is it—you having to come back to bury Grant?"

"It's where he wanted to be," Tyler said simply. His

father had insisted he didn't want to return to Marsh Plains, not until the last month of his life. He'd given Tyler the deeds to the cemetery plot and asked to be buried in the town where he'd been born. Guilt weighed on him when he'd realized his father had probably never returned because he'd known how Tyler was eaten up inside over the past. "I plan to lease the Double B," Tyler added abruptly, placing several bills on the counter. "I've already talked to Annie."

Jake scratched his head. "You're taking a lease on the place? That's one of the nicest pieces of ground in this area. Annie's always been a good gal, but. . .." he let his voice trail off, as if he'd said more than he intended.

"She let the place get too much ahead of her," Tyler said coolly, dipping his spoon into his ice cream float. "It needs a lot of work."

"Annie did the best she could under the circumstances," Jake said quickly. "She's a hard worker, but after the fire, well—we don't see too much of her these days. Danny comes into town for whatever she might need, groceries and whatnot. I hope you're going to keep him on. It'd be a real shame if he was turned away after devoting himself to Anna and the Double B the way he has. As for her, folks pretty much let Anna have her privacy. Seems that's the way she wants it."

Carefully, he put down his spoon. "I know there was a fire. What happened?"

"She got hurt bad." Jake reached for the bills and stepped away from the counter. "You might better speak with Annie to get the facts. All I know is one of the barns burned and she got caught in the middle of it trying to get her horses out. That gal's had a hard row to hoe since Martin died. She certainly needs a break in this life." Jake rang up the sale and closed the cash register. "Now, it's getting on toward eleven, so I'm going to finish closing up. Take your time with that float."

"Thanks, Jake, for your hospitality and the float." Tyler wondered at the older man's almost protective attitude when he'd asked about Annie, but he knew he wasn't getting any more information from him tonight.

Ω

The finer details of the lease agreement were hammered out later that week. Anna stared at the sheaf of papers on the small table against the wall as she waited for Tyler to join her in the foyer. They had a meeting with her lawyer in thirty minutes and she felt jittery with nerves, hoping she was doing the right thing.

Anna picked up the papers. For such a simple matter as a lease, there was a lot of paperwork involved.

During their work on the lease and accompanying agreement, Anna learned Tyler had participated in rodeo and reining competitions throughout the years, garnering several impressive championships. He also mentioned casually that he'd recently sold his interest in two large dude ranches in the mid-west. He seemed to have extensive plans for renovation at the ranch, and Anna couldn't help but wonder about the money he had at his disposal. Was he planning on dumping money into the Double B in the hope that eventually she'd sell it to him? Didn't he know she'd do everything possible to hang onto this place?

Nervously, she adjusted the skirt she'd changed into for the meeting. It wasn't fancy, but it was more business-like than her usual attire of jeans. Now she wondered if she should have stuck to jeans, she didn't want Tyler to think she was going out of her way to look nice for him. She shook her head in confusion. He wouldn't care what she wore. All that mattered to him was their business arrangement. All that should matter to her was this business arrangement, so she'd better not worry about personal details. This lease was a means to an end.

Anna looked at her watch, thinking of the pile of boxes waiting for her upstairs. She still had to move about half of her belongings to the guesthouse out back.

"I'm ready," Tyler said behind her.

Anna ran her hand quickly over her cheek, making sure her makeup was in place, then turned to face him, staring at his suit jacket and dark pants. She'd never seen him in a suit and she couldn't help but compare this Tyler to the young man she'd given her heart to years ago. Why couldn't she get over the memories that repeatedly slammed her?

Tyler moved forward and stood very close to her. "You look really nice, Annie," he said, his voice husky and deep.

She opened her mouth with a ready retort, but the look in his eyes made her stop. As she pulled back and looked down at the papers, the fresh scent of the soap clinging to him made her grip the papers in heightened awareness. Carefully, she eased her fingers open, smoothing the rumpled edges of paper.

"Thank you," she said coolly, determined to keep things on an even keel. "When I wear my camouflage makeup, it's harder for people to see the scarring. If you're ready, we can go."

He didn't say anything further, for which she was glad. They left the house and walked toward the driveway and the car Tyler had on lease. Tyler opened the door for her. Before she got inside, Anna met his eyes. She felt as if the air was being squeezed out of her lungs. It had to be due to tiredness. She hadn't been sleeping well, and she'd risen earlier than usual this morning. But she couldn't deny it was because of her reaction to Tyler as a man. Part of her wanted to reach up and grip him by the shoulders, move close and lay her cheek on his chest. Stop it, she chided herself. Don't even think about looking back. Six years was a long time.

Tyler lifted one hand toward her face and startled, Anna arched back.

"Your hair is snagged on your earring." Gently, he unthreaded the hair. "Nice earrings."

Anna touched the earrings, for the moment having forgotten which ones she'd chosen. Her fingers traced the light filigree pattern and the rough garnet stone. "They were Martin's favorite," she said quietly. She had thought for one crazy moment he intended to touch her cheek. Angry that she was actually trembling, Anna turned her head away as she settled in her seat. "Thanks for taking care of that," she said crisply.

"No problem, Annie." He insisted on calling her Annie. She'd already reminded him several times to call her Anna, but it hadn't mattered. In the end, she told herself it made no difference what he called her, theirs would be a working relationship. If he could handle them working together, then so could she. Somehow.

"Do you have everything?" he asked.

She met his glance, and stiffened her shoulders. She could do this. "Yes." She hoped she was ready, because very soon she would be committing herself to a year-long lease with a man who clearly wanted her ranch. A man she used to love and for whom she still felt an attraction. Knowing she had to take affirmative action, Anna pulled her car door closed.

"Let's go."

Ω

The drive into town was silent. Anna couldn't help but wonder if Tyler's silence could be attributed to arrogant unconcern for the events unfolding. His slight frown gave no clue to his thoughts. How could he not be plagued by doubt or worry that they could be in such close proximity for months and make this work? Even sitting beside him in the car she kept suffering flashbacks. She didn't want to remember how he used to look out for her, how he used to kiss and touch her. . .the close friendship they'd shared until it deepened, for a few short weeks, into something more. She put her hand up to her forehead and rubbed gently.

Fifteen minutes later they arrived at the attorney's office. In the middle of town, Randal France's office was in a busy office complex with a dozen other lawyers. Anna stared at the four-story gray building and moistened her lips. She glanced across the parking lot, which was almost full, but since it was only ten-thirty in the morning, there weren't a great deal of people leaving as would have been the case during the lunch hour.

Tyler opened his door and exited the vehicle. Anna stared at the building. Randal's office was on the first floor, second door on the right as you entered the building. One receptionist, and then his private secretary, and the waiting room. Anna had been in Randal's office a dozen times, so there was really no need for anxiety but Anna could help wondering if she was making the right choice. Despair played at the back of her mind. She wondered if she'd ever feel normal again, facing strangers.

She thought of Martin and the dead end her life had turned into. She jumped slightly when Tyler opened her car door. She stared at him, seeing the mild inquiry on his face. She took a deep breath. He had no idea the crazy fears jumping around in her head, and that's the way she intended to keep it. They walked up the short sidewalk into the building. Once inside she approached the reception desk.

"Anna Barlow," she said, looking to her left down the

hallway where two women and a man stood talking. "We have an appointment." On the right, Anna saw the corridor to her lawyer's office was empty. Some of the tension eased from her shoulders as they were told they could go right in.

Once inside her lawyer's office, Anna handed the secretary behind the desk the papers. "It will be a few minutes," said the young girl. "Please take a seat." Stiffly, Anna sat beside Tyler in the otherwise empty waiting room.

"Is this the right thing to do?" The words almost forced themselves from her mouth. She stared at him with mounting tension when he didn't answer right away.

He narrowed his eyes. "Are you thinking of backing out?"

Anna looked around the room, then at the closed door beyond Tyler's shoulder, feeling her heart beating in a desperate kind of way. "I'm wondering if this is too rushed. Maybe we should go over the terms again."

"Annie, if you've got concerns about the lease, let's address them in the lawyer's office. I want everything clear and above board."

She nodded jerkily. She almost felt like she had pre-marital jitters. Pre-lease jitters. She clamped her lips together to keep back the nervous laughter. "The ranch is too important for me to take chances. My grandfather would probably kill me if he knew what I was doing."

Tyler's face remained expressionless. She wanted to scream at him to at least crack a smile, but the butterflies were having a field day in her stomach. At least if they'd gone right in she'd have something on which to focus.

Anna tapped her fingers. "I hate waiting."

"Who's your lawyer?"

"Randal France."

"He used to be a judge," Tyler said flatly, suddenly

rising.

Anna nodded, surprised when he began to pace. "He's been retired for quite a few years and now practices law part time. We—that is, Martin, always used him for anything that came up." She suddenly realized his face had gone pale and his lips were compressed tightly. "Are you okay?" she asked, concerned.

"Mr. France will be with you any moment," the secretary interrupted, then the woman gathered together several papers and left the room.

"You don't look that well," Anna said.

"I'm fine," he muttered, running a finger under his collar and pulling slightly at his gray striped tie.

"This shouldn't take too long," she said, amazed that she was offering him reassurance.

The door opened and Randal France entered the room, wearing a severe black suit and black tie, and at six-foot-three, looking very imposing. "Hello," he said, his eyes sharp. Anna had met Randal when she'd first come to the Double B. He'd handled the case when Martin formally adopted her. Although well into his sixties, he was a handsome man with a sharp wit and a way of looking through any person intent on evading the truth, no doubt a leftover from his years as a family court judge. He approached her. "Anna, how are you? It's been so long since I've seen you."

"I'm doing okay, Randal." She was conscious of the heat of Tyler's hand on her elbow as she rose to her feet and took Randal's extended hand. "How's Marnie? Is she keeping up on her riding?" Casually, she took a step away from Tyler.

"Of course, you know how much my daughter loves horses." Randal smiled. "You should come out to the house one of these days. I know she'd be glad to see you. She took several blue ribbons this year."

"She's always been a talented rider," Anna said, not committing to a visit. She half-turned toward Tyler. "I'd like to introduce you to Tyler Stanton. As you know, we're here to sign the lease agreement."

Randal turned to Tyler. "Tyler Stanton," he said. The two men exchanged a look Anna couldn't decipher, almost a measuring up on both sides. "It's been a long time, son."

"You know each other?" Anna asked.

Tyler stepped forward and took the hand the older man extended, and then glanced at her. "Briefly. A long time ago."

"I seem to recall you swore never to be back in front of me again," Randal said musingly.

"At least not under the same circumstances as our last meeting, Judge," Tyler came back, a slight smile now easing across his lips. Anna saw that his color had returned to normal and she became intensely curious as to what their past association might have been.

"That's a relief," Randal said. "For the record, I'm retired. I'm not a judge anymore."

Anna watched Tyler's brow go up. "You'll always be Judge France to me."

"What a coincidence," Anna murmured, not sure how to take this. Had that been the reason Tyler had looked ill, when he'd realized whose office they were in?

"Please come inside and take a seat."

They followed Randal into his office, a spacious room with floor-to-ceiling bookcases and a large wooden table with chairs occupying the center of the room.

"I have the copy of the agreement Anna faxed to me," Randal continued. "With the exception of some minor changes in wording which I've made, I feel it's a well-thought-out document benefiting both parties." He looked up from the papers and directed his glance to

Tyler. "I assume you've had your lawyer go over this?"

Tyler nodded. "Yes."

He handed each of them a copy. "Take a look at the minor changes I made on page two. If there's any other changes either of you would like made, now is the time to let me know."

"Annie?" Tyler said. "Didn't you have some questions about this?"

Anna stared at him, then at the papers, her mind blank as to her earlier concerns about signing. She looked at Randal. "To be honest, I was getting a little nervous." She pressed her palms down on the table surface. "It's not that I have any specific concerns, it's just this entire lease idea has been moving very fast. I thought about Martin and how mad he'd be that it came down to this." Anna cleared her throat. "You know how he felt about the ranch. I feel as if I've failed."

Randal nodded in understanding. "I can understand your worry, Anna," he said. "We both know how close Martin was to the ranch, but you also know he'd want you to do whatever's in your best interests. You're an intelligent woman, Anna, and you're used to being in full control. Now, handing some of that control over to another person can feel daunting. Let me remind you we did insert that escape clause, which works for either party if you feel the lease isn't working. You can get out of it with minimal notice, after the first six months. However, we're still presuming you're both reasonable people and can work out any concerns the other might have."

Some of the tension eased in Anna and she nodded in agreement.

"I've also inserted language, which Tyler's lawyer agreed with, if after ninety days you'd like to reevaluate the lease, you both have that option." He looked at her across the table. "Anna, do you have specific questions or concerns not covered?"

"I just want to make sure the property is protected."

"Under the lease agreement, you'll retain full rights to your property. The money you receive can be put aside for taxes and whatever else you might need. If you need investment advice, I can steer you in the direction of a good financial adviser. But if you have concerns other than the ones I've addressed, now is the time to say so."

"No, just what we talked about, and of course Danny."

"I'm sure Tyler understands your wanting to look out for Danny's welfare."

"Yes, we talked about it. I'm okay with the contract now. At first, it just seemed so final."

Randal looked at Tyler. "Tyler?"

"I'm ready to sign."

"Then if you're in agreement, you can both do so."

Tyler perused the papers, signed them and slid his copy across the desk toward Anna. Very carefully, she read the papers. She initialed the first sheet as Tyler had done and penned her full name on the last page's signature line. Carefully, she placed her pen on the polished tabletop and looked at Tyler.

"We're in business," he said, smiling at her.

Anna nodded in acknowledgement, pressing her palms into her lap under the table. As she stood, the men rose also and she reached out to shake hands with Randal. "Thanks for your time."

"I'm always here, Anna, if you need me." His glance encompassed them both. "I look forward to hearing wonderful news about the Double B. I'll have my secretary make each of you copies for your files."

"Thank you, Judge," Tyler said. Once they each had their copies he escorted her into the outer office, his hand burning through the material at her shoulder as he touched her briefly. Anna kept her eyes straight ahead, dismayed by her reaction to his closeness.

Outside in the hallway, the quiet of the lawyer's office was left behind. Anna rolled her papers, keeping her gaze away from Tyler as she hid her trembling hands. How could his proximity give rise to so much reckless wanting? Reckless, because she'd surely gotten over him a long time ago. It had to be a fluke, a residue of the old attraction. She had to figure out how to squash it for her own piece of mind.

"Let's get out of here."

The rate of Anna's heart slowed. He sounded very matter-of-fact and she realized she was making a fuss out of nothing. Steadying herself, clutching her copy of the lease, she looked at him. "Yes."

Just then someone jostled her and she turned. A man apologized, and Anna was once more back in the real world as she noticed the man's glance linger on her face. Feeling stiff, she nevertheless managed a smile as he muttered an apology, and walked away.

As if he knew about the mixed feelings in her head, Tyler grabbed her hand and tucked it carefully in his own, pulling her close to his side. "How about lunch before we go back?" he asked quietly.

She stared at him, her mind beginning to race and knew her hand jerked in his. She said the first thing that came into her head. "Somewhere quiet?" She swallowed with difficulty. "Maybe you'll tell me how you know Judge France." There was no break in Tyler's stride, but Anna sensed something different about him, and it distracted her from her own fears and wanting to return immediately to the ranch. Apparently, she didn't know everything there was to know about him, not if the tension she now felt was any indication. What secrets could he be hiding?

Chapter Three

TYLER EASED THE CAR through the late morning traffic, his mind going over the meeting they'd just left. He'd been thrown a curve to find himself once more in Judge France's presence. He hadn't seen the Judge since he was a kid and in trouble with the law.

Judge France had been one of several people who had stepped in and helped him out. The entire town probably knew his past history, and he'd always thought Annie was aware of it, but she'd never mentioned it. He hadn't brought it up, not when she'd looked at him years ago like he was ten feet tall. He hadn't wanted to do anything to hurt or disillusion her. He'd done enough of that to people when he was younger. His mother and later her family had washed their hands of him, no doubt thinking he'd come to a bad end, but luckily for him, his father had taken him in hand.

"The light's green."

Tyler looked up at the streetlight, then drove through the intersection, telling himself to pay attention before he caused an accident. He'd seen Annie's careful scrutiny of the building where her lawyer worked, and then the way she'd avoided letting the receptionist see the scarred side of her face. She wore makeup which concealed the worst of the scarring, so he wondered if her responses were unconscious. Her vulnerability affected him. Part of him wanted to shield her from the hurt of someone's stares, the murmurs, but he also knew it was unrealistic to think he could protect her or even that she wanted him to. She'd been on her own long enough, he sensed she wouldn't want any interference from him, however well-intentioned.

Something had stirred in him when that guy almost ran into her in the office. Maybe it was old-fashioned, but he'd felt protective, even though she'd stiffened away from him. Maybe she'd been expecting the guy to say something. He'd had a moment where he thought about pulling her closer, and he'd felt caught up in her scent, which was familiar and sweet, reminiscent of the old days.

He pulled into a parking area and turned off the car. "I know this hasn't been easy," he said, drumming his fingers on the steering wheel. "It was probably hard as hell, putting the ranch up for lease, but if you're honest, you'll admit this arrangement can work for both of us."

"I have high hopes."

Some of the tension eased inside Tyler. "Good. Let's go inside, order lunch and then we can talk."

Tyler exited the car and walked around to open Annie's door. She didn't move.

"We're eating here?" She looked through the windshield at the fancy curved doorway of the restaurant, as if she'd just realized where he'd parked.

Tyler looked over his shoulder. "I remember this place as one of the nicer places in town. The food always used to be decent."

"It's the most heavily trafficked restaurant in town," she said, her voice stiff. "Or at least it used to be."

He bent toward her, shading his eyes against the sun so he could see her better. Her face had paled and she held her hands clenched together as she leaned back against the seat. "I thought I could do this, but I can't." Several strands of hair fell across her cheek. Tyler wanted to feel the soft texture between his fingers but he gripped the metal of the car door instead.

Annie raised one hand to her cheek, then dropped it and darted him a glance, her eyes holding the sheen of moisture. "This doesn't make sense to you, but it's just too hard, especially—" she stopped.

"Especially?"

"Looking the way you do, compared to the way I look."

Tyler shook his head and straightened. "You're still on that, aren't you?" he asked impatiently. "Your looks, your face, just like it was six years ago. Back then you didn't have scars, but if you didn't have your makeup perfect I remember you wouldn't go into a place. Christ, Annie, you still don't realize you've always been more than a face."

"You don't understand."

Tyler crossed his arms. "No, I don't." He stared across the parking lot at the restaurant. "What I understand is some things don't change. You're still doing what you want, not what's good for me. . .for us . . . the ranch."

"What are you talking about?"

"This is the hottest spot in town. It's a great place to show up together, get the talk going about us, about the ranch. Small town gossip and all that."

"That's why you came here?"

Tyler pulled his dark glasses from his pocket,

avoiding her doubtful expression. "Of course, why else?" He paused. "Sure you don't want to go in? I hear they've got chocolate desserts people kill for."

She looked at him with startled surprise, then looked at the restaurant again, where people entered and exited. She'd always had a sweet tooth for chocolate.

Tyler's heart pounded at the lie he'd told, wondering if he was pushing too hard, but then she stepped from the car, ignoring his proffered hand. Slowly, she stood, her face still white but a determined set to her jaw.

Tyler walked beside Annie to the restaurant, silently applauding her courage. Once inside the building he kept on the alert for anyone who might be inclined to stare at her, not quite sure what he'd do if that happened. In truth, he was afraid this whole idea might backfire in his face and she'd throw the lease in his face.

The headwaiter approached them with a smile. "Good afternoon. May I seat you and the young lady?"

Tyler glanced around the crowded room, all too aware of the tension in Annie. He wondered if she was even aware how stiffly she held herself. He looked at the headwaiter's nametag and said pleasantly, "Harlin, how are you today? This is Anna Barlow and I'm Tyler Stanton. We'd like a private table."

Harlin nodded his head and gave Annie a smile. "Ms. Barlow, Mr. Stanton, I'm pleased to make your acquaintance. As you can see we're very busy today, but I'm sure we can find you a table."

Annie looked around the dining room. "Yes, I'd like to sit out on the balcony. It overlooks the lake, doesn't it?" she asked, and Tyler noticed how her fingers gripped the small purse she carried.

"Certainly, and it's a beautiful day for dining outside," Harlin replied smoothly. "Come with me please."

After they were seated and Martin took their order,

Tyler wondered if Annie had deliberately chosen a corner table with no one on her right side.

As Annie looked around Tyler thought she looked a little less tense. "Maybe I needed this," she murmured as she looked out over the lake, surprising him. "A little exposure." She folded her napkin in half. "I'm doing the best I can," she said, turning to him. "I make no excuses for shying away from public places. I told you how it was."

"I thought I understood, but I guess I really didn't." He'd probably never understand the full extent of the hurt that she held inside, her sensitivity to a glance from a stranger.

She carefully placed her napkin in her lap. "Now, before we talk business," she said, "tell me how you know Judge France." She looked at him with a lifted brow. "You did promise to tell me."

Tyler looked at her with surprise. "That sounds like a challenge, as if you expect anything but honesty."

She took a drink from her water glass, then pushed wisps of auburn-tinted hair out of her eyes as Harlin brought their drinks and lunch. When he left, she said bluntly, "I have to wonder about your motives, since you lied to get me in here."

Tyler didn't blink. "Am I wrong? Isn't this a great place to start?"

"You think quick on your feet, Tyler, you always did. But don't lie to me again."

He understood the warning and nodded his head in response.

Tyler lifted his glass, watching Annie expectantly. After a slight hesitation, she raised her glass also. "To a successful union," he said solemnly.

Her eyelids flickered almost nervously and he watched her full lips move, but she didn't smile. Her glass lightly touched his. "And for whatever tomorrow brings," she added softly, "may we both have the courage to face it. I want this venture to be a success."

Tyler lifted his glass and took a deep swallow, then he carefully placed it on the table. "One way or the other I plan to be successful. If you've got the cash, you can pull any string and make things happen. Money is power."

She looked troubled. "That sounds so—"

"Realistic?"

"Cynical and bitter come to mind."

Tyler straightened his sleeve cuffs. "I admit freely to a certain bitterness regarding the past, but don't let anyone fool you it makes a difference having money. You're less likely to be pushed around."

"And yet you've returned to this area. I still find that hard to believe."

"It's something along the lines of more of the hair of the dog that bit you, or rather, the dog that turned on my father." He lifted his glass, then abruptly put it back down. Taking a deep breath, he started again. "You know part of the reason I came back. The other part is my father always said he didn't want to return, but I think he did and maybe I knew he wanted to come back, but ignored it." He leaned forward and lowered his voice. "Just before he died he asked to return, but it was too late. I had him flown in so he could be buried here."

She looked stunned. "Tyler, I'm so sorry. I had no idea you lost Grant so recently."

"It was a small memorial service, and a few locals attended that my dad knew a long time." He sat back in his chair and tapped his fingers against the table. "It'll be interesting to stick around and see if the town is as unforgiving as I remember," he added carelessly.

"I've never found this town like that."

"You weren't escorted to the bus station and forced

to get on a bus."

Annie's face paled. "Is that what happened?"

Tyler looked toward the inner dining room. "You know the answer to that." He lifted his drink and took a long swallow, remembering the shove the deputy had given his father so he stumbled and fell against the bus steps.

"No, I didn't," she said quietly, "but you've just given it to me."

"Martin and the sheriff were friends. Are you claiming you didn't tell them to make sure we left town?"

Annie sighed. "It doesn't matter anymore, now does it? It's in the past, but you're not happy with how you think the town treated you," she said quietly. "Did you ever think it might have only been a few short-sighted people?"

Tyler mulled over his late night stop at Jake Oakey's Ice Cream Parlor. Jake had been okay to him, but he was only one man. "I don't know." He looked at her plate. "You haven't touched your food."

"I will. It looks very good."

She took a bite of her salad. Tyler watched her catch a drip of dressing on her bottom lip with her tongue. He felt an urge to lean forward and touch her mouth with his, then he thought of other things he'd like to do beyond a kiss. Frowning, he looked down at his own steak.

Gruffly, Tyler said, "You asked me how I knew Judge France. Before you came to the Double B, I was a smart-mouthed kid who'd decided to quit school. I lived with my mother. My last scrape with the law Judge France gave me an ultimatum. Live with my father and keep my nose clean or end up in juvenile detention." He stared at her. "I thought back then you might have known about my background. By the time you arrived, I'd straightened myself out." He smiled without humor. "When the trouble happened six years ago, everybody was ready to believe Martin over a Stanton."

"Martin made sure I knew about your background," Annie said softly. "I think he thought it was a way to protect me from you."

Tyler felt his heart trip, then hammer loudly. "You defied Martin and went on seeing me?"

She shrugged and looked away from him. Tyler thought he caught a glimpse of pain on her face.

"How did you keep the ranch going when you stopped competing?" he asked abruptly, troubled by what she'd admitted.

"I've taken in a limited amount of training." At his surprised look, she said, "You thought I severed all contact with anyone outside the ranch?" Her eyes took on a distant look. "I wanted to. I didn't want to see anyone. I took on just enough training to keep me going. . .people who knew what to expect when they came here. Mostly, people approached Danny and he'd tell me. This year there's been a lot of expenses with the house and it's depleted me financially."

"You went through everything Martin left you?" he asked skeptically.

"I—I, yes." Annie twisted her fingers together and looked away from him.

Watching her closely, Tyler said, "As hard as it is for me to believe, I have this gut feeling he didn't leave you much. How can that be?"

She started to shake her head in denial, but then she let out a sigh. "He wouldn't have done it on purpose," she said defensively. "Things happened. He'd had some bad luck and he was sick, then he made some bad investments. His accountant said he was overextended but I know Martin, I'm sure he expected to be on top again. If he hadn't died, everything would have been okay. He'd have pulled out of it."

"What about your barrel winnings?" He knew she'd done very well.

"Gone." She lifted her chin. "It's common knowledge that I paid back the breeding fee that was collected fraudulently. At sixty thousand, it pretty much wiped me out."

Tyler sat back and swore. They'd all been caught in Martin's trap. "As unscrupulous as he could be at times, how could Martin do that to you? He had to know the truth would come out."

"I don't care how much in debt he was, it wasn't Martin," she said angrily. "He wouldn't switch horses. This was his ranch, his sweat and blood. His pride. You don't go and ruin your life's work, not for sixty grand. It's a drop in the bucket compared to the money he had coming in."

Tyler leaned closer. "How do you know? Did he tell you he was innocent?"

"He suffered a massive stroke and never came out of the coma. We'll never know who was responsible."

Bitterly, he looked at the spark of anger in Annie's eyes. She'd never believe it was Martin and he would always know it had to be. "We'll never agree on this," he said in a low voice. "And unless new information turns up, I'll never be able to piece together what did happen. It will always be the Stanton scandal."

"Honestly, Tyler, I don't know what to believe. Sometimes I wonder if we should leave the past where it belongs." Unhappily, she added, "I know for you that's not an option."

Tyler looked at their plates, the food hardly touched. Maybe this hadn't been a good idea, not when it led to rehashing the past. "Are you ready to go?" he asked.

With a look of relief, Annie nodded.

Tyler took care of the bill and together they left the deck and reentered the dining room. Tyler saw several people glance up from their tables and he could almost sense their curiosity as he and Annie wended their way through the tables. He hadn't felt this self-conscious since he'd been a gangly teenager, and he knew it stemmed from a certain protectiveness toward Annie. He felt her stiffness as he guided her in the same manner as when they'd arrived, his hand at her elbow. He felt a sudden resistance as she stopped. He looked down at her, thinking that no matter what she thought of her face, with her eyes large and luminous, her body poised gracefully, she was a woman who would always be noticed.

"Anna," a man's voice exclaimed, and Tyler realized one of the diners had put out his hand and stopped Annie.

Annie lifted her hand and touched the man's arm. "Gill, so wonderful to see you." She turned to Tyler. "Tyler, I'd like to introduce you to Gill and his wife Tara Dakins. They own the ranch just the other side of Bridgeton, Twenty Percent Acres, do you remember it?"

Gill Dakins, a man somewhere in his fifties, face weathered and body lean of build, rose to his feet. He immediately embraced Annie and then shook hands with Tyler.

"Anna, I haven't seen you in so long." His sidelong glance at Tyler was sharp and inquisitive.

Tara rose to her feet and likewise embraced Annie. "My dear, I'm so happy to see you."

"It's wonderful to run into such dear old friends," Annie said, and to Tyler, her voice sounded genuine, without strain. "Since we did run into you, you should be the first to hear the good news. Tyler will be leasing the

Double B."

"My dear Anna," Tara said, "it must be so difficult for you to lease the ranch, but I'm sure you've given it careful thought."

Tyler marveled at the apparent ease with which Annie smiled. He knew that leasing the ranch had to be eating at her. Martin would have hated it. He'd probably have let it fall into the ground before he let anyone else run it. Especially a Stanton.

"It will give the ranch the boost it needs," Annie said now. "We came here to celebrate with lunch." Annie threw him a pleased smile and Tyler's insides tightened. She hadn't smiled at him like that in six years and now it was only for the benefit of her friends.

"Tyler, you're a lucky man," Gill said. "Anna's one of the best horsewomen on the east coast. I hope this means we'll be seeing you back on the circuit?" he asked Annie.

Annie looked startled. "Not this year," she said. "We have a lot of work ahead of us. We'll be concentrating on the ranch."

Tara turned to him and it seemed to Tyler her smile wavered. She put a hand up to her throat and her face went white. "I—I didn't catch your last name."

"Stanton," he said, watching her dark eyes narrow.

"Grant Stanton's son?" Gill asked, clearly surprised.

Tyler had known this awkward moment would arrive, no doubt one of many awkward moments. He shoved a fist into his pants pocket. "The same."

Tara stared at him, her blue eyes now like chips of ice. "I see."

Tyler clenched his jaw, wondering what Tara Dakins thought she saw. He had nothing to apologize for, but he still felt the sting of the past. "I guess you knew my father?" No sense in beating around the bush.

"Yes, who doesn't know the story?" her voice was

brittle and Tyler clenched his jaw.

"Depends what story you're recalling. I'm wondering why I don't remember you," Tyler added.

"Gill only recently retired and bought the ranch," Annie said quickly, stepping forward as her chin went up a notch. She turned to Gill. "We're going to work the ranch together, and I'm behind Tyler one hundred percent. You'll be hearing a lot more of the Stanton name. I intended to give you a call, Gill, so I'm glad we ran into each other. If there's any business you'd like to send our way, you know how to find us. I'll leave it up to you."

The older man's surprised looked smoothed out. "A partnership sounds ideal."

Tyler thought that after his initial surprise, Gill didn't seem put off by the news that he'd be the one running the ranch. But then again, it was early days yet.

"We expect to be up to full operation within the next few months. Not only barrel racers," Tyler added, "but cutting horses also."

"That's Tyler's specialty and he's got the championships to prove it."

Tyler marveled at the note of pride Annie injected into her voice. She gripped his wrist and turned it so she could see his watch. "We have to go," she said apologetically. She placed a hand on Tara's arm. "I hope you'll stop by the ranch. It would be nice to see you again."

Tara smiled stiffly. "I'll try to do that Anna." Her glance moved to Tyler and then quickly back to Annie. "I'd love to see you."

Tyler couldn't help but think Tara Dakins wouldn't stop by unless she was certain he was absent.

Tara hugged Annie and nodded coolly to him. Cynically, he supposed she could have just ignored him altogether. He felt a slight tremor shake Annie, and then another. Final goodbyes were exchanged and they walked the length of the dining room, then up the steps and outside. Tyler had no time to ponder Tara's coolness as Annie suddenly began to walk very quickly toward the car.

He reached his hand out to her. "Whoa, hold up." She kept going until she reached the car, then stopped and leaned against the back of it, her breath coming hard and fast as she pressed a hand to her stomach. With concern, Tyler pulled her upright, holding her by the arms. "What's the matter? What is it, Annie?" he asked urgently.

"I had to get out of there."

He noticed now that some of her makeup had rubbed off and the scars stood out in bright relief against her skin. Sympathy rose in Tyler, but he hid it, knowing she wouldn't appreciate it.

Placing one arm around her shoulders, he opened the car passenger door. "Come on, sit down a minute and relax. You look like you're going to fall over. Maybe we'd better find a doctor. Do you think you're having an allergic reaction to something you ate?"

She lifted her hand to her mouth and looked at him. "No doctor," she said huskily. "I need some air."

When her shaking had subsided, he said. "What happened?"

"I was afraid," she admitted, then shook her head, eyes closed. "It's ridiculous and I'm embarrassed to even admit it, but I thought I might get sick."

Confused, Tyler looked down at her bent head. "You were scared of your friends?"

"Not just scared of them. . . scared spit-less. Being in that area with all those people I felt overwhelmed. I could feel them staring at me."

Tyler started to tell her there wasn't anyone staring, but then stopped. She wouldn't believe him and he didn't know that for sure anyway. He tightened his arms about her, the gesture involuntary. Again, he felt like an insensitive jerk for not realizing what it would do to her. "Annie, you did a great job, stopping and talking with old friends. If anyone was staring, they were wondering who that laughing, poised woman was."

She shot him an incredulous look. "One of us is wearing rose-colored glasses."

"I know what I saw," he said stubbornly.

She pressed her fingers against her temples. "It really doesn't matter. I got through it," she said, looking at him. "Gill and Tara aren't merely old friends. Gill is the man to talk to in this area about any type of livestock."

"Well, that might be a closed door if his wife has anything to say about it," he said ruefully. "I sensed a definite chill."

Annie sighed. "I know, and I don't understand it. She and Gill were really supportive after Martin died, and then after the fire—the accident. I think she's just worried about me."

"She's worried I'll cheat you," he said grimly. "Either that or she has a personal ax to grind."

When her eyes met his Tyler felt snared in those clear greenish depths. He figured by coming back to Marsh Plains he was stirring up memories people would rather forget. . .that Annie would rather forget.

"I've never known Tara to be unfair," Annie said, "but let me tell you Gill is a businessman first and foremost, with connections up the kazoo. By next weekend, all the big players in New York will know the Double B is back on the map. So you see," she gave a small smile, "you were right about going into the restaurant."

It suddenly hit Tyler the enormity of what she'd done. Sensitive to people seeing her face, she'd nevertheless already started getting the word out that she was behind him in this venture. "It would be a boost to have Gill's recommendation," he said thoughtfully. "You did a great job, Annie." He squeezed her shoulders, glad that her color had returned to normal. "Still feeling sick?" he asked.

"No, I'm better."

Tyler closed the door and walked around to his side of the car. He pulled open his door and seated himself. Reaching into his jacket pocket Tyler retrieved his sunglasses and played with them as he watched Annie thoughtfully. "There's one other thing I need to know," he said quietly. "I need to know about the fire." Since he'd first seen her, it had been uppermost in his mind. As her mouth tightened, Tyler wondered if she'd tell him to mind his own business. With her hand gripping the door handle, she looked ready to bolt.

Ω

Anna had known the questions would come from Tyler at some point, but she'd hoped to be prepared when the time came and not feel so emotionally shaky. She closed her eyes for a brief instant, once again seeing the flames, hearing the horses scream.

She looked away from him, clenching her fingers in her lap. God, why did he want to know? "It was long after you'd left, it has nothing to do with you," she said irritably, resenting the intrusion. "You left, remember? That gives you no rights as far as what's happened in the last six years."

He stared at her hard, his mouth grim. "Maybe you're right, but we're going to be working together and we'll see a lot of each other. I feel I have the right to know what happened."

"You want to know what's made me this way? That's funny, since you shattered what little confidence I had when you left." She waved her hand. "Forget it. What happened was an accident. The doctors tell me there's nothing more they can do for my face. I've had laser surgery, but I have to live with it, learn to adjust. End of story."

"The scarring is what's made you so reclusive?"

Impatiently, she looked at him. "Isn't that enough?"

"I'm just trying to figure this out."

"There is no figuring it out! There's no mystery. Four years ago I made a mistake. We'd been baling hay for two weeks, trying to beat the predicted rain. The last cutting of hay was baled and put in the barn, even though I knew it was too wet. One night I woke up. Even up at the house I could hear my horses screaming." She put her head down. "I was tired. . .so damned tired. The hay heated up. The technical term is the Maillard Reaction," she added, her mouth twisting. "It heated and burned down the barn with the horses inside. I ran down there in my nightgown and tried to get them out. The stall latches were so hot they burned the skin off my fingers, but I couldn't stop, the screaming was terrible, the fear in the horses."

Tears ran slowly down her cheeks. "It's my fault six champion barrel racers died. My lovely, lovely horses."

She saw Tyler's mouth go slack, saw the shock register in his blue eyes. She pushed her hair back and turned to look at the parking lot instead, not wanting to see the horror and disbelief on his face. She'd seen it first hand and the shock of that night still lingered with her.

"Danny found me, but to this day he won't talk about it. I didn't know anything until I woke in the hospital. I remember being groggy, yet filled with an overwhelming dread. There were bandages on my face and hands. Thinking I was blind, I flipped out and they had to sedate me. I'd been badly burned and most of my hair was gone." Anna took several calming breaths. "So now you know. Every time I look in the mirror, I hear my horses and I smell the stench. I get sick."

"Oh, Annie, God—I'm so sorry." She heard the break in his voice, almost like it mattered to him that she was hurting. She shook her head. Of course he'd experience horror, he wasn't an unfeeling person, but he'd walked away so easily six years ago. You don't walk away from someone you care about, and he'd left without a word to see if she was okay. He would never know the devastation and betrayal she'd felt. The hurt of his leaving still lived with her, and her own private guilt would never go away.

"It's not like I haven't tried to be normal," she added softly. "Months after the fire and several reconstructive surgeries I went to watch a small horse show in the area. It was the first one I'd attended since leaving the hospital. I was trying to get some normalcy back in my life. A friend of mine, Sara, talked me into going." Annie wet her lips, feeling a tightness in her chest. "A child sitting near us started crying uncontrollably. I discovered the reason soon enough when the child's mother stared at me, at the newly healed scars on my face. Humiliated, feeling center stage, I sat through the remainder of the event, all too aware of the rude whispers and stares.

Sara hustled me out of there afterwards, but we both cried all the way home and I never attended another event. They know me in town and the shelter where Sara works, but I don't venture other places without a lot of thought. Before the fire I'd never worry about entering a strange place. I always knew someone or I'd be recognized from my barrel-racing days. People were happy to strike up a conversation and I always took my looks for granted. I admit I even used them to my advantage. Now it's too late to be sorry."

He shifted in his seat and Anna felt his heat where his arm touched hers. The air changed, became almost charged. Anna looked up at him and the breath left her body as his head dipped toward hers. He watched her with serious intent and he urged her slightly closer. Anna looked at his mouth, hers going dry. A kiss, she thought. . . would they share a kiss of comfort, one meant to soothe away the hurt or one for old time's sake? Even as the crazy notion formed, a slight frown pulled at his dark brows and he pulled back. The spell. . . the moment was broken and she watched numbly as he pushed his dark glasses further up on his nose and started the car.

As they left the parking lot, Anna gripped the door handle so she didn't touch her face. She knew why he'd pulled back and there was no sense in crying over something that could never be fixed. They could never get involved again. They had both moved beyond that innocent, trusting time and place they were in six years ago. She just wished it didn't hurt so much.

❈ Chapter Four ❈

THE NEXT MORNING ANNA fumbled for the telephone as it rang, startling her from a sound sleep. She looked for her clock on the bedside table, but it wasn't there. Trying to shake the sleep from her mind, she remembered she was in the small bedroom in the guesthouse, and the clock was now on a shelf across the room because she hadn't finished unpacking. The bright red numbers showed it to be six-thirty in the morning.

Groggily, Anna brought the receiver to her ear. "Hello."

"Anna, it's Sara. Oops, you sound like you just woke up. I'm sorry."

Anna pushed herself up against the oak headboard, her brain slowly connecting the name with the voice. "Sara, I'm so glad to hear from you." She smiled. "And yes, you did wake me up, but I had to get up anyway." She wiped the sleep from her eyes. "What's going on?"

"I'm going to burst if I don't tell someone. I got that promotion."

Anna sat up straighter. "Sara, you deserve it for all your hard work at the shelter."

"Well, I am excited and I couldn't wait to tell you. I still can't believe I won out over the other candidates."

"You made it happen," Anna reminded her gently. "You're one determined lady."

"I was wondering if you're going to be around? I'd really like to stop and see you. It's been a while since we touched base."

"I'll be around all morning."

"I don't have to be in to work until later. We could grab a bite and catch up. In fact, I'll bring bagels and cream cheese. Hey, before I hang up, any luck with the ad for the ranch?"

"It's all set up. Tyler Stanton has signed a lease for a year. He trains cutting horses. I can still do my thing and he'll bring in his own business."

"His name is Tyler? That sounds like a name from a commercial or a soap opera. Is he like one of those cowboys you see in magazines, tall, dark and mysterious looking?"

Anna laughed. "Sara, you're such a romantic."

"One of us has to be," Sara said dryly. "So I would venture a guess he's sixty plus and married with grandkids?"

Anna twined the telephone cord around her fingers, picturing Tyler in her mind's eye. There was nothing grandfatherly about him, but Sara hadn't been around six years ago, so she wouldn't know that. "Well, actually, he's more like the cowboys you see at the rodeo."

"Maybe you two will hit it off and he'll sweep you off your feet," Sara said, her voice excited.

Anna bit her lip and stifled a moan. Tyler had swept her off her feet once, but it hadn't lasted. She gripped the phone receiver. "I'll see you later."

She replaced the receiver and stared out the window at the early morning horizon, streaks of orange feathering the sky. She wondered if it would be easier if she was more like Sara, eternally romantic and optimistic. Maybe if she'd had the courage to jump back on her feet after the fire she wouldn't feel like her life had stalled. She'd let her fear and insecurity stifle her, limiting her life. Now she had to free herself from those mistakes.

Annie swung her feet over the side of the bed, quickly shoving boxes aside so she had a clear path to the kitchen and her small bathroom.

Tyler had mentioned last night he had horses arriving today. As Anna dressed, she felt a tingle of excitement mixed with a measure of trepidation. She'd been a top rider at one time, but she'd been out of touch for the last two years. It was one thing training horses for pleasure, but she wasn't certain she still had the skill to mold a horse into a topnotch barrel racer. What if she messed up?

Anna buttoned her cotton shirt, then pulled a lightweight sweatshirt over her head, stepped into an old pair of jeans and walked into the small living room. As she stretched, she looked toward the kitchen and groaned, unsure which boxes held the coffee, tea and condiments.

She stifled a yawn as she walked across the small area rug to the dining room window that gave a view of the house. The kitchen lights were lit, as she'd expected. Tyler had always gotten up early in the mornings, like he couldn't wait to get started on the day. Apparently that hadn't changed. She wouldn't be surprised if he'd already left for the barn. As Anna pulled on her boots, a tightness grew in her chest. For the next year at least, she would be seeing Tyler probably every day.

Anna hurried across the dew wet grass, hugging her

herself against the cool morning air. She opened the back door to the house and stepped inside the small alcove, the heavenly smell of brewed coffee greeting her.

The kitchen door opened as she hesitated by the back door.

"Good morning, Annie," Tyler said with a welcoming smile.

A sense of anticipation filled her, catching her off guard. Awkwardly, she said, "Can I get some coffee? I haven't unpacked everything yet."

"Sure, come on in." He stepped aside.

With his white T-shirt and worn jeans, he could have been any other man off the street, yet he had a presence about him, an air of power. Anna took a quick gulp and stared at his clean shaven face, the neatly brushed back hair. She recalled its fine texture, the way he looked with it tumbled on his forehead after they'd made love. The scent of him seemed in her nostrils, memory tugged sharply, and for a moment, she felt again, the brush of fingertips against her breast.

She almost choked, then began breathing deeply. Anna berated herself for going there. What quality was there about him that exuded strength? What did she find so attractive about him, even after all this time? Suddenly, the kitchen seemed crowded as she stepped inside. The round kitchen table had papers scattered across it, and a paper plate with the remnants of toast also sat there. She caught a hint of cinnamon in the air.

"Still wolfing down cinnamon-sugared toast?"

He smiled slightly. "Some things you never get over."

He'd obviously been working, even this early in the morning. She turned to him and they almost bumped into each other so she retreated to the counter. "I don't want to interrupt your paperwork, I just need a little coffee to get me by."

He shrugged, opening the cabinet overhead and lifting out two cups. "The work will keep. Take a seat."

"Who'd have thought life would come back in a circle like this?" she muttered, feeling edgy as Tyler fixed her coffee. Six years ago he'd left, and her life had felt like it ended when she'd lost both him and Martin, but now he was here again in this kitchen, and for a moment it was like he'd never left.

Tyler seemed to go still, then he turned and placed a cup of steaming coffee before her. "No, not a circle, more a linear path we just keep moving along."

She gripped her mug. "So you're saying we never come back to the place where we were previously?"

His look was level. "There may be a resemblance on the surface, but nothing is ever the same."

"Right. We're not two hot-headed kids thinking we're in love. It isn't the same." Nervously, Anna took a sip of her coffee, one teaspoon of sugar, black. He'd remembered. Jerkily, she came to her feet. "I'm expecting a friend. If you don't mind, I'll take a small container back with me to the house and leave you in peace." She raised her cup. "Thanks for the coffee." She poured a small amount of coffee crystals into a plastic container, covered it and then turned to find Tyler blocking her way. Her heart pounded as she stared into his eyes, surprised by the yearning that gripped her. She wanted to stop remembering the way his arms used to hold her so tightly or the feel of his mouth on hers. She swallowed, her glance darting to the door behind him.

"Annie," he said. "You're welcome to anything in the house. You have to know that, so don't ask."

"Anna," she corrected huskily. Her fingers clenched on the plastic container and she placed her cup of coffee on the counter. Impulsively, she reached out and gripped his hand. "Thank you." Suddenly discomfited by her own impetuous action, she moved back, but Tyler lightly gripped her hand.

His head dipped toward her, the caring in his gaze stirring an emotional need she'd kept banked and hidden even from herself. The tang of cinnamon seemed all around her, making desire curl as tight as a fist in her stomach. His mouth touched her cheek and then the corner of her mouth. Confused, she pulled back and blurted, "I thought—" and she stopped.

"You thought what?"

"The other day in the car, you backed off," she said tensely, feeling the heat move up her neck. Suddenly it was incredibly important that she understand why he hadn't kissed her.

His expression became guarded. "Calling a halt was best for both of us. You were under stress and I was disgusted with myself for taking advantage."

Some of that earlier hurt calmed, slid away. "I thought it was this." Diffidently, she indicated her cheek.

His expression showed surprise, then a hint of anger. "Annie, whether you believe it or not, I don't see that when I look at you. And neither will any man who cares about you."

Anna felt her jaw go slack, and a trickle of hope touched her. What did she want, she wondered desperately? Did she want to pick up where they left off, or just to feel whole again? Maybe it was all wrapped up together.

As she stared into his eyes, she had so many memories from their time together. Perhaps, she thought, a real kiss would be anticlimactic, a disappointment. Surely the memories had grown out of proportion with time.

Perhaps Tyler had the same thoughts, because he bent his head and she lifted her face toward his. Their lips met for the first time in six years. Heat struck deeply in her stomach, a sharp sensation of pleasure mingled with pain. Anna lost herself, feeling as if she were pulled back in time as she tasted his mouth. When he straightened, she followed him, murmuring a soft protest.

Tyler's fingers lightly touched her cheek and stiffly, Anna pulled back, looking anywhere but at Tyler, wishing the sizzle his nearness produced would just go away. How could she have done that. . . so completely lost herself—even for only a moment or so? She felt as if she was struggling to breathe. She didn't want him to know that he still had this power over her. Dammit, it wasn't fair. After all this time they should have been through with each other.

"Hello? Anna?" Sara's voice came from the hallway. She had forgotten Sara was on her way over, and she'd neglected to tell her to come to the guesthouse.

"In the kitchen!" she called, knowing her voice sounded strained, but there was no easy way to describe her state of mind as she stepped back, still watching Tyler. She smoothed her hands down over her shirt, running her tongue over her lips, tasting the cinnamon again. A flash of emotion teased at her, and she wanted to reach for him again, even knowing Sara was about to step into the kitchen. Confused, Anna wondered what Tyler thought, but his face was blank. Had this been an experiment for him?

Sara breezed into the kitchen, carrying two white paper bags. She stopped dead in her tracks, her long skirt swirling around her slim legs, then she placed the bags on the closest counter and hugged Anna, laughing as she pushed her wispy blond hair out of her eyes and looked around at Tyler, one brow raised.

"Hello and good morning." She looked back at Anna. "Aren't you going to introduce us?"

Feeling as if her face was stiff, Anna said, "Sara Whitehall, Tyler Stanton. Tyler's leasing the ranch for a year. Sara is a good friend."

"Hello Sara," Tyler said, looking up from the table to give Sara a smile as he gathered his papers. Seeing the bemused look on her friend's face, Anna could imagine her reaction to that smile. She'd felt it herself.

"Nice to meet you Tyler," Sara said. "Anna mentioned she was thinking of leasing the ranch but I've been away and missed everything. This happened quickly. You two must have really clicked," she added, looking at Anna.

"You're right, everything just fell into place," Anna said, her smile feeling stiff. "I forgot to tell you I'm in the guest house now. I just stopped over to get some coffee, so we can head back over there."

"Don't leave on my account," Tyler protested, already heading out the door. He paused in the open doorway. "Annie, will you have time later to meet me down at the barns? I'd like to go over the plans I have."

She nodded, gratified that he wanted to share his plans with her. "I think that's a good idea." She looked at her watch. "I can get some unpacking done and meet you in the barns by noon."

"It's a date, then." The words seemed to fall naturally from his lips, but Anna knew better than to take them literally. She couldn't seem to stop watching him.

Tyler lifted a hand. "See you later. Nice meeting you Sara."

"Likewise," Sara murmured, watching him leave.

The door closed behind Tyler and Anna saw him pass the window on his way to the barn.

Sara hooked her arm with Anna's, effectively drawing her attention away from the window. "He's seems a nice guy," Sara remarked casually. "He does look like a cowboy from the movies and he calls you Annie. Of course, the way you're watching him, like he's your last drink of water in a desert makes me curious. I won't pursue that if you don't want to talk—but I hope you will."

Anna wasn't surprised to see an assessing look in her friend's eye. Sara had a knack for sizing people up, though she'd once admitted to Anna that it was unfortunate that knack didn't extend to her own relationships.

"First, tell me about the promotion!" Anna sat down at the table. "It's been a long time coming, and you've certainly worked hard enough."

Sara reached for the bag she'd brought. "Let's dig into these mini bagels." Sara quickly and efficiently emptied the bag onto plates as Anna gathered silverware. "My boss put in my name for the promotion, but there were a couple others up for consideration."

"But you've been there the longest, and you're the most devoted person to that women's shelter I've seen there. My gosh, the hours alone should show your dedication."

Sara smiled. "You're such a good friend. Actually, we each had some preliminary interviews for the position, and I honestly didn't know I was going to get it until the very end."

"So I bet they saw your warm hearted, real concern for the women and that was the deciding factor." Anna spread cream cheese onto a blueberry bagel.

Sara laughed with amusement. "Well, they tend to go more by the statistics, work reports, that kind of thing." She held out her coffee cup as Anna filled it. "Actually, the deciding factor was several of the women from the shelter, the regulars, got together and put in a good word for me." She hesitated. "They actually kind of interrupted the last interview I was on."

"I knew it. They just love you down there."

"Well, I have to tell you, it really brought tears to my eyes, they were so sincere."

Anna grabbed her friend's hand. "Well, I'm glad you got it. You're the right person to be in charge."

"What about you, Anna," Sara asked quietly, "how do you feel about not being in charge?"

Anna stared at her friend, her uncertainty in her face.

"Come on, now," Sara said gently, "it's your turn for updates. And I mean update me on everything," she added meaningfully.

Anna told her what had occurred in the last week. "As you might've guessed," she added hesitantly, "Tyler and I knew each other years ago. He used to work for Martin."

"Boyfriend and girlfriend?" Sara asked, eyes wide.

Restlessly, Anna moved over to the sink and poured herself a glass of cold water. With her back to the counter, she admitted, "It was a bit more intense than that. I thought he was the only one for me. Of course, I was only nineteen, and that's how you tend to think at nineteen. Tyler was twenty-one."

"Well, I did notice you could have sliced the air it was so thick when I bopped in. I seem to have a knack for making an entrance at the wrong time." Sara sighed, putting her chin on her hand as she stared at her.

"Tyler left."

"And he broke your heart," Sara said softly.

Anna didn't bother to deny Sara's statement. How could she? It was the truth. "We hurt each other."

"Anna, how can you stand to be around the man you once loved? To remember what you meant to each other? You must be pretty desperate to even consider this."

Anna looked away. "Desperate is the right word, but

the lease will bide me some time, maybe even save the ranch, but I'll admit I'm scared. What if this is a waste of time and I lose the ranch anyway? I know Tyler wants this place. I'm not sure how far he'll go to get it."

"Then you might be taking an awful risk," Sara said, concerned. "Do you think he'll do something underhanded?"

"No. He wouldn't do that." There was no question in Anna's mind, but then she backpedaled. "He couldn't have changed that much."

Sara leaned forward and said urgently, "Then why are you worried? You've signed the lease and you're locked in for a year. You're being given the chance to do the work you love. Maybe it's on a bigger scale than you've been doing, but don't let fear paralyze you. Take small steps and see how it goes."

"You don't understand," Anna said stubbornly.

"I understand fear allows us to go only so far. If you want your life back that might mean battling the fear. If you want it bad enough, you work at it every day." Sara's face broke into a smile. "If I had the chance to fix or go back to whatever you and Tyler had before, I'd sure as heck reach for that opportunity with both hands."

"It's not such a simple fix. We can't just go back."

"Whatever you choose to do, your life is changing, kiddo, and it's about time. Break out of that vacuum you're in." She shook her head. "I've seen this so many times working at the shelter. Women are hurt and they don't want to take that chance to rebuild their lives, but you can't remain stagnant. You move beyond this and get stronger, whether it's alone or with someone else by your side."

Anna gave her a skeptical glance. "If I don't fall on my face."

Sara shook her arm in exasperation. "How many

times have you been thrown from a horse?" she demanded.

"This year?" Anna asked, puzzled.

"My point exactly. This year. . . your entire life. . .too many times to count. It hasn't stopped you from riding, has it?"

"Of course not."

"Don't let the fear of a fall cripple you. Get back on and ride to win."

Anna had to smile over the analogy. "Are we likening Tyler to a horse?"

Sara laughed and rolled her eyes. "I'm not touching that one."

Long after Sara had left, Anna mulled over her friend's words. She longed for some kind of normalcy, and perhaps a healing. She knew that only by healing could she make her life her own again, but surely Sara was oversimplifying things. It couldn't be as easy as picking up her life where she'd left it before the fire. She doubted that even with the passage of time all the hurts could be overcome.

❊ Chapter Five ❊

TYLER TOOK ANOTHER TURN around the barn and looked again at his watch. Twelve-twenty. Where was Annie? Was she still catching up with her friend Sara? He wanted to get started. Maybe she was upset over that kiss and wouldn't show up.

It had started out innocently, but having her close had been like old times, and he'd given in to the desire riding him. It had felt so good to hold her. The quickening of her breath, the softness of her body against his. . . he realized how much he'd missed that. They'd never had the chance to say goodbye. One minute they'd been falling in love, and the next moment scandal had ripped them apart.

Tyler looked out over the pasture. Was he looking disaster in the teeth, thinking about Annie this way? She'd done him in once, dammit, he couldn't open himself to caring about her again. Martin had all but ruined them—both of them. He pushed his fist against the wall. Annie had suffered too. She'd learned to stand on her own two feet, but at what cost. They'd both moved too far apart. A sick ache in his gut told him things could never go back to what they were.

Tyler looked around the barn, struck by feeling very much at home. Could it work? He had very definite plans about the changes he wanted to implement, but he also wanted Annie's feedback. He'd been measuring and planning all morning, keeping him moving from the barn to the outbuildings and back to the barn. The house would be next, but right now he envisioned all kinds of improvements without essentially changing the barn layout already in place. He thought Annie would probably go along with what he wanted since he wasn't making drastic changes.

The rustic contours could be stained a light gray, giving the entire place a facelift. He stared with satisfaction at his animals grazing in the pasture. They were an athletic crop of horses and he was interested in hearing Annie's opinion on the bunch.

He'd even received a call from Gill Dakins to let him know he was sending him a potential client, possibly two. The client wasn't from the immediate area, but as Annie had predicted, Gill was a businessman and didn't share his wife Tara's antipathy for the Stanton name. Even so, Tyler was cautious about anticipating too much too soon.

He walked from the barn to the house, noticing the swing between two sturdy wooden poles alongside the path. He saw himself pushing Annie on that swing, her laughter loud with delight. He'd grabbed her mid swing and held her against him, teasingly rubbing his whisker rough cheek against her softly curved one.

Tyler strode toward the swing, the chain cold and hard as he gripped it. He pulled it toward him, trying to recall the last time he'd sat on a swing just out of pure joy. Memory eluded him. He'd worked like a dog in the last six years, he hadn't given himself time to sit on swings or much time to relax. All that had stopped when he'd left here.

"That's Miz Anna's swing."

Tyler shoved the swing away, watching it careen into the wooden post. He pivoted on his heel to face Danny. The other man had always had a knack for quietly appearing. "I remember pushing her on this swing."

The other man looked off toward the mountains, his brow furrowed. "She doesn't sit on it no more." He fell silent a moment. "She rides and rides, all day and sometimes into the night, but that swing, no, she don't sit on that."

"Do you recall the good times, Danny, before I left?"

Danny gave a short nod. "Sure do, but that was a long time. It's been bad times now for Miz Anna, Tyler."

"But now it'll get better. I plan to fix this place up. There'll be people here again."

Danny shook his head. "I don't know. This is her place and now maybe it's not. She doesn't want people all over."

"The ranch can be great again, if we work at it. That's my goal, you know, to make it a big name like before. Maybe bigger. She'll be happy with it in time."

"And then you go away," Danny said flatly. "What happens when you go away?"

Tyler narrowed his eyes, but the other man's face looked guileless. "It doesn't have to be like that. There wasn't a choice back then."

Danny stared at his boots and scuffed them in the dirt, but his voice came out very definitely. "Mama says there's always choices."

Remembering he'd said something similar to Annie, Tyler nodded. "You're right, Danny." He wondered if there was something different he could have done six years ago. "Sometimes people just get so angry you forget everything else." Tyler looked at Danny searchingly. "How has Annie gotten along these last years? Do you help her with the training?"

"No, she does the training all by herself. I take care of the barn and horses." He started to back away. "I gotta see if Miz Anna needs me. I'm leaving soon."

"If you like, I can tell her you're leaving. I'm going to see her."

Danny looked toward the house. "I don't know. If Miz Anna don't see me, she'll worry."

"Do you check in with her every time you leave?"

Danny's sudden, furtive glance raised Tyler's curiosity. "She always says she's okay, but I make sure, ever since that time she got sick. I got her to the hospital."

"You're talking about the fire?"

"No! Talking about the fire hurts Miz Anna so I never, ever talk about it."

Tyler took a deep breath. "Okay, you don't want to hurt her. Why don't you go home, I'll let Annie know you've left."

Danny frowned a little, and Tyler wondered if he trusted him to tell her. Then, with a quick nod, Danny loped down the path toward the barn, but had only gone ten feet when he spun around and looked back at Tyler. "Tell Miz Anna I checked the Iris patch. Those flowers down there have lots of buds this year." His grin was huge. "I'm going to pick her a big bunch when they open. She likes them. You promise to tell her?"

Tyler nodded. "I'll make sure to tell her." Tyler moved in the opposite direction toward the house while Danny set off once again at a lope. Danny's mind had twists and turns he'd never been able to fully understand and this time was no exception. Tyler began to wonder what Danny knew about the scandal six years ago.

As the trees gave way the house came in sight and an uncanny sense of belonging filled Tyler, stopping him in his tracks.

In all the years he'd worked here and lived various places out west, he'd never felt a connection with any one place. It stymied him. The ranch house with the mountains as a backdrop was beautiful, but he'd seen other similarly eye-catching places. Nothing compared to the mountains and vistas out west, but right here and now, they faded just a bit in his memory. He did like the way the great maples and oak trees grew behind the house and sheltered it from the fierce northeasterly wind in the winter. The verandah ran the length of the house, the wooden rockers and chairs placed here and there. It's like he expected to see laughing kids erupt from around the corner of the house any moment. It would be a great place to raise a family.

Annie's children.

Tyler blinked hard. Ridiculous. It was a house. He made himself notice, not for the first time, how the paint had faded and most of the windows needed caulking and the trim had split. This place was going to take a lot of work to bring it back.

The Double B represented a challenge. Maybe working on it would lessen the hard ache inside that had never quite left him alone. But Tyler had also been aware of a gradual shift in his thinking all week. Maybe it had something to do with seeing the town and the people through the passage of time. He wanted to erase any memory in this town that the Stanton name meant trouble, but he hadn't counted on people like old Jake Oakley, whose kindness he'd let slip away from him through the years.

Tyler walked up the front path to the house and stepped onto the verandah. The latch stuck as he opened the door, catching on the wood casing. Mentally, he added that to his repair list as he walked through the quiet house. Going to the side window in the kitchen, he spotted Annie's truck parked beside the guesthouse.

Tyler walked back outside, across the side lawn and toward the smaller structure. It was actually in better shape than he'd first expected. Partially sheltered by oaks and a smattering of apple trees, the guesthouse wasn't as weathered as the main house, though he could see it would still need some attention before the winter months. He knocked on the front door, and receiving no response, walked around the back.

Ducking his head under a piece of loose trim that hung down, Tyler reached for the back door handle and found the door slightly ajar. Pushing it open, he walked inside. The kitchen was full of boxes and crates that spilled over into the living room area. Tyler stepped around several unopened boxes and halted in his tracks as a soft scrabbling noise caught his attention. Annie lay sprawled on the floor, her face to the wall and her arm extended into the cavity of a cabinet. He watched her a moment, transfixed. She was totally consumed in what she was doing, her forehead furrowed as she peered into the hole where the cabinet drawers used to be. She lay on her side, jeans molded to her long legs, moving her feet every now and then as if for balance as she moved her arm in and out of the cabinet hole.

He stepped into the room, leaving the door open. A swish of air followed him inside, and something crackled under his boots. Tyler looked down and saw several dry oak leaves had spilled onto the floor.

Annie twisted around quickly, her sweatshirt riding up over her ribs, affording him a glimpse of smooth skin. Tyler clenched his hands into fists, then deliberately opened them again and rubbed his palms along the side of his jeans.

"Tyler, you startled me!" She was breathless as she pulled ineffectively at the edge of her shirt. He could still see her flat stomach and the curve of her ribs.

"What are you doing under there?" he asked gruffly, skimming over her bare feet and slender ankles. There was something intimate about Annie's bare feet. Out of nowhere, he suddenly remembered how ticklish she was.

"The kitchen sink is backed up. I think I'm finally making some headway, though. Turn the water on, will you?" Her voice still carried that breathless quality that fascinated him. If he closed his eyes he could imagine her whispering in his ear. "It's right behind you," she added, slightly impatient when he didn't move.

Heat touched his face. He twisted back toward the faucet and turned the water on full bore. "Why didn't you tell me there was a problem?" he asked curtly, staring at the tight pull of her jeans across her legs. She shrugged and retrieved the metal plumbing snake, using a rag to wipe it before she coiled it.

"It seems to be going down okay now. I went under the house to look at the layout of the pipes."

"Geez Annie." He knew there was just enough room to squirm into the crawl space. Tyler shuddered. Apparently she had no fear of spiders and snakes. He'd seen plenty of both when he'd inspected this house and the main house. "Why didn't you tell me there was a problem? I would have taken care of it."

She looked nonplussed, as if not understanding his irritation. "I guess I'm just used to dealing with this type of situation so I tackled it. Anyway, I'm responsible for this place. It's not in your contract."

Tyler narrowed his eyes, but could see she had a point. He still felt as if he should have helped her out. He stepped forward. "I wouldn't mind helping you out. Let me take a look."

Pushing her tools aside, she placed the snake on the floor. "It's running freely now," she said defensively. "I worked the snake past the elbows and used up almost the entire fifty feet before the clog broke."

Tyler bent on one knee and looked into the hole. Sure enough, where the cap was off he could see the water going through just fine.

"See? All clear."

He reached in and screwed the plastic cap back on the pipe, then used the wrench to tighten it. He sat up and leaned back against the wall, side-by-side with Annie. This close, he could see the slight dusting of freckles across her nose, but only on the unblemished side of her face. He studied those freckles with great interest. His glance shifted from her perfectly nice nose to her eyes, then her face. She was waiting for him to applaud her efforts, but he felt annoyed that she'd fixed the problem without telling him.

"You could have come to me, but I guess you did handle it on your own." Tyler looked away from her, struggling with the urge to pull her forward and drop a kiss on her mouth. He rubbed his hands on his jeans. "Next time tell me."

"Are you sorry you missed crawling into that space with the two-inch spiders?" she asked dryly, amusement curving her lips. "Do you still have a thing for spiders?"

A creep of sensation jumped across his back. "I can't say I missed that, but I still think I'm responsible for any general repairs and upkeep while the lease is in effect."

She narrowed her eyes and her hands clenched at her sides. She pushed herself up along the wall. "Maybe next time I'll take you up on it and save the big, bad parts for you."

Tyler looked at the dirty smudges on her hands and

arms, the long dark streak across her forehead. "It's a new experience to see you like this," he murmured, "not one I'd have missed, but I'd have called in a plumber."

Annie balled up the dirty rag in her hand and tossed it at him. "If you call in a plumber, it's seventy bucks for the call. After he cuts the line, snakes it and puts it all back together, you're talking a couple hundred or maybe even two-fifty. That's a lot of money to blow when it's something you can fix yourself."

"I guess we'll agree to disagree," he said, lifting a cabinet drawer and sliding it back in place.

"My pipe wrench is still in there." She put the snake on the floor, knelt down and reached her arm in the lowest opening. As she fished around on the floor inside the cabinet for the wrench, her movement brought her close to him. Tyler stared at the fine silkiness of her hair, the almost black lashes that seemed incredibly long. She muttered an apology when her elbow jabbed him in the chest.

Their eyes were mere inches apart when she pulled the wrench out. Tyler stared into her eyes, falling into the old fascination with the green and hazel flecks in the irises. She blinked and quickly pulled herself back from him, then bent over and hoisted the silvery coil of the snake onto her shoulder. "I'll put this away and then we can go down to the barns. Sorry for running late," she mumbled.

Tyler noticed the sandwiches on a plate on the counter behind her. They'd been loosely covered with plastic wrap to keep them from getting stale. His stomach chose that moment to rumble. Annie looked at him in startled surprise. He started laughing and she began to laugh also.

He leveled an intensely serious look at her. "I don't know any other woman who would have crawled under the house or snaked the sink line."

Annie lifted a brow. After a moment, she said, "Maybe you've been seeing the wrong kind of women."

"Are you asking me if there have been others?"

Annie hesitated. "I don't want to know." She backed up against the counter. "People move on, lives change."

"You've changed," Tyler said, not wanting to talk about the past. "I never expected to see you wrangling anything, especially a plumbing snake."

She shrugged. "You're right—six years ago I wouldn't have crawled under there and risked getting cobwebs in my hair." Her expression looked slightly bemused. "As far as that goes, I wouldn't even have known where to find the plumbing."

"We're both different people." Tyler wondered if she'd turn her back on him now, like she had then. This time, would he let pride and anger get in the way and walk away so easily? "Can we eat those sandwiches?" he added abruptly, eyeing them hungrily.

Annie's eyes flickered and she squared her shoulders, as if she would challenge him for abruptly changing the subject, but then she simply nodded. "That's why I made them. Let me get washed up."

On impulse and giving in to need, Tyler leaned in close and kissed Annie's mouth. Startled, her eyes met his, very close, their depths deep green with surprise, and then a hint of sultry satisfaction.

"When opportunity presents itself, I hate to miss it."

"Well, maybe next time you should at least ask," she said softly, dipping her head down.

Tyler wiped his palms on his jeans, but kept his voice low. "Annie, you know I've never been one to ask for anything." Temptation rode him to do more than put his mouth on hers.

"Yes, I remember." It sounded almost like a whisper,

but he felt as if he'd just been accused him of something. He took a half step back, reminding himself it was a bad idea to try mixing business with pleasure.

Ω

After cleaning up and a quick lunch, Anna walked with determination beside Tyler on the narrow path to the barn. She kept telling herself to relax, but her body wasn't listening. She gave him a sideways glance and grimaced. The attraction she felt for him wouldn't leave her alone, causing thoughts to run helter-skelter through her head. In the kitchen earlier, her skin had fairly jumped with sexual awareness and he'd just stared at her with that intent gaze of his, no doubt thinking she was a mess. Maybe she should have let him take care of the clogged line. But old habits die hard, and with money being scarce the last few years, she'd tried to fix anything that cropped up. Only as a last resort had she called in professionals.

"Danny left earlier," Tyler said. "He was pretty adamant that I tell you. He seemed to think you'd be worried about him."

Anna smiled, thinking fondly of Danny. "He likes to check in and out."

"He also mentioned a flower patch. Irises."

"He brings me flowers. He's done it ever since—well, since Martin died."

"Danny seems to think you worry about where he is, but I have a notion he's keeping tabs on you," Tyler said slowly, frowning. "He mentioned he took you to the hospital once. When was that?"

Evasively, Anna said, "It was a long time ago. Danny keeps an eye on everything around here. I'd have been lost without him."

"Did you ever notice he's always hanging around? I'm not saying he's stalking you, but −"

Anna looked at him, affronted. "You think he's

spying on me?"

"All I'm saying is his preoccupation with you seems a little over the top."

Anna stopped. "You know he's not like other people, but he takes his job here very seriously. Everything he does is with the best intentions." She faced him squarely, a tight feeling in her chest. "Don't look for trouble where there's none. If you hurt Danny, I'll take it personally."

"I'm not after him, but if something has the potential to throw a wrench in my plans, I'll address it. Do you find that unreasonable?"

Anna said more calmly, "I'm sure you'll soon realize there's nothing to worry about and that Danny's an asset to this ranch. Now if we can continue to the barn, I have plans to meet with Sara this afternoon."

As the barn came into view and the pasture beyond now dotted with unfamiliar horses, Anna welcomed the distraction. "Your horses are already here," she said with pleased surprise.

"They arrived a few hours ago. I thought we could take a look at them together later."

Inexplicably, Anna's heart rate quickened the closer they drew to the pasture lot. There were several grays, she counted three blacks, a tall bay and a chestnut filly the color of warm honey. It had been so long since the pasture was filled with horses, she couldn't help but think this was a good start.

"You put them in the pasture that has the good fencing?" she asked anxiously.

"Yeah. I've got a small crew coming in tomorrow to start on the rest of the fence."

She gave him a tentative smile. "You don't know how wonderful it is to see livestock once more in the fields."

"They're having a great time on the grass," he said. "I've been figuring up how much hay we'll need to make it through this winter," Tyler went on conversationally. "I'm making plans to lime and fertilize also."

"More hay, liming and fertilizing?" she mused, staring at the grazing horses. They seemed quite content in their new surroundings. "That sounds like long-term planning, as if you're thinking of staying longer than the one year."

"I have to think long term until plans indicate otherwise," he said, shrugging his shoulders. "The land certainly needs fertilizing. I want to bring everything up to par. If this works out, maybe I'll lease it next year too. I like to leave my options open." He shaded his eyes to glance at the mountains in the distance.

Anna knew it was too early for her to even think about letting him lease it next year.

"How much hay did you put in before you had to buy from outside sources?"

"The last two years I've had hay brought in for my mare." She looked away from him. "After the fire, I stopped cutting the hay."

"You had a neighbor cut it for you before that?" he asked.

"No, Danny and I cut and raked most of it, then I had someone bale it." She saw his surprised look. "I told you, I had to take care of whatever I could on my own. I couldn't afford to hire people."

"I guess I'm amazed at what you've taken on. I notice there's about twenty acres that have been left untouched. If I fertilize and reseed it, next year there should be a nice cutting off it. The way the grass is growing this spring, it won't be long before I can start."

"I guess it's your choice what you decide to do," she said, lifting a shoulder in a shrug. Anna knew he'd never agreed with the way Martin ran the ranch. He'd felt they should modernize and expand but Martin had been happy with the old ways. She had to wonder if Martin's finances would have fared better if he'd been willing to bend a little.

"What other plans do you have?" she asked, quickening her pace as they drew level with the area where the barn and foreman's cottage used to stand. But Tyler stopped and looked out over the clearing, so Anna wrapped her arms around herself and waited. She hated this spot. It brought back too many painful memories. She turned away from it.

"I spoke on the phone with the building inspector about permits," he said.

"Why?" It was all she could manage. Uncomfortably, she stuffed her fists in her jeans pockets. She didn't want to think of the cottage and attached barn that used to stand there. She lifted her gaze and stared at a flock of birds overhead instead.

Tyler walked into the clearing, halting at the stone foundation just visible at ground level, the entrance to the cottage where white lilacs still grew. Anna did not move any closer, she couldn't. This site held too much memory and pain. Even now, she heard a ghostly reminder of screams.

"This foundation is in relatively good shape," he added, touching the toe of his boot to a few stones. "I thought about erecting an outbuilding on this spot. What do you think?"

Anna tried to shut out the raw memory of flames lighting a night sky, the horses --

"It'll probably raise my taxes and I think it's a poor idea." She hated the churlishness in her voice, but she had to leave the immediate area. She turned and hurried toward the barn. If he wanted to build a hundred sheds on old foundations, so be it, but she wouldn't be a part of it.

She stopped in the open barn door, trying to control

her breathing, not wanting to look wild-eyed and teary. Tyler came up behind her and grabbed her shoulder. "Annie."

Quickly, she blinked, backing away from him. "Feel free to make your plans," she said tautly, keeping her body stiff. Anna watched the breeze play through his hair, splaying the fine strands across his forehead. He wouldn't understand what she herself couldn't explain. "I don't know what's wrong. Maybe there's too many ghosts for me to sit idly by while you change everything." Part of her wanted to keep the Double B as it was while the rational part knew things never remained the same.

The sound of hooves hitting boards reverberated throughout the barn. They both spun around. Anna hurried into the barn, her feet knowing every crevice of the shadowy interior by heart. The barn, redolent of hay and horses, filled her nostrils, the earthy scent familiar and beloved. She'd spent so much time in this barn that it had become a sanctuary, as this ranch had become her sanctuary. Her hiding place.

When she drew level with the last stall, the horse inside whinnied loudly.

"Spirit, why are you in here all by yourself?" The gray's small pointed ears pricked forward and she hung her head over the stall door. Anna traced her fingers over the horse's velvety lips as they had done a thousand times before, then she cupped the soft nose in her palms.

She twisted around to look at Tyler. "She hates being inside. Did you put her in here because your horses are in her pasture?"

"Early this morning she acted like she had a touch of colic. I put her inside to keep an eye on her. I figured if she started having trouble, I'd have the vet come around. Luckily, she seems okay." He lifted a dark brow. "Believe it or not I didn't put her in here to curtail her freedom."

Heat moved up Anna's neck. "Sorry I jumped to conclusions."

He lifted his hand and gently pushed wisps of hair behind her ear. Anna held back the shiver his touch created. She watched his eyes, barely daring to take a breath. She didn't want him to have the power to move her, to make her relive the old emotion.

"I hate it that you make me remember how it used to be between us," she said tautly, but she didn't try to evade him. The touch of his mouth was feather soft at first, then more insistent, almost frightening in its raw appeal. She had the sinking suspicion she could kiss him all day and then into the night, and still want more. She put her palms against the solid wood behind her as his mouth, once, twice, touched her lips and she breathed in his clean scent. Part of her started to burn, and that's the way it had always been with Tyler. There was pain in remembering what they'd lost. She hadn't allowed anyone close in such a long time. She hadn't been ready. Tyler's closeness, his kiss showed her with shattering ease how wonderful and pleasant the experience could be. Anna kissed him back.

His hands, big and calloused, moved gently on her shoulders.

Her horse nudged her shoulder, grounding her in reality. She twisted away and stumbled a few steps to the center of the aisle. "Getting involved will hurt both of us and it'll ruin everything."

He stared at her quietly and she held her breath, wanting so desperately to say the hell with it and kiss him again. Finally, when she was sure she couldn't handle the silence, he blinked and gave a short nod of acknowledgement.

"You've got a point," he said tightly. "We're on the right track with the ranch, we can't afford to mess it up."

He turned and stood in the door opening, silhouetted by the light outside. Several moments passed and she fought with herself to keep from going after him as she wanted to do.

"If you're still interested," he finally said, "I'll tell you the rest of my plans."

Anna wiped her damp palms on her jeans and clenched her fists. "Yes, of course I want to hear everything." She walked toward him and wondered how he could sound so normal. Why had he kissed her? Was it just the moment? Introducing emotion or going into an affair would change everything. She wasn't the type of woman for an affair. She wouldn't be able to walk away. She'd been hurt so much the first time.

She stuffed her hands in her back pockets as she drew level with him. "So what other plans do you have?"

"I want to reduce the size of the box stalls and increase the number of stalls."

"They're big and roomy," she protested. "I always felt that was a plus."

"They're too big. It's one thing if you've got mares with foals by their sides, but we don't need all that space for the operation we're going to be running. If we cut the size of the stall, I'll have more room to take in outside horses. Also, we'll have horses on rough board, so I'm going to start erecting run-in sheds."

"How many horses are you planning on boarding?" she asked, trying to keep her voice even, but the turmoil was churning her stomach into a nervous knot.

"Upwards of twenty, plus my own."

Anna looked at him with disbelief. "I don't care how tiny you make the stalls, we don't have enough room for that many horses."

"You make it sound like I'm cramming them in the box stalls. Each stall will run up to ten by twelve. Trust me, Annie, I know what I'm doing."

Trust him. The man she used to love, who'd turned his back on her? "Where will you put the rest of the horses, then?"

"I'd like to add on to the indoor riding arena, subject to your approval, of course. Plans are being drawn up right now to put box stalls around the entire outside perimeter so that in the winter we can continue to work the horses and have a bit of heat. I'm bringing in machinery to drag the arena floor, then I'll truck in some decent material for footing."

"I'm sure you've thought of this, but you're going to need hay storage for all these animals."

"There'll be storage area above the arena and also the second floor of the barn. I'm also checking around the area to bring in some round bales for the rough boarders."

"It sounds like you've taken everything into consideration." He'd obviously given this a lot of thought.

"Do you have any ideas you'd like to add?" he asked.

Anna looked at him in surprise. "My head is swimming with all the plans you've made. Offhand, I'd say you've thought of everything."

"I know it sounds like I'm making big changes, but if you let yourself think of the possibilities, this can really take off. You can participate as much as you like, or not at all. I just wanted you to know what I planned."

"I appreciate that, Tyler. Sara pointed out to me the rut I'm in, and I'm going to do my best to change that." She'd try, that was all she could do. "After the fire I had thirteen operations on my face and scalp and my life had literally ground to a halt. I'm not creating excuses, but I know it's going to take me a little while to get acclimated."

"Take whatever time you need." His voice sounded rough with what she recognized was concern.

"Do you ever miss it?" she blurted. "The way it used to be? The way we used to be?"

He looked startled, and Anna wished she'd kept her mouth shut. Why stir up trouble?

"I miss what we lost—what Martin took away," he said in a hard voice, turning on his boot heel. "And unfortunately or not, it seems that Martin will always be between us, Annie."

She caught her breath, pain lancing through her. They'd both been marked by a past they could never change, or forget. "He was hard and he made his own rules, but he was never selfish with me," she said in a low voice.

"Then you were the only one that saw that side of him," he said grimly. "There was many a day I was ready to walk off."

"If you hated him so much, why did you stay?" she demanded, stung.

"I never hated him. In the beginning, I didn't have a choice. The court ordered me to live with my father. I did learn a lot from Martin but I stayed on longer because of you." His eyes were shadowed and intent. "Only because of you. I knew I wouldn't be able to see you unless I worked here. Martin guarded you jealously."

Anna gripped a wooden beam and the rough wood bit into her fingers. He spoke the truth. Martin had watched over her to the extent of excluding people from her life. "You never told me how you felt about him. Don't you think I had a right to know?"

"I never wanted to alienate you from Martin. In the end it didn't matter anyway, now did it?" he said grimly.

"The decision I made that night to stay with Martin was difficult, but you didn't give me a chance to explain."

She lifted her chin. "There were things you didn't know, circumstances I'd promised not to reveal. My hands were tied." She knew he'd never believe her if she told him now. It would be too much after the fact, Martin's illness, his last days.

Impatiently, Anna turned away. "This is useless. Not everything is black and white." She frowned. "There's something I've never understood. Six years ago I knew neither you nor Grant could have done what you'd been accused of, and yet you never gave me the same consideration. You never stopped to ask why I had to stay with Martin. Didn't you ever think about that?" She shook her head before he could answer. "Maybe you really didn't know me after all, Tyler." The years rolled back as she lived through the remembered pain. "You're not the only one who felt cheated."

Helpless in her anger and the wasted years, Anna exited the barn. Her eyes burned as she stared at clouds scattered willy-nilly in an otherwise blue sky. Tyler came up behind her and she turned to face him.

"No matter what Martin might have been, Tyler, one thing he taught me was I don't have to prove anything to you or anyone else."

"That's right. You don't, but I guess this conversation is six years too late. We've both survived and gone separate ways."

"But our paths have crossed again." She swung away from him in confusion, wishing she felt like she'd moved on. "If this meeting is over, I'm going to the house to take a shower."

"It's over for now," he said, his expression grim. Perhaps he did regret that he'd never contacted her. Anna knew it no longer mattered.

She walked back to the house. She'd thought she'd given up all dreams of loving and being loved, but now she realized those dreams were still buried deep inside, along with thoughts of loving Tyler. His return was creating havoc out of the order she'd managed to create for herself. With his return, Anna felt as if all the old emotions had been resurrected. Had she been a fool to let him in her life once more? No. She reminded herself he was merely a means to an end. Saving the ranch was her first priority.

❄ Chapter Six ❄

LATER THAT AFTERNOON ANNA studied the milky blue glass laid out on her new workbench. The breeze pushed gently against her back, the sun shaded just enough so she didn't feel its direct heat. She'd set up a temporary work area under a small pavilion that had at one time been used for outdoor picnics. It would serve her needs until the snow came then she'd have to figure out something else for her stained glass. She had almost completed her biggest glass project so far, a painstakingly detailed scene of the ranch and surrounding hills.

Anna leaned her hip against the table edge and stared across lots at the barn and pastures. She spotted her mare Spirit, her pale gray coat in stark contrast to the rich green grass where she grazed. Anna felt fortunate to have Spirit. Her horse had been pastured outside the night of the fire, otherwise she too would have been lost to her. It was a painful reminder of things loved and easily lost.

Anna could see Danny down by the paddocks. Starkly, she knew if it hadn't been for him two years ago, she'd never have made it out alive. To this day she still didn't know how he'd pulled her from the fire without injury to himself, and on the few occasions she'd tried to talk to him about it, he'd become upset and confused, so she'd left it alone. It had been easier that way, not talking about the fire, the loss.

Carefully, Anna marked the glass with her grease pencil, put her protective goggles in place and flicked the power switch on her cutting saw. It was a tricky cut because of the awkward size of the glass and the intricate curves she had to follow. Once the cut was complete, she turned off the motor and lifted the glass. The breeze turned into a small gust and the glass moved, shifted sideways and she lost her grip on one side. The newly cut glass slid along her arm and Anna bit back a cry as a corner sliced into the fleshy part of her arm. She went perfectly still, afraid of losing her now precarious hold with her uninjured hand. Trying not to panic, she quickly looked around, but she could no longer see Danny.

"Danny! Danny! I need help."

"Annie?" Tyler's voice was suddenly behind her.

She remained still as relief moved through her. "Tyler, I lost my grip on this glass and it's against my arm."

"Don't move." His arm came around her from behind and she felt his breath on her ear, then heard his indrawn breath when he angled his head and apparently saw where the glass had sliced into her arm. The weight of the glass lifted and her arm began to bleed, warm and wet down her wrist and over her fingers. It took Anna a moment to move as Tyler placed the glass on the workbench. Gratefully, she leaned against him a moment as he lay the glass down.

"Be careful," she cautioned, looking around him to inspect the glass. "If you knock the edges it will chip the glass."

"The glass be damned!" The harshness of his voice surprised her. For the first time Anna looked at him and realized how white his face had gone.

"It's a perfect cut," she said indignantly, then suddenly felt pain, immense and throbbing, shoot the length of her arm. "Oh." She gripped the arm above the cut.

Tyler grabbed her by her good wrist. "Do you have something clean to wrap that arm? It's bleeding pretty good."

Feeling slightly dazed, Anna looked down at her arm, trying to push back the queasiness and pull herself together. "There's clean rags in the table drawer, but it's okay, really."

"Yeah, it looks okay," he said caustically. Quickly, he pulled out a long white cloth and ripped it into several pieces, pressed it over the cut and grabbing her hand, he placed her fingers against the material. For a moment, she felt lightheaded as the arm throbbed with each beat of her heart.

"Come on," he said, putting an arm around her and urging her forward.

Anna planted her feet. "The bleeding will stop. Let's give it a minute."

"You may have chips of glass embedded in there. You're going to the hospital."

"No. It'll be okay in a little while."

He set his jaw. "Are you nuts? I've seen enough cuts to know this one needs stitching. I'm taking you even if I have to carry you." He reached down behind her knees and at her shoulders to do just that.

Anna jumped back and put out her good hand in alarm.

"Leave Miz Anna alone." Danny's voice sounded low and demanding behind them and they both turned.

Danny stood still, jaw set as he stared hard at Tyler. "Let her go."

"It's all right, Danny," Anna said quickly, surprised by Danny's aggressive stance.

"She has to have her arm sewn up." Tyler turned his back on Danny and faced her again. "I'm taking you to the hospital."

"She doesn't want to go." Danny stepped closer to Tyler.

Without him moving a muscle, Anna sensed the threat in Tyler. She stepped between the two men and calmly said, "Danny, Tyler's probably right. I cut my arm so I have to have it seen to." She held it in front of her and Danny's face suddenly went white as he saw her arm for the first time. His eyes rolled back in his head and she feared he'd fall down, but he shook himself, gaining control, and said, albeit weakly, "Miz Anna, you gotta get that fixed."

"We're wasting time. Let's go." Tyler gripped her uninjured forearm.

"I'll go, I'll go, but not to the hospital. We can go to Doc Barnum's in town."

He must have seen the hard resolution in her face, because he didn't argue, just pulled her gently toward him. "Let's go before that soaks through. Keep pressure on it," he barked.

She tried to turn back to the house. "Wait, let me put on my makeup—"

"Dammit, Annie, we're leaving now!"

"Right now," Danny said, nodding quickly. "I can take you. It's really bleeding."

Seeing the blood soak through the cloth, Anna closed her mouth on further protest.

Jaw tight, Tyler said, "You stay here Danny, keep an eye on things for me. I promise to take good care of

Annie."

Danny stood still, his glance settling indecisively on Tyler.

"Tyler's right, Danny, we need you here."

After an incredibly tense moment, he finally nodded. "Okay."

Anna and Tyler hurried across the grass and out to the front of the house where Tyler's truck and car were parked. Danny hurried to open the car door and helped her inside.

"I'm fine," she protested, keeping her gaze away from the red soaking the rag. "Tyler, let's take the truck instead. I'm afraid there'll be blood all over this car."

Ignoring her, he closed her door and hurried around to the front, then immediately started the car. The wheels spit gravel as they drove out the driveway and onto the street. Anna turned and caught one last sight of Danny standing where they'd left him. She chewed her lip, hoping Danny's concern for her didn't end up costing him his job.

Ω

Danny paced back and forth. He counted off on his fingers. One: check the horses. Two; water. Three; hay. He stared after the car, but all he could see was a big cloud of dust. Miz Anna. Four; bring the horses inside. He bit at his lip until he tasted blood. He had to take care of the farm while Miz Anna was gone.

Danny pushed his hands through his hair. The car was gone, the dust too. Miz Anna depended on him, Mama told him that all the time. He would do things right so she wouldn't be disappointed in him. He never wanted her to be disappointed in him again.

Ω

Anna looked over at the speedometer. "You'll end up with a ticket if you don't slow down."

Tyler glanced at her, his gaze sweeping the blood soaked cloth. "Ticket be damned."

She smiled weakly. "That's what you said about the glass."

His head whipped around, then back to the road ahead, brows drawn in a dark frown. He eased up slightly on the gas. "This isn't funny. You may have severed something."

"I'm not laughing. It's just—" she shrugged and looked out the window, fighting emotion. How could she tell him his concern brought a lump to her throat and if she didn't laugh she'd cry?

"How are you holding up?" he asked several moments later. "Feeling lightheaded?"

"I'm fine. The doctor's office is off the main drag on Cranberry Street, small green house set back from the road." She bit her lip. "You'd better call him first so he's expecting us."

"Do you know the phone number?"

He dialed the number and told the doctor's office what had happened and that they were on their way over. He seemed to be listening to something detailed on the other end, but didn't share it with her.

Tyler drove quickly and efficiently, but by the time they pulled up outside the office, Anna was biting her lips as the pain intensified, making her afraid she'd lose her lunch.

Tyler jumped out of the car and ran around to open her door, supporting her up the short walk to the side door. Lynn, Doc Barnum's nurse and wife, opened the door and ushered them inside. When she saw Tyler, she lost her smile. "Tyler!" she exclaimed. "I heard you were back."

"Hello Lynn."

Anna suddenly remembered Tyler and Lynn had dated a few times before she and Tyler had gotten together. She turned to Tyler, but he looked more distracted than interested in a conversation.

"Lynn is married to Bobby, Doc Barnum," Anna said.

Lynn took Anna's arm. "Anna," she said with warm concern. "Come right in and we'll take a look at that arm."

By now Anna was feeling decidedly wobbly, but determined not to lean on Tyler more than necessary. It was a relief to sit on the examination table but she continued to watch Lynn and Tyler covertly, wondering for a brief, jealous moment if there were any lingering feelings between the two of them.

With barely a glance in Tyler's directly, Doc Barnum entered the room. Anna sat perfectly still as he pulled back the blood soaked cloth.

"Anna," he said, "what have you done?"

Beside him, Lynn pursed her lips and said, "It's a good thing you got here so fast, that's a nasty gash."

"It'll have to be stitched," the doctor said, gently touching and prodding around the gash. "I told Tyler you'd have to go to the emergency room if it was too deep."

Anna met Tyler's glance and read the very real worry clouding his eyes.

"Will there be scarring?" he asked.

"The doctor does a nice job of stitching," Lynn said reassuringly. "There might be a thin line for a while but it'll fade with time."

Anna had the urge to laugh, but clamped her lips shut, afraid it might turn into more than a laugh. What did a little scarring on her arm matter?

"We'll have to clean this out and then you'll need a

tetanus shot," the doctor murmured.

"Well, you've got me here," Anna said staunchly, "you might as well do the works."

"That's the spirit," Lynn said. She looked at Tyler. "If you want to wash up, you can help me gather everything the doctor will need."

"Okay." He looked at Anna. "I'll be right back, will you be okay?"

"I'm fine." Tensely, Anna watched Tyler follow Lynn out of the room, and she had to wonder at the purposeful look on Lynn's face.

Ω

After showing Tyler where to wash up, Lynn pulled supplies from a locked cabinet and handed him several rolls of plastic wrapped dressing.

"This is what you needed help with?" he asked with surprise.

Lynn grabbed him by the sleeve and pushed the door closed between the two rooms. "No. I could do this blindfolded. I want to talk to you."

Tyler waited.

"The word around is you're moving back into the Double B."

Tyler narrowed his eyes. "Good news travels fast. I already have."

Lynn's brow went up. "Don't take that tone with me, remember we grew up together and I think I know you pretty well."

"Yeah, so is that good or bad?"

"You tell me."

"It seems that maybe you've already formed an opinion."

She gave an impolite snort. "My opinion in this doesn't count for squat. All I remember is you were always the wild, independent sort."

"People change," he said shortly, wondering where this was going. He and Lynn had dated in the past, but nothing serious. Once he'd decided on Annie, that had been it.

"I know you're a decent guy, despite a few rough edges, but my point is, I don't want to see Anna get hurt. She's been through a lot. As nice a guy as you are, I think you could hurt her."

"Hell, Lynn, what makes you think that? Is this because of what happened six years ago?" he asked, his voice hard.

"I don't know what happened—Anna never said a word to anyone. I just know you left, she changed, and since the accident, she's even more vulnerable. Everyone in town gives her the space she needs, but if she ever asks, we'd be there for her."

"Can you get to the point?"

Lynn put her hand on her hip and cocked her brow. "If you're getting involved, make sure you stick around this time."

"Shit, Lynn, that wasn't my fault. I don't know your recollection of that time, but I didn't have much choice."

Lynn sighed. "Tyler, I've always liked you, but I like Anna too, and I can't watch you walk back into her life after all this time and not say something."

"Okay, you've said it, not that I think it's your business. Now can we get back in there?" he asked impatiently, looking toward the room where he'd left Annie, resenting that he'd been cast as the bad guy.

She looked at him a moment and her expression changed, as if she was seeing something she hadn't noticed before. She nodded, and then she did a complete turnaround and smiled at him. "Yes, let's get back to Anna. After all, she's the reason you're here. Maybe I've got you all wrong, Tyler."

Ω

Four days later Anna walked to the barn early in the morning. She'd managed to do some light unpacking the last couple days and generally take it easy, but the arm the doctor had stitched no longer throbbed and as long as she was reasonably careful she could resume normal activity.

She was still surprised by Tyler's concern on the day she'd been hurt, amazed by the way he'd waited around, looking anxious while the doctor stitched her up. It had almost felt like a blast from her past, the time she'd twisted her ankle and he'd carried her all the way from the barn to the house.

Martin hadn't been pleased that day to see her in Tyler's arms, but Anna knew that's when she'd begun to fall in love with him. Funny how she recalled stuff like the stray curl at the edge of his temple, the ferocity in his expression when she got hurt. Too bad it hadn't stayed that simple and easy between them.

Anna walked to the barn and found Tyler riding in the outside ring. The animal was beautiful and sleek, its coat a deep black. By the look of the horse's powerful hindquarters, she knew he'd be great on barrels. She wondered if Tyler would let her give him a try.

Anna moved to the old upturned barrel between the barn and the pen, where she'd sat countless times and watched Martin work his horses in the riding pen. Tyler had always been an exceptional rider, his hands light and easy on the horse's mouth, his seat quiet as he moved like fluid silk with the animal. He had a natural grace, almost like he'd been born in the saddle. Anna knew he planned to bring in cattle so he could begin his training on the cutting horses, and her excitement began to rise. Finally, the Double B would be back on track, no longer a breeding ranch, but at least a real working ranch once more. She was only beginning to realize how much she'd missed being part of that. She only knew it was good to feel alive again.

Tyler brought the horse to the middle of the pen and dismounted. Anna stood and dusted off the seat of her jeans and ducked through the wooden rails. "Great ride!" Enthusiastically, she moved forward to stroke the horse's nose.

Tyler leaned down to loosen the saddle's cinch strap. "He's got lots of heart and he likes to play, he should do well."

Anna stroked the soft muzzle. "Some things never change, do they? You still look for horses with that extra edge."

Tyler lifted a brow, but then shrugged, as if it were a given. "I've found the best cutting horses like to play, they're curious and full of life. I want to bring that out when they zero in on a cow. Wouldn't you rather play than work?" He gave her a searching look, his eyes deeply blue in his suntanned face. "I seem to remember you going for the same type of horse." The message in his eyes said something else. She recalled how they used to play as lovers, making love out in the middle of nowhere or wrapped in the sheets of his bed on a miserable, rainy day.

With difficulty, Anna turned her attention to the horse. "Spirit loves to play and test me. I admit I love the challenge of channeling that energy."

"Exactly." He lifted the saddle and swung it from the horse's back. "How are you feeling today, Annie?"

Anna lifted her bandaged arm. "Like there's nothing I can't handle." She'd never handled Tyler, he'd always been his own man. Maybe that had been her downfall, thinking she could handle him.

One corner of his mouth lifted. "I'll bet you can take on just about anything these days. You've really changed from the girl I remember."

Anna met his gaze squarely and dipped her head in acknowledgement. "Despite the obvious physical changes, you're right."

Tyler placed the saddle on a rail and began to brush the black's neck. "So what do you think of this guy?"

"He's gorgeous. I bet he'd be great on barrels."

"Yeah," he said with a grin, "but you can't have him. I had an idea I'd like to run by you, if you're interested. Once your stitches are out and you're feeling up to it, I'd like to keep mornings free so we can work together with the horses."

Anna studied him intently, her mouth dry. "Work together?" Spend time together like they used to.

Maybe Tyler was having the same sense of déjà vu, because he suddenly became very focused on the horse. "Exercise them. I also have a client who bought a mare for her twelve-year-old daughter. She needs someone to work with them on barrels and gymkhana events. If you think you'd be interested, I'll let her know."

The idea thrilled her, and then the next moment the anxiety set in. "Are they local people?"

"They're new in the area, but heard about us through a friend of a friend."

Anna gripped her hands together and chewed her lip, then swallowed with difficulty. "What if they expect something—someone different?" Strangers. Why was she afraid of strangers? A woman and her little girl.

Tyler gave her a level glance. "They know your reputation. If they're not satisfied, then they can go somewhere else."

"But Tyler, we're building a business. Maybe if they

won't work with me, you could—"

Tyler looped his horse's reins through his hand. "It'll be okay, Annie. They work with you or go elsewhere. Simple."

Simple. Black and white, no shades in between. Tyler had not changed. He'd always found compromise unacceptable.

"Okay." Anna thought about that. "There's another thing we have to go over. I need to know how much room we'll have for additional horses, just in case we start getting calls."

"Good idea. We'll have to run over the plans later this afternoon or maybe tonight." Tyler grabbed a hoof pick from a grooming box and lifted his horse's front hoof. "By the way, I've been in contact with a potential client referred by your friend Gill Dakins."

Pleased with the news and on familiar ground, she smiled at him. "That's a good sign, as I'm sure you know. The horse community is a small one when it comes to information getting around."

"I know that first hand," he said dryly, but he smiled. "He's interested in bringing some horses in for training." He picked up another hoof and began to clean it, his back to her. "Which brings me to something else. I thought if you'd like to try your hand at reining some time, we could play around with it. I can give you some pointers." He dropped the hoof and stood upright. "You're an excellent rider, I know you'll be good at it."

Anna knew her skill level, but felt pleased by the compliment nonetheless. "I've played around with reining to some degree, but never on a professionally trained cutting horse. I'd love to try it."

"Good. Gill Dakins gave me the name of a stock dealer, Jerry Wills. I'm going to go look at his steers today. If he's got something I can use, I'll buy enough to get started on the reining. Let me put Dudley out and I'll fill you in on everyone's feeding schedules so we're consistent." He unsnapped the crossties.

"His name is Dudley?" Anna asked with a raised brow, smiling.

Tyler shrugged. "That's his registered name, if you can believe that."

"Dudley." Anna surveyed the handsome animal from head to toe. "He sure doesn't look like a Dudley. I'd say more like a Star Prince or a King's Ransom."

"Well, when people see him in action they'll realize there's more to him than just a name." Tyler dropped the brushes back in the grooming box. "This guy's won more in competition than any other horse I own."

Anna stepped up to the horse and gently rubbed the underside of his jaw. "You'll wow everyone so much that they won't dare make fun of you, Dud," she promised.

"Is that what they do?" Tyler asked from behind her, his voice deadly quiet.

Anna stiffened, then twisted around to face him, one hand on the horse's shoulder. "What?" she asked warily.

"Do people make fun of you?"

She went perfectly still, no words coming readily to mind. Dudley moved his feet impatiently, then began to paw the dirt floor. Anna stepped back. "It has happened," she admitted in a low voice, staring at the opposite wall.

"Annie—"

She cut him off with a chopping motion of her hand. "Tyler, you'll never understand. I'm treated differently, people can't help it. Sometimes they're downright cruel in their curiosity. It's different if kids ask questions, but adults can be incredibly insensitive."

"When?"

"One time I was in town and a woman I knew said it was a shame I couldn't feel anything on my right cheek.

She asked if I had burn scars on other parts of my body."

"Curiosity?"

"Maybe. But I thought at the time there was more. She was someone I'd gone up against in competition and we'd never really gotten along. It's almost like she was pleased about what had happened."

"Maybe she was someone who you can't judge everyone by. Maybe something about her was off anyway."

Anna paused, frowning. "I never thought of it like that. All I knew at the time was it really hurt."

"Whether it was one insensitive person or not—I wish I could fix it." Tyler touched her arm, a momentary contact, but burning all the same.

"You can't. It's got to come from me. I have to become immune to the hurt or ignore conversations that stop when I enter a room. It's my insecurity, and there's nothing you can do to make it better. It's not up to you to fix it."

Tyler's hand lifted and stroked her cheek, the gesture keeping Anna immobile. She still felt on uncertain ground with him, as if they were teetering too close to where they'd left off six years ago. She stepped back, not liking the vulnerability she felt.

"I know there's nothing I can do, Annie, but I wish there was." He turned and led the horse outside.

Anna battled a hot burning in her throat coupled with an uneasy feeling of gratitude. Why feel empowered because of a few simple words from Tyler? Surely forgiveness didn't come that easy? The hurt from his leaving couldn't just dissolve.

By the time Tyler walked back inside, Anna had composed herself and was moving some pitchforks out of the way into a corner.

"Whoa," Tyler said, removing the handles from her

grasp. "You're not supposed to be lifting anything with that hand. You don't want to take a chance on the stitches pulling out."

"I'm fine," she protested. "It hardly bothers me. Anyway, they'll be coming out in six days."

"We're not taking chances," he said firmly. "If you're ready, I'll show you the feeding schedule." He walked over to the metal grain bins that had been brought in the day before and pushed up the lid. "I have grain rations and supplements written down in this notebook," he said, indicating a clipboard hanging on the front of the bin. "And there's separate bins for oats, flaked corn and pellets. If you have any questions let me know."

Anna ran her fingertip over the notes he'd written, his handwriting large and bold on the lined paper. "It looks pretty straightforward."

"Everyone's been fed already." He hesitated. "I plan to take a ride and check out some of the horses. I'd ask you to go, but it's probably not a good idea because of your arm."

"I'd love go for a ride," she said firmly. "If I'm careful, there shouldn't be a problem. I'll be fine," she added for extra emphasis when he still hesitated. She turned and lifted Spirit's bridle from the hook. "You can saddle my mare for me if that makes you feel better," she added, tongue in cheek.

He smiled slightly. "I almost forgot how stubborn you can be."

They stared at each other a moment. Memories flitted through Anna, some sweet, others somber. "What happened six years ago?" she blurted. "Why did we let each other go so easily?"

She turned around abruptly, giving Tyler her back. "Forget it," she mumbled, embarrassed at her own wayward mouth. How could she have said that? It was old history. "I'll get your horse," she threw over her shoulder, hoping he'd let her comment go.

Anna approached the muscled dark bay gelding in the stall next to her horse. She opened his stall door and spoke to him softly, admiring his elegant head as she buckled the chinstrap of his halter. She heard the scuff of a footfall behind her and turned to find Tyler standing outside the stall watching her. He reached past her and snapped on the lead line. "I don't want you to bump your arm."

Anna stepped from the stall, Tyler and the horse behind her.

"Letting go wasn't easy, Annie, not unless ripping your guts out is easy."

Anna's mouth went dry. She saw him again that last night as the deputies led him from the cottage. His eyes angry and bright, his body stiff with resentment whereas moments before he'd made such sweet love to her. He'd looked furious with her, as if it had been her fault the sheriff had come for him.

"It wasn't easy," she admitted. "It taught me not to take anything for granted."

"We both learned something." Tyler brushed the horse's hindquarters. "This is Frisco," he said abruptly, obviously not wanting to talk further about the past. "You can start riding him when your arm is better."

"He's a fine looking animal." She followed his lead. "Is he yours or a boarder?"

Tyler threaded his fingers through the horse's coarse black forelock. "Frisco is my guy." Tyler began to rub a rubber curry comb over the horse.

Anna entered her mare's stall. After tying her horse, she lightly curried her and then grabbed the brush, enjoying the feel of it gliding over Spirit's gray coat.

"I've raised Spirit from birth," she said, raising her

voice. "She's such a game horse. Anything I ask of her, she's there. Crazy, but sometimes I think she can read my mind."

"If you're lucky, you have one, maybe two horses like that in your life," Tyler said.

Anna ran her hands down Spirit's legs.

"I'll take care of her feet," he said. "I don't know if you've been in the tack room, but each horse has their own tack. The names are written on tape under the saddle horn. I have no problem with you riding any of the horses," he added.

"I'll forewarn you that I will take you up on the offer," she said lightly, following him into the tack room. Since the last time she'd been in here, more than half a dozen saddles had been added. As she stared at the saddletrees along the wall and the polished wainscoting, she smiled reminiscently. "Martin once told me he built this tack room himself, you know. He was really good with his hands."

"He did a good job, Annie," Tyler said, looking around. "This place was built to last. It's rare to find this type of workmanship. Martin and I might not have agreed on a lot of things, but I know what kind of work he could do, on and off a horse."

As Tyler hefted Spirit's saddle on his hip, Anna followed him from the room, admiring him for admitting as much as he had about Martin.

Anna watched him place the bright blue saddle pad on Spirit's back, then the saddle. He tightened the girth and pulled the leather through the ring, then dropped the stirrup back in place. Anna led her horse from the barn and out into the sunlight, thoughtfully stroking Spirit's neck as she watched Tyler slip his horse's bridle in place.

When his horse was saddled Tyler grabbed his hat from a hook inside the door and exited the barn. Anna was surprised to see a camera in his hands. Coming to a standstill, he took several pictures of the mountains beyond the pasture. Anna waited patiently, surprised by this new facet of Tyler. When she'd known him he'd never shown any interest in photography.

Anna leaned back against her mare and stared up at the clear sky, then heard a series of clicks beside her. She looked at Tyler and found he'd turned the camera on her and snapped a picture. Anna choked on a startled breath and shielded her cheek with a cupped hand, the movement instinctive and too late. She dropped her hand.

"Save your film," she snapped.

Tyler's expression turned wary. Instantly, she felt guilty, but then wondered why she should feel guilty, she hadn't stuck a camera in someone's face and invaded their privacy. She quickly turned away. "I don't appreciate having my picture taken." She swiped at her cheek, the mountains a blur in the distance. It was ridiculous to be so sensitive. She thought he understood her sensitivity, but now realized she couldn't expect anyone else to understand how she felt about her face.

Tyler made an impatient sound. "Hell, that was thoughtless. I'm sorry. I should have asked."

She turned back to him. "Why did you do that?" she demanded.

"It was the way you looked with that horse beside you. It was a picture I had to take."

Anna snorted in disbelief and glared at him, but the genuine concern on his face made her realize she was acting out of proportion. She tried to rein in her anger, her sense of outrage at being caught off guard. "M-maybe I overreacted," she finally admitted gruffly.

Tyler mounted his horse and Anna tried to get control of herself. She felt totally out of control where the scarring was concerned. Sensing her turmoil, Spirit uncharacteristically danced away from her. Anna lifted a hand to soothe the mare.

Tyler sat watching her. "Are you sure you still want to go for a ride? I'd never hurt you deliberately," he added in a low voice.

Anna caught her breath. She could contradict that statement, but it was an old wound she didn't want to revisit. He had hurt her once by turning his back when she'd needed him the most. "Forget it." Quickly, Anna mounted her mare, who was still acting restless, and urged her into a trot. She needed action, something to clear her head of blue eyes and the man that was once again turning her life upside down.

Anna stopped her mare after about a hundred yards at the first turnoff and looked back at Tyler. "Do you want to head down into the valley or go higher?"

"Higher," he said.

He pulled his hat lower but she could feel his eyes piercing her.

"How's the trail to the summit?"

Anna's breath caught short in her throat. How they used to race up there! "I've kept it pretty clear of debris, but the path is still narrow just beyond those hemlocks up ahead. It's mostly grass cover and it's a nice, easy run to stretch their legs."

"I remember how you used to ride like hell through there."

"With Martin yelling at me to slow down." She smiled over the memory, then sized up his horse. "Your guy has longer legs, but my girl has stamina." Fondly, she patted Spirit's neck.

"Let's test that theory," he said, and nudged his horse into a smooth lope.

Anna followed him. When the trail widened she drew

level and gave a triumphant laugh as she and Spirit raced past, saluting Tyler as she took the lead. He followed her as they reached the crest of the hill and for a moment it might have been six years ago . . .two kids wanting nothing more than the wind in their face and a fast horse beneath them.

She slowed Spirit to a trot and then a walk. With a quickening of breath, she acknowledged once again an intense love for the fresh morning breeze and the ability to ride her horse as she pleased. From her vantage point she looked at the ranch laid out below them, the early spring grass, the sun promising it would be a banner day. Everything felt perfect right now, as if she'd been able to turn the clock back to a happier time.

Anna watched Tyler dismount, distracted as she stared at his straight back and the way his jeans fit across his behind. Feeling as if she'd done this before, she swung her leg over the saddle and jumped to the ground, sitting on a large rock as she deliberately turned her attention to his horses in the pasture below.

"This was always the best spot on the ranch," Tyler said, coming to stand beside her.

Bittersweet memories wound around her as their glances met. She couldn't hold that glance so she looked away, recalling the first time they'd made love. It had been on this hill, just past dusk and not a soul around for miles. Anna pushed her hair away from her face as a soft breeze swirled it around her head. She wondered if he remembered that hushed day, the trees sheltering above, the lush, green ferns beckoning. With a self-deprecating groan, Anna wondered why she'd ridden to this spot. Did she want to stir up the pain of the past, or just try to move beyond it?

"I have such a love for this ranch," she said abruptly, uncomfortable with the bombardment of memories.

"Sometimes even I don't understand it."

Tyler scanned the ranch below them and shrugged his shoulders. "You have a special connection with the land. You always did, like it possessed you or something."

"You say that like you can't fathom such a connection to trees and soil. Martin told me once it's been in his family for five generations." She gave a short laugh. "And now I'm barely hanging on to it. That hurts like hell to admit."

"It's your family, too," Tyler reminded her. "Your heritage."

Anna acknowledged he was right, but she'd always been too aware she was Martin's illegitimate granddaughter and while it hadn't mattered to Martin, it had to her. Back in high school, amid a frenzy of parties and proms, she'd kept quiet about her background as she'd tried so hard to fit in. "Sometimes I think I'll wake up and find out this has been one big joke. Maybe I'm still eleven and just going into foster care."

"This is no dream, Annie," he said soberly.

"When Martin died and the responsibility of the ranch was suddenly thrust on me, I wasn't prepared for it." She'd wanted someone to lean on.

"When you're thrown a curve you learn to deal with it." His mouth looked hard and Anna knew he was thinking about the way he'd left town. He blamed Martin and he blamed her. "Instead of being angry at the change in circumstances, be glad we're going to bring the ranch back," he said, turning to her. "People will come here again for quality horses. They won't forget the Barlow name."

"Sometimes people have short memories," she said dryly, looping the reins up through her mare's bridle so she didn't trip. She moved to stand beside Tyler, knowing Spirit wouldn't wander far. "I'll be the first to admit I hate change."

"Nothing is static." He lifted a brow. "Think about where you were five years ago and where you are now."

"I was here, of course, with a full riding and training schedule and a fairly successful career." But she'd been alone. The few relationships she'd had, she'd let die a natural death. Anna wondered now if she'd really tried to move beyond her first love. Beyond Tyler. Anna stared at the familiar shadow of dark beard, the once reckless, loving eyes now tempered by time and experience.

"Where do you see yourself five years from now?" His voice held a challenge.

She laughed at the unexpectedness of his question but inside a small bitterness welled. If he'd asked her that six years ago, she'd have said they'd be married, have kids and horses, their own ranch. She'd wanted it all. "My dreams aren't the usual career woman's plan," she said blithely, stalling.

"It doesn't have to be anyone's idea but yours—whatever makes you happy."

Martin had always wanted more for her than her simple dream of kids and marriage. He hadn't wanted her involved with Tyler or any of the local boys.

"You're free to do whatever you want, Annie." Tyler stepped close and lifted a hand to her cheek, then his fingers speared into her hair. She felt that touch through every fiber, each muscle and sinew resonating with feeling. As she looked into his eyes she became very aware of his heat and scent. Right now, she knew what she wanted, and it wasn't talking about long ago dreams. Want for Tyler speared into every part of her.

"Maybe you'll decide to find a cowboy to fill your dreams."

She held perfectly still, concentrating on the sensation his fingers created as he cupped the back of her head.

Tingles moved down her neck, and she despaired at her own vulnerability. "I'm not waiting for a cowboy to come knocking on my door and make me happy." Defiant, she pushed back slightly from him.

"You're smart. Depending on others to keep you happy leaves you open to disappointment."

"Smart or realistic?" she murmured. Anna had a hard time deciding, almost mesmerized by Tyler's closeness, his eyes serious and intent. She wanted to be in his arms, as crazy and insane as that idea might be. Her fingers flexed as the thought leapt into her brain.

As if he read those thoughts, Tyler pulled her. Anna lifted her arms, encircling his neck. It felt good to be this close to him again. . .crazy, wild and abandoned.

They couldn't go back, but perhaps they could grab a little bit of time and caring for themselves. His head dipped toward her, his breath warm on her cheek, and Anna turned the unmarred side of her face to him. She wondered if she'd melt right then and there. She wanted him close and that confused and delighted her. How could she be afraid and yet yearn for the man in the same instant? She remembered the touch of his mouth, the way it had made her feel and forget. Heat rose another notch between them. She was a woman with needs, and those needs spoke strongly when this man was close. Was it merely memory playing her or was it real feeling for who they were today, two people who had been hurt?

She tipped her head back and looked into his eyes, enjoying the brush of his lean and work muscled body so close to hers. An intensity of heat moved through Anna as her breathing came fast and hard, slipping past her control.

The attraction deepened, sucking her in. She wanted more from this man. She'd had a small taste of his kisses since he'd returned, and she couldn't help but wonder how much he'd be willing to give. Would he want to be the cowboy at her door? She reached up and pulled his head down, momentarily satisfied when his mouth met hers, but all too soon wanting more. Despite the wanting, she felt stiff, conscious of her scarring. No man had been this close since the fire, the very idea had made her queasy. She closed her eyes now, not wanting to see the awareness of how her face looked in his eyes. For the moment she could pretend she was the same as any other woman being kissed by an attractive man. Tyler. She groaned deep in her throat.

His arms were hard around her, then his hands cupping her jeans, bringing her closer to his heat. Touching him aided the explosion of her senses. Anna felt incredibly needy, her hands trembling as she moved them up his chest, glorying in the hard muscle, the chest wall that moved as rapidly as her own. He was more muscled than six years ago, his body hardened by experience and time. He grasped her face between his big palms, pulling her mouth from his chest where she was intent on pressing a line of kisses, holding her as he dropped his mouth to hers once more.

Finally, Anna came up for air, drawing in deep gulps of it, looking around, the trees brilliant with green leaves just budding, the sun warm on the new grass. The enticing bed of ferns just a stone's throw behind them.

"Annie," Tyler muttered. He pulled her over toward a big rock and he sat, opened his legs and pulled her between them and her body began to shake with reaction. She had to get a grip on herself, her emotions, but control seemed a long way off. With a small sound, she accepted the truth that she was just as attracted to him as she always had been. Maybe she'd never stopped loving him. That made her stomach muscles cramp, but she couldn't sort it out right now.

Anna leaned forward and delicately traced his mouth with the tip of her tongue. His hard body was against hers, the grass a carpet under their boots. They could drop the short distance to the ground. Anna read the same thought in his eyes. They complimented each other, heating each other to boiling point, but beyond that what did they really know about each other anymore? Would she regret taking Tyler as a lover. . .again?

His hands moved under her sweatshirt, up her ribs until the breath came fast between her lips. He pulled it over her head, flinging it behind him. Then his hands moved to the buttons on her shirt and slowly, one by one, he undid them. Anna held her breath, afraid to move, hardly daring to believe she was contemplating going through with making love with Tyler on the top of this summit, in front of God and everyone. She felt nineteen again, anxious and hardly able to wait to be close to Tyler.

Almost in slow motion, she watched her shirt fall at her feet. Her brassiere of thin straps and lace, covered very little. His gaze heated her as his fingertips caressed her skin. When his mouth replaced his fingertips, she thought surely her legs would collapse. With hands that shook she unbuttoned the remainder of his shirt and pushed it back from his shoulders. His collarbone felt hard beneath her palms, the light dusting of hair on his chest hiding nothing of the lean muscle beneath the skin.

"Tyler," she whispered. "Tyler." His mouth swallowed her words, the seduction of his lips took her thoughts, but she gave them willingly.

The grass was springy beneath their bodies, cool until he rolled and brought her on top of him, careful of her bandaged arm. She lay sprawled across him, but he held her close, their bodies naked from the waist up. Anna sat up and kicked off her boots. Tyler pulled her back, undid the button of her jeans and worked them down her hips, the denim rough across the skin of her legs as he pushed them down her ankles. She helped him, then tugged his own jeans down. As she pulled her lace panties down, she lost her balance with them twined around her ankles and she fell on him with a whoomph, laughing, but he caught her and pulled her tightly against him, his boxers the only barrier between them, and really no barrier at all. She rubbed against him, closing her eyes to concentrate on the sensation, letting it rocket through her. The air swirled around them, and it was foreign and yet familiar to have the warm breeze on her naked backside.

Tyler's hands cupped her hips and pulled her close. He bumped against her and she pulled down the waistband of his boxers. She looked down at him and caught her breath, then she sank down, feeling him, clenching her teeth in agony, the pleasure so great and so expected, yet unexpected. Tears sprang to her eyes and she buried her face in his neck, feeling the clench of his legs as he thrust upward and she met him, all thought leaving as she allowed her very essence to be lost in the moment. As the sun beat down upon her head they burned together, just like it was old times, their bodies once more cradled by feathery ferns.

Ω

Tyler felt like he'd run a marathon, but the lazy movement of Annie's fingers on his scalp was hypnotic, calming him on the inside. For a moment, he wanted to remain like this forever, relaxed and at peace, as if this was how it was meant to be. The pines towered above them, forming a canopy where the sun filtered through, speckling Annie's bare skin as it cast shadows on the grass. He touched her skin, ran his palm over her shoulder, watching the movement of his fingers, fascinated by her light tan, the hint of her ribs as she inhaled and exhaled. She was beautiful, slim yet fit, her body strong and for that he was glad. She'd taken as much as she'd given.

He was shocked that their lovemaking felt like they'd never been apart. Their coming together had been almost an agony of feeling, a torrent of memory shaking him up. Uneasily, Tyler wondered how they'd lost this six years ago. Had they given up too easily as Annie had suggested? Would they give up again?

Tyler closed his mouth on the words that wanted to erupt. *I want you in my life.* How could he think they'd have a life together? The past would always be in the way. Talking about it would break the frail bond that existed between them. He clenched his jaw, staring at the white clouds feathered like mare tails in the blue sky. He wouldn't revisit the past, not when he wanted to ride out this euphoria another few minutes. *Let it go, Tyler, let it go...*

"Why so grim?" Annie asked, pulling her shirt around her shoulders as she sat up. To Tyler, it seemed a defensive gesture. "Are you thinking this was a mistake?"

Tyler looked at her, her hair tossed, feathers of it soft against her cheek. For a moment, she looked like his Annie. . . the one he'd fallen in love with. The Annie he'd have done anything for. She'd always been perceptive about his feelings and thoughts, and he was amazed that the passage of time hadn't changed that. Right now he wanted to dodge the question, not really sure in his heart what had happened. . .what was happening. "Do you think it is?" He reached for his clothes.

Annie watched him intently, but Tyler didn't want to talk about it. He wanted things to go back the way they were before they'd made love. He didn't know where they were going, and he hated going anywhere without a road map, without a destination in mind. He felt like he'd been blown off the map. He'd deliberately put her out of his mind for years, for Gods sakes, why this instant reconnection as if a day hadn't passed? Dammit, he felt as rattled by her as when he'd been twenty-one. His body remembered her.

"It's a mistake if we don't care about each other," she said slowly, as if choosing her words.

The emotion in her eyes was like a punch in the gut. He saw her vulnerability, yet her wariness.

"We parted so abruptly back then I think there's left over feelings we've got to deal with. Maybe we needed to do this," she added, waving her hand over the area where they'd made love, the ferns crushed into the earth. "There's nothing wrong with revisiting that residue of caring. But maybe this chapter needs to be closed so we can now move on with our personal lives."

Impatiently, almost angrily, Tyler thrust his shirt buttons through the holes. He didn't want to think of it as some kind of closure, but he didn't see how they could go forward either.

"Can't you talk to me, Tyler?"

He turned to her. "Annie, the past is dogging our every step. I can't forget my father or that he never got over what happened. Neither one of us can forget but we need to work together for the livelihood of the ranch."

"It will work," she said almost fiercely. "Between the two of us we'll figure this out. As for the rest, people will come around. They'll see you for the professional you are. The ranch will once more be a success."

"Let's hope you're right."

"They have to respect your knowledge. And besides, you were born and raised here, that counts for something."

Tyler couldn't help the mocking laugh that escaped

him. "It never did before. There's no reason to think the town gives two hoots about a Stanton. Look at Tara Dakins' reaction to me being here."

"She's one person. What about Randal France and Lynn Barnum?"

He shook his head, unwilling to be sidetracked. "We'll see what happens in the next few months. All I know is my return is business. It's not a homecoming party."

Looking disgusted, Annie shook her head. "No one is saying it should be a party." She came to her feet slowly and began to dress.

Tyler watched her, his mouth going dry as she reached for her brassiere, then her shirt again where she'd let it slide to the ground. It had been so unique, empowering to make love with Annie. As she slid the last button in place, he wondered how they would go on from this moment. He didn't regret his words, they were reality, but he could see by the sadness in her face she didn't agree with him. "Do you expect me to get sentimental about being back here? My feelings are nothing close to sentimental."

"Nobody twisted your arm." She turned toward her horse.

Tyler thrust a hand through his hair. He didn't want her leaving with things so unsettled between them. "Don't go." He moved to stand in front of her, but when she looked up at him expectantly, he wasn't sure how to begin or even what he wanted to say.

There was regret on her face. "We're on opposite sides of the fence." She stepped around him. "Nothing has changed."

Tyler reached down and scooped up his black shirt and quickly pulled it on his shoulders, following her as she caught up with Spirit.

She unthreaded the reins, jammed her foot in the

stirrup and mounted.

Annie looked down at him. "I don't regret what happened but the timing's off. I guess we don't have anything to build on."

Tyler couldn't deny the same thought.

"I've done most of the talking!" Annie said, exasperated, "Say something! I know darned well you've got an opinion."

Tyler recognized some of Annie's spark from the old days, and he couldn't help but smile. Desire rose again and he almost reached up to pull her down. "Step off that horse and I'll have plenty to say." The smile lurking in her eyes told him he'd touched a familiar chord. He could almost see the wheels churning in her head, and he wondered if she'd slide into his arms. He stepped closer, knowing if she dismounted, he'd pull her back to the ferns and there'd be no turning back for either of them.

His body still vibrated with the memory of their lovemaking. What would it hurt to find that satisfaction in each other's arms again?

A half smile lifted her mouth. "It would be so easy, wouldn't it? Swing my leg over this saddle and jump down. Walk into your arms." She looked toward the trees and her expression grew pensive. "But then I think of the aftermath, the problems we could be creating down the road with everything so unresolved between us." Her glance met his. "We don't know each other anymore and maybe we're starting over backwards."

"Dammit, Annie, we know each other as well as any other two people. Do you want promises that I might not be able to keep?"

She straightened and picked up the reins, but he caught the hurt in her eyes. Turning the mare's hindquarters to him, Annie looked back over her shoulder. "That's the last thing I'd ask," she said softly.

"We jumped into this too fast and I haven't got a clue where to go from here, but I can make sure it doesn't happen again. I'll see you around."

"Annie!"

She nudged her mare into a lope away from Tyler and it took all his control not to jump on his horse and chase her down. She had a mind of her own and he'd said the wrong thing, but he'd been honest with her.

Annie seemed to think they needed time. They'd already had six years, but he didn't know how much more it would take to heal the hurts they both held. Grimly, he feared they might never heal.

❄ Chapter Seven ❄

WHEN TYLER RETURNED TO the barn twenty minutes later he found Danny sitting on the fence rail, chewing on a piece of grass and staring vacantly across the empty pasture lot. As Tyler drew closer and dismounted from his horse, Danny finally looked up and acknowledged his presence with a quick nod. Slowly, he dropped his feet to the ground and approached him.

Tyler stifled an impatient groan, not sure he was up for a conversation with anyone. He needed time to think about what had happened up there on that hillside with Annie and right now his brain felt like it was short-circuiting. Annie wasn't the same as he remembered, and he felt as tangled up inside as a bad roll of baling twine. After their lovemaking, he'd been on an incredible high, but with the way they'd parted and with doubt setting in, he felt about as wonderful as a day old hangover.

He kept seeing Annie's head drop back, the heavy strands of hair splaying across his arm, heard her sighs as he kissed her again and again. . ..

"Miz Anna said I was to wait for you." Danny rubbed his hands down the sides of his jeans and watched him expectantly. "No matter how long it took, I was to wait."

"Danny, why don't you come into the barn?" Tyler led his horse inside. Quickly and efficiently, he unsaddled the gelding and brushed him down.

Danny watched him closely and then walked with him as he led Frisco to the outside paddock and released him. Tyler rested his boot on the fence rail and looked out over the pasture. Finally, he turned to the other man. "You know, Danny, this is a big ranch. By next week, I'll start cutting hay and there's a load of other chores that have to be done. I'll need a good man to work for me."

"That's why I have to talk to you. Miz Anna said you're the boss now and I'm to listen to you."

Tyler looked at Danny speculatively. "We've known each other a good long time, haven't we, Danny? We were friends once."

Looking confused, Danny stared at the ground.

"Danny," Tyler said patiently, "if you're going to work for me, I don't want any problems. I have to know what's going on with the ranch, no matter how big or small a problem. That means there are no secrets. And I won't have you interfering between Annie and I."

"No problems, no mistakes. I do my work," Danny said, his jaw now clenched. "You won't have to fire me."

Tyler stared at the other man's guileless pale blue eyes. "Did Annie say you'd be fired if you made a mistake?" He didn't believe that.

Danny's blue eyes went wide with shock. "No, No. I'll do a good job and you won't fire me."

"Who said you'd be fired?" Tyler asked again.

Tyler watched Danny nervously clench his hands. "Mr. Martin told me to be quiet and if I make any more mistakes, I get fired."

Tyler frowned. "You're talking years ago, Danny. Do you remember the day my father and I left?"

Danny quickly shook his head. "No. I gotta go." Without another word he turned and walked away. After about forty feet, he stopped and looked at Tyler over his shoulder. "I'll be on time tomorrow morning and I'll work hard, but I don't remember anything about Mr. Martin." Quickly, he walked away.

Frowning, Tyler watched him hurry up the road until he disappeared and he wondered if Danny knew something about what had happened six years ago. Maybe Martin had threatened to fire him if he told anyone the truth. With a sick twisting in his gut, Tyler knew he'd have to find out what Danny knew, even if only for his own peace of mind. The problem would be getting that information without scaring Danny away.

Ω

Much later that evening Tyler heard a car door slam and looked out the office window. He'd turned on the outside light earlier so Annie didn't come home to a dark house, and now he could see her battered pickup truck in the driveway they shared.

Tyler left the papers he'd been going over and exited the office. Throwing open the front door and walking across the lawn between the houses, he called her name.

Annie stood by her front door, and now she turned, a small bag clutched to her chest. "Tyler, you startled me."

"Sorry. Can you come over to the house?" he asked.

She retraced her steps and then crossed the lawn towards him. "Is something wrong?" she asked, her voice hushed in the semi-dark. "It's pretty late."

"We need to talk."

She hesitated a moment, but then she nodded. "Sure."

Tyler led the way back to the house, holding the door as she stepped inside the foyer. He closed the door behind her and noticed her quick glance around.

"It looks bare in here without your certificates and ribbons," he remarked.

"I've packed it all away in boxes. With you leasing the house it's more fitting for your awards to be up there."

"I'd like to collect trophies that show our collective effort," he said quietly, reaching behind her to switch on a wall sconce. She smelled as fresh as the outdoors, and Tyler wanted to catch her close to him and kiss her like he had this morning.

Annie stepped away, shaking the hair off her forehead as she turned in a half circle, her eyes large in her pale face. "That would be a wonderful coup, of course, but I don't imagine I'll return to competition."

"I hate to see good talent wasted," he said. "Have you ever shown Spirit?"

"No. We've only played at barrels from time to time."

"I think she'd do well."

"I'm not ready for setting up schedules, thinking about show timelines or being in the public eye. I don't know if I'll ever have the confidence to show again." He saw a flicker of interest in her eyes but she merely shrugged a shoulder. "I loved competition, but sometimes it's just the right time to stop. Like Martin used to say; know when to cut your losses and move on."

"That can be a tough philosophy to follow, but it's your choice." Martin had played hardball all his life, and he'd expected Annie to fall into line. Tyler had often suspected that even his early friendship with Annie had set Martin against him to some degree. "Something else I've been thinking about today is putting out press releases to let people know we're open for business. And," he studied her intently, "what do you think of having an open house to kick things off? We'd invite the public, not just horse people—the general public for a fun, informative day here at the ranch. We could have a barbecue, have some reining demos going on. I know it could go either way," he added. "People will show up or they'll decide to stay away. I'm hoping curiosity will win out and they'll come."

"The open house sounds like a great idea, but what about the renovations you've just started?"

"I have a bigger work crew coming in so the renovations won't take too long," he said. "I want to have the open house in the next month or so, maybe earlier if I can pull it together." He glanced at his watch. "I've already come up with some ideas. Why don't we talk about it while I whip up a late night dinner? Have you eaten?"

She hesitated a moment. "Sara and I caught a late lunch together in town." He thought she'd refuse, but then a ghost of a smile appeared on Annie's face. "Now there's an enticing thought, a man to make me dinner. Will it be hot dogs and beans?"

Like old times. Tyler almost said the words, but he stopped himself in time, his thoughts flashing back to six years ago. Back then, all he'd mastered was hot dogs and beans. The memory created a dull ache in his chest.

"No," he said lightly. "I was thinking about a juicy steak and Greek salad. I like cooking once in a while. . .nothing fancy, but I'll guarantee it's edible."

Annie laughed. "The word edible did the trick," she said.

"Come into the kitchen."

"I'll set the plates and silverware out," she said, slipping past him as he held the kitchen door.

Tyler followed, enjoying the light, fresh scent lingering in her wake.

As Annie gathered plates and eating utensils from the cabinets and drawers Tyler opened the refrigerator and removed the salad and steaks he'd promised her. With an economy of movement, he placed the steaks under the broiler and turned the dial.

"So how is Sara—and the new job?"

"She's dived in with both feet. More responsibility, which means a bigger time commitment. But she's loving it." She lifted a brow. "Sara told me you plan to give them a donation."

"It's a good cause."

"It is." She smiled at him.

He took a deep breath, determined to tell Annie the real reason he'd invited her over. He turned to face her just as she pulled her sweatshirt over her head. The movement pulled her T-shirt underneath up, exposing her ribs and outlining her breasts, then she tugged it off her head. As she pushed her shirt back down and smoothed her hair, he cleared his throat, trying to recall what he'd wanted to say. He wasn't going to get very far if all he could think about was how good it had felt to touch her this morning.

"Annie, it feels like we've gone too fast." He had a hard time forcing the words out.

She balled up the sweatshirt, her shoulders stiff as she stared at him with a guarded expression. "If you're referring to this morning," she said stiffly, "I've never—that is—"

"I just want you to understand I don't want to ruin our relationship," he cut in, "any type of relationship, before we even get started. What would you say to getting to know each other at a slower pace?"

"You mean go back to square one?" she asked cautiously, leaning her hip against the table.

Hope filtered through Tyler. "Yes. We get to know

one another again." He pulled a chair away from the table and invited Annie to sit down, then he opened the broiler and turned the steaks as he waited for her answer.

"I don't know. It didn't work out for us six years ago, why think now is any different?"

"We're different. We're not the same people we were back then."

"Even if we decided to start seeing each other," her voice sounded cautious, "how will we able to keep a personal relationship separate from business?"

Tyler looked at her with surprise. "You'd want to keep our relationship a secret?"

"This ranch's livelihood is important." Her voice held quiet acceptance. "We don't want to do anything to jeopardize it."

Tyler studied her closely. "You think if people know we're dating it would hurt your reputation? You want to put the ranch before us?" It felt like a slap from the past.

She looked at him incredulously. "No. All I'm saying is people might see a personal involvement between us as unprofessional. Let's at least keep it quiet until after the open house. I'll feel like I'm on display if people suspect we're involved."

"I'm not allowing anyone's opinions to keep me from seeing you, nor will it be a secret."

"I don't want it to affect your business," she said stubbornly. "Tyler, what drove you away is what ultimately brought you back here. You've admitted yourself that it bothers you how quickly everyone believed Martin and not you or Grant."

"My dad had an incident in his past that the sheriff blew out of proportion and the rest of the department just fell in line like sheep. I can't handle that narrow-minded thinking. I had to come back to make things right. It's what I needed to do for my dad. Maybe I need to prove to myself I can be a success here. I'll never leave with my tail between my legs again."

He watched her unwaveringly, reading the emotions that chased across her face; the lingering doubt she couldn't hide. Finally, she gave a slight nod of her head.

"Okay, we can try it your way."

"We'll keep things simple and platonic until the time is right." Tyler placed a steak on each plate.

Anna pushed her utensils around, hearing his voice almost from a distance. "Platonic?"

Tyler paused with his fork halfway to his mouth, a piece of rare steak dangling from the fork. "It seems the best solution, nothing to complicate the growing relationship."

She nodded. "Sounds logical. How long do you think we should keep it simple?" she asked, trying to keep her expression only mildly interested. "Six months. . . a year?" She popped a piece of steak into her mouth, ignoring the consternation darkening his face as she chewed the meat. "This steak is very good." Squirming in her seat, she put her fork down. "We could set our sights on six months."

"A hundred and eighty days." His voice came out flat.

Anna lifted her glass and watched him over the rim, doing her best to suppress a grin. She was enjoying herself, her earlier hesitation for the moment forgotten. "Well yes, if you base it on a thirty-day month. Technically, it's more. What do you think?"

He suddenly narrowed his eyes. "I think you're having a laugh at my expense."

She grinned outright. "And if I am?"

"I deserve it for coming up with such an asinine idea." Standing, he leaned across the table and dropped a quick kiss on her cheek. He sat back down and took a deep swallow of his drink. "Even when we were kids there was nothing platonic about our friendship."

"It is a noble idea," she assured him, suddenly feeling breathless, resisting the urge to touch her scarred cheek. He'd kissed her so nonchalantly. Two weeks ago she couldn't have imagined anyone touching it, much less putting their lips against the skin.

"Yeah," he said, "I'm a noble kind of guy."

Anna ignored the underlying sarcasm and smiled at him. "Yes, you are." She indicated the steak. "We can add cook to the list of what I know about you. Did you learn how to cook out there? What did you do in California?" It was more than idle curiosity. "I feel like I need to fill in the empty years."

"Nothing spectacular. I worked and took night classes for awhile but I had to drop out."

"You always dreamed of going to school for computer engineering, but you weren't able to finish your degree?"

"My dad needed me and it was around that time I got this idea to start my own company. Everybody and his brother is into internet marketing. Twenty-year-olds making hundreds of thousands of dollars."

Anna stopped chewing and stared at him, fascinated. She swallowed. "Is that what you did?"

He nodded. "I developed a unique software application that scrambles credit card numbers."

"I'm completely computer illiterate," she confessed, "So I'm easily impressed."

Tyler smiled at her. "I had my own tech company in our shoebox size apartment. It was a pretty wild ride for a while. I sold the company and I made a lot of money," he added, his voice sounding quite deliberate. "I followed the circuit for awhile, played at some rodeo and riding. Later on I invested in three properties in Montana that Dad and I converted into dude ranches."

"So you've had a good measure of success." Anna

suddenly felt tense and uncertain. It was so different from her life, which had taken a nosedive. "Were you happy?"

His eyes held a mocking light. "I had a ton of money to spend, what do you think?"

"Were you happy?"

Tyler put down his knife and fork with a clatter. "I worked my ass off and fell into bed at night so I didn't have to think about this place. Is that what you want to hear?"

His harshness made Anna feel as if she were under attack. "Only if it's true. I wondered so many times if you missed being here." *If you missed me.*

Tyler looked away, his jaw working. "Every day and every night, but I put that wanting out of my mind." He looked back at her. "I put a lot of wants out of my mind. I let my business take precedence and I had my dad to look after."

"You never really told me what happened to Grant," she said softly, almost afraid to know. *He'd died too young.*

"Annie." His voice held a warning.

"I need to know."

"After we left he started drinking. It's like no matter what was going on in our lives, whatever success we had, he couldn't forget this place." Tyler put his head back and Anna could see the strain on his face. "Near the end he begged me to bring him back here, but before I could his liver gave out. He was buried here in Marsh Plains like he wanted."

She bit her lips, shaking her head over Tyler's loss. "And you still blame all of us," she added quietly, seeing it in his face.

Tyler let out a deep breath. "Annie, I honestly don't know where blames lies. Nobody but my dad lifted that glass to his mouth, but what happened here ate at him."

He stood and walked over to the refrigerator. Opening the door, he pulled two sodas from the shelf. "Something's bugging at me. I think Danny knows something," he said abruptly. "He was waiting for me by the barn when I got back this morning."

"I told him he should talk with you about work. Why would you think he knows something? What's wrong?" she asked, worried.

"I don't know." He frowned and sat down again. "I get the feeling he's hiding something."

Anna shook her head. "No, not Danny." She reached for his hand and gripped it. "I know Danny. He'd never deliberately hurt me. Since the fire he shows up every morning for work. Some weeks I couldn't pay him, but he still worked. I know he cares about this place."

"About you," Tyler said with emphasis.

"Me, the ranch—it's all the same."

"No, it's not, at least, not to Danny." Tyler looked exasperated. "Annie, I didn't want to get into six years ago, but let's look at the facts. I know it wasn't my dad, so it had to be Martin or Danny. They were always here with the horses and they had access. For whatever reason, something went wrong." He gave her a pointed glance. "Danny's always been half in love with you. Maybe he figured out a way to get rid of me."

"No!" Anna jumped to her feet. "What you're suggesting is wrong, all wrong."

"It makes more sense than anything else I can figure out."

"Leave Danny out of this."

"Explain why the mare's owner had a foal that he was certain wasn't sired by the Double B's top stallion, for which he paid a heavy stud fee."

"Lucky Ace was a pure black quarter horse stallion known for throwing black foals. Once in a while you'd end up with a bay, but in his fifteen years standing here at stud, eighty percent of his offspring were black."

"How was the mare's owner so certain it wasn't Lucky Ace's foal? Was there testing done?"

"It wasn't necessary. The foal was clearly a spotted Appaloosa." At his stunned look, Anna exclaimed, "Didn't you know that?"

Tyler sat back in his chair. "No. Back then during the so-called investigations the accusations were flying and there was a lot of confusion. The sheriff wouldn't tell me anything and I sure as hell couldn't afford a lawyer. It was never mentioned the foal was spotted."

"We had an outside stallion in at the time. He was a strawberry roan appaloosa."

"I remember. He was only here a few days before Martin shipped him back. So someone bred that mare to the App. Someone wanted to either hurt the Double B or my father's reputation as breeding manager." Tyler looked at her and the deadly seriousness in his eyes sent a chill up her back. "You know I have to find out the truth. I can't let it rest."

Apprehension crept over Annie, and her shoulders drooped. "I know." Tyler would dig until he found the truth. It was the type of man he was. In the past she'd applauded his tenacity. She pushed her plate away. "Do what you have to do, Tyler. Maybe it's past time for all this to be resolved." Maybe then they could get on with their lives. "That's what you came back here for, anyway."

He didn't deny it. "You realize that whatever I find, it might drive us apart. Do you want to take that chance?"

"Yes." She said it quickly, bravely, before she changed her mind, knowing in that moment it was what he needed to hear. He'd been unjustly accused and he needed to clear his and Grant's name. Inside, she was afraid what he would find and how it would affect them. But why be afraid when she knew Martin and Danny had to be blameless?

Tyler pushed the steak platter closer. "Would you like something else?"

"No, I've had enough." She stood, moved to the sink and turned on the water. "I'll help you clean up."

Tyler came to stand beside her, his elbow brushing hers. "No, it's late. You go home, take a shower and relax, I can handle this." Turning his head, Tyler kissed her lightly on the mouth. Anna leaned into him, disappointed by the brevity of the kiss. As if reading her thoughts, Tyler smiled and bent toward her again. Slowly, his mouth touched hers, causing heat to build. It amazed her the effect his closeness had on her.

Anna wanted to forget everything they'd talked about and spend the night in his arms. It would be so easy to slip into that pattern. She pulled back and looked into deep blue eyes framed by dark lashes. She turned sideways. "I enjoyed our dinner, but I have to leave."

She took two steps away from him, and she thought he'd try to stop her as he followed her, but instead he lifted her bag where she'd left it on the counter. "Don't forget this," he said.

"My camouflage makeup." She accepted the bag. Feeling somewhat awkward, Anna concentrated on a wooden plaque hanging on the wall just beyond his shoulder. Home is where the heart is. "Sara gets it through the shelter from a woman who specializes in masking skin problems."

"That's great, Annie, if it makes you feel better," he said, his voice quiet.

She looked at him with a frown. "It's more than great. It's a lifesaver."

He didn't say anything and she remembered what he'd said about the scars not being important to the man who loved her. She searched his face, afraid he might have lied to make her feel better. A lie of kindness from a man who no longer loved her. What did he feel for her?

She murmured goodnight and Tyler let her go this time.

As she walked back to the guesthouse, she pondered all that had occurred today. She felt only a step away from caring deeply for Tyler once more. When she'd fallen in love with Tyler six years ago, she'd thought her life was perfect, but now she wondered if she'd discover her idea of perfect was no longer the same. She and Tyler were no longer the same.

❅ Chapter Eight ❅

ANNA AND TYLER WALKED toward the barn in the early morning, as they'd been doing all week. Tyler's arm brushed hers casually and for Anna the contact was like a hot brand, the effect resonating throughout her body. She'd become accustomed to working with Tyler, but at times redefining their relationship had been exhausting.

"What's on the agenda for today?" she asked, flexing her fingers. "I'm itching to get my hands on that pretty little quarter mare that came in. She's got lots of spirit and agility." She'd watched them unload her two days ago and she knew today she'd have the opportunity to see Tyler interact with the mare.

He smiled. "I knew you'd like her. I'll talk to the owner. I plan to work her into my reining schedule, but we've both been around long enough to recognize that mare's as athletic as they come." He looked at his watch. "I've got more steers arriving late morning, so I'll have to miss our ride today," he said regretfully.

Anna had looked forward to their morning rides all week. "That's okay," she said lightly, masking her disappointment, "there's always tomorrow."

Tyler turned to look at her. "You didn't forget Angela Mortimer and her daughter Carol will be here this morning?"

Anna curled her fists and stuffed them in her back jeans pockets. "Of course not." How could she? She'd been running on nerves all morning, able to think of little else except the upcoming meeting. She looked at her watch. "They should be here in about forty minutes."

"Do you want me to stick around?"

For moral support, Anna thought, grateful. "Don't be silly. I can handle it." She could handle whatever life threw her way. So why then did her legs feel shaky?

"Maybe we can get together this afternoon and go over some plans for the open house. I'm thinking about starting to put the word out."

Anna looked at him in surprise. "So you are serious about it?"

"I wouldn't have suggested it otherwise. I'm taking out some ads in the papers and I've approached some of them about doing a feature. I want to pull this together in the next few weeks."

Anna swallowed, staring at the ground. "That's awful quick."

"Yes."

As they passed several piles of carefully stacked lumber, Anna deliberately directed her attention to the large shed the construction crew had finished erecting only yesterday. She stopped in her tracks and drew a fortifying breath. "It's so strange to see something in that clearing when it's been empty for the last two years," she murmured thoughtfully, her feelings mixed that he'd chosen to erect the structure in the same location where the cottage had stood. The cottage where Tyler and his father had lived. The cottage where they'd made love that last night.

"Come over and take a look," he invited, holding his hand out to her. "Come on."

Anna hung back, shading her eyes against the sun. "That's okay, I can see it from here."

Tyler walked over to the two men applying stain to the shed's exterior and spoke with them for several moments. When he returned to her side, he held out several sprays of lilac from the bushes that had survived the fire two years ago. Touched, Anna stared at his offering, then slowly accepted the flowers. "Thank you." Tentatively, she inhaled their scent.

"It will house tools and small equipment like push mowers, rakes and shovels."

Anna lifted her head and gave the building her careful consideration. "It'll save time running back to the barn for tools," she said. "We always had a storage problem."

"The best part is in the winter there's room on the back side to stockpile sand when the roads are iced over."

"You're thinking ahead." She turned on her heel and directed her attention to the barns just ahead. "And that gray stain on the buildings looks so elegant. It really makes them stand out."

He lifted a brow inquiringly. "Then I take it you approve of the changes?"

"Yes, though I admit at first I was resistant. It was hard to imagine the buildings anything other than that weathered brown color they've been since I came here. I'm amazed how a little stain can make such a big difference. The place already looks so much happier." She laughed at his grimace. "Well, it looks better than three weeks ago."

"And what about the open house?" he asked. "Can I

count on your help?"

Anna still hesitated. She knew an open house would mean a lot of people and a lot of planning. "I'll help out on the sidelines."

"What do you think about giving a riding demonstration?"

She shook her head. "No."

"Think about it," he urged.

"Boss." Tony Hastings, the new barn manager called out as they drew closer to the paddock and barns.

Anna moved several paces away from Tyler and turned to greet Tony.

"Good morning Anna." Tony had an easy smile on his weathered face. He turned to Tyler, pushing his dark blond hair back in an exasperated gesture. "There's a guy looking for work."

"We've hired everyone we need for now," Tyler said.

"I know, but he says he's got to talk to you. His name is Mario and he's waiting in the office."

Tyler glanced at her. "This will only take a few minutes."

She shrugged. "I'll get started on the barn chores."

Together, they walked into the barn and she immediately noticed a short, stocky man standing in the aisle outside the office. He looked to be somewhere in his late fifties, his dark clothes worn white in places and his face very thin. He looked hard-pressed to say the least and she couldn't help but wonder what his story might be. Tyler shook hands with the man and she heard him explain they weren't hiring right now.

"I hear you're expanding," the man said quickly, with a faint accent. "Everybody in town is talking about it. Don't you have some work for me?"

Anna pulled a wheelbarrow out of its cubby, then gathered her rake and pitchfork as she surreptitiously kept an eye on the two men.

"Thanks for enquiring, Mario, but I can't help you," Tyler said firmly.

The man's shoulders slumped. "Can I leave my name in case something opens up? I'm staying at the "Y" in town, and my family is at the shelter. The woman there, she said to come and see you about work," Mario added.

Sara, Anna thought, wondering how Tyler would feel about Sara telling people Tyler might hire them on.

"Have you asked around town about work?" Tyler asked.

"Yes," the older man said with quiet dignity. "I'm trying to take care of my family, but I'm only out of prison two months and people don't want to hire me. I thought you'd be different," he muttered.

Anna swallowed quickly, her glance glued to Tyler. Even if Tyler chose to ignore it, she recognized the desperation in the man's voice.

"Why would I be different?" There was no mistaking the ice in Tyler's voice.

"I hear talk," Mario said. With a sharp nod, he turned away.

Tyler frowned as Mario left the barn, then he looked up and caught Anna watching him. Anna looked away, staring at the faint pink scar on her arm. She had forgotten to put a band aid on the healing scar. Tyler had insisted on taking her back to the doctor's office yesterday and he'd again shown concern while her stitches were removed. Why couldn't he show the same concern for this man who obviously needed work?

Anna turned away, disappointment causing her to jab her pitchfork into the straw. Sifting the bedding, she wondered where the man would go. She pushed back a sour taste of frustration. Tyler was a businessman. He had to draw the line somewhere between profit and compassion. Maybe it wasn't realistic of her to wish he'd take his eye off the bottom dollar and just hire the man because he could.

Ω

Anna held her breath as the small group approached her—a woman somewhere in her thirties, a teenage girl and a young boy who zigzagged up the path as he ran ahead. The woman was elegantly dressed in a dark red pantsuit while the young girl wore jeans, a baseball cap and an oversize lime green T-shirt. Black-haired and slender, she dragged the toes of her sneakers in the dirt. Anna stifled a groan. The young girl looked bored, as if she'd rather be anywhere but here.

The boy, who looked to be about five, jumped on the paddock fence rail when he reached Anna and hung there by his hands, head tilted back as he stared at her with wide eyes. Her throat closed with tension as she realized she and Tyler could have had a child this age by now. Quickly, she told herself to breathe and relax.

"I win!" declared the young boy.

Anna couldn't help but laugh at his triumphant grin. "What have you won?"

"The race. I reached you first so I win." He said it in a matter of fact way, as if she should understand what he meant. Anna had to smile, but didn't mention that no one else seemed to be in the race.

He jumped down and raced back toward his mother.

"Hello," Anna said as the other two drew nearer.

The older woman smiled and held out her hand. "You must be Anna. I'm Angela and this is my daughter Carol. The one running on adrenaline is my son Justin."

"I'm happy to meet all of you," Anna said pleasantly. She turned to Carol. "You're interested in riding lessons?"

The young girl shrugged in an offhand manner. "I

already know how to ride." She flipped her hair over her shoulder.

Angela touched her daughter's arm and said quietly, "Carol's been riding at a local stable for the last two summers. We bought her a horse last fall and she's begun to enter competition, but I think she should have some formal training. Mr. Stanton thought maybe you could help us."

"What do you think about that, Carol?" Anna wanted to gauge Carol's interest.

"I don't need lessons."

Anna looked at her and considered her. "Let me ask you this. What kind of competition are you entering?"

She shrugged. "Barrels, some games."

"How does your horse do in these competitions?"

"We haven't won anything, if that's what you mean."

Anna smiled at her. "No, what I mean is does she complete the course? Do you ever have problems getting her to listen?"

"She doesn't always do what I tell her," Carol admitted reluctantly.

"Hmm. Maybe your horse needs lessons. I'd be happy to evaluate her for a few days and then we can decide how to proceed."

"Do you have a horse?" Carol asked suddenly, and Anna noticed her staring across the pasture at the grazing horses.

"Of course." She pointed to the spot where Spirit grazed way up on the hill. "That gray mare up there is my horse."

"What has she won?"

"She's never been placed in competition," Anna said quietly. "It's a long story, but I don't compete anymore. Having said that, I do have several barrel racing championships to my credit. I have an idea. Let's go out to the pasture and bring my mare into the ring for a demonstration."

As they left the others in the barn area, Carol looked at her doubtfully. "Don't you want to bring some grain or something?"

"Well, with some horses I'd have to do that, but I've raised Spirit from a foal and I'm very familiar to her. She's never been harmed and there's no reason for her to run away. She likes our rides together."

Carol jogged beside her. "I have to bribe Lady to catch her. She does like our trail rides, though," she added hastily.

Anna shrugged. "Maybe her previous owner soured her in the ring. Training in the form of play time is something we can work on with her." Anna took the lead rope and halter from Carol's hands and draped it over her own shoulder. "Be careful not to wave this around or you could scare the horses. What I usually do is let the halter and lead rest on my shoulder until I'm right up close to the horse."

Anna stood by the gateway and called her horse, then whistled. Spirit lifted her head and then slowly made her way toward them. Carol followed her as she moved to meet Spirit. Anna spoke to the mare as she draped the lead line over the horse's neck and then snapped the halter in place. Turning, she gave Carol the lead line.

"There you go. You can take her into the barn." Anna felt the faint tremor in Carol's hands. "She's a pretty quiet mare," she said casually. "Let's get her saddled." They walked back to the barn and after a quick brush down led the mare to the arena. Once inside the ring Anna mounted, then sat still, conscious of several pairs of eyes watching her. She suffered from a momentary case of nerves, but then she settled down. If she acted nervous, Spirit would pick up on it and act accordingly.

"I'm going to warm my mare up with some walking, trotting and circles, then I'll give you a short demonstration on barrels. We have three barrels set up in the ring, and this will give you an idea of what to expect."

Anna concentrated on Spirit, pouring her energy into her mare's movements. After the warm up, she cantered down one side of the ring, sat deeply for a rollback on the haunches, and then sprinted back to her point of beginning. Standing still a moment, she waited for the dust to settle, then urged Spirit forward into the barrel course.

She clung to her mare around each tight turn, then looked ahead to the next barrel, until finally they raced toward the finish. When they stood still and she rubbed Spirit's withers, Anna swallowed several times as emotion choked her. Spirit had just given her one of her best rides ever, she knew it without having to look at a stop watch. After a moment, she looked up to speak to Carol, and was surprised to see others had come to stand around the perimeter of the ring. She scanned the faces. Tony, Danny, Gill Dakins, two stable workers and Tyler. The big grin on Tyler's face made her stomach do a flip-flop. He gave her the thumbs-up sign and slowly turned away, speaking to Gill.

Bemused, Anna looked at Carol, whose face had been transformed by an expression of awe. "I want to learn to ride like that," the teenager said as she climbed through the fence to stand at Spirit's shoulder. "Will you teach me?"

The sparkle in Carol's eyes created a thrill of excitement in Anna at the prospect of teaching again. "That's why you're here," she said. "We can begin any time."

"I can't wait to get started," Carol said, and Anna marveled at the change in her from when she'd arrived only a short time ago.

Ω

Several hours later Anna saddled a bay gelding by the name of Dealer for an exercise session. As she led the horse into the riding ring, she saw Tyler's truck pull into the parking area beside the barn. Anna latched the gate, watching Tyler exit the truck carrying a small cardboard box. He waved at her and strode in her direction. Running a hand down Dealer's satiny neck, Anna eyed the box curiously.

When Tyler stopped outside the paddock Anna heard a curious mewling sound and realized it came from the box. He tipped the box slightly so she could see the three kittens curled together inside, one gray and two striped orange balls of fur. As Dealer stretched his nose inquiringly toward the box, Anna exclaimed, "Where did you find them? They're so small."

"Somebody dumped them on the road. I figured they'd get hit if I didn't pick them up. The pet store in town really didn't want them since they've already got too many, so. . .." With a sheepish grin, he shrugged. "I thought they'd make good mousers in the barn when they're old enough."

"Mr. Stanton, where do you want the cat food?"

Astonished, Anna looked past Tyler as Mario appeared behind him carrying a bag of kitten chow.

"Mario, there's an old wooden crate in the tack room. Get a towel out of the rag box and line the crate, then put the kittens in there. The cat food can go in the feed bin for now."

Tyler handed the box over to Mario while Anna looked on. Tyler caught her expression of surprise and he grinned slightly. "Mario," he said, and the man turned back. "Meet Anna Barlow."

"Hi, Mario," she said, looking back and forth between them.

"Anna." Mario dipped his head and shifted the box to his right side. "I must take care of these kittens. Excuse me." He walked back to the barn.

Anna stared at Tyler, waiting for an explanation. All this time she'd thought he'd turned Mario away. "You introduced me as Anna," she said, instead of asking him why he'd changed his mind about Mario.

"Annie is my name for you," he said, one brow lifted. "I'm not sharing."

A shiver traveled across her shoulders. It was almost like he'd said he wasn't sharing her, she was all his. She had the strongest urge to throw her arms around Tyler and cover his face with kisses. Distracted, she blurted, "I thought you sent Mario away."

"It turns out Mario knows horses, which is why Sara sent him over. I gave him a ride into town and we got talking. I changed my mind." He shrugged it off as if it was nothing. "So how did the meeting with Angela and her daughter go?"

Anna smiled. "Actually it was Angela, Carol and her little brother Justin. I think it turned out to everyone's satisfaction. Carol's horse is being trucked over tomorrow morning. I'll let her settle in for a day or so and we'll take it from there."

"Good." He stared at her intently. "You had a great ride on Spirit today. Gill Dakins wanted to know if I thought you'd consider selling her."

Anna answered without hesitation. "Not in a million years. She's an incredible horse and he knows that." She laughed. "In the past, he's asked me countless times if I'd sell her and the answers always the same. That ride this morning was almost like. . .." She let her voice trail off, chewing her lip as uncertainty pulled at her. How did she describe the feeling of everything being in perfect attunement?

"Like old times?" he inserted softly.

Anna crossed her arms. "Maybe that's close, but even that seems inadequate. It was an incredible feeling. Spirit's mother was one of my top horses and she was only getting started in competition when I lost her." She would never forgive herself for the horses she'd lost, but it was done. "I'd rather discuss the future. Is Mario going to be working with Danny?"

"On and off. Tomorrow I plan to have him working on the grounds but I did catch Danny in the barn and introduced them."

"You probably know Danny isn't good with abrupt changes. It's best if you ease him into it."

Tyler raised a brow. "You worry too much about him."

Defensively, Anna said, "One thing I know about Danny, Tyler, is that he needs to feel safe."

"He's a man, Annie. He wouldn't appreciate your worry. Come on. . .I worked with him too, remember. You're not giving him enough credit. He can handle himself."

Anna sighed with uncertainty. "Maybe you're right. It's just that he's done so much for me, I don't want him shortchanged and I certainly don't want to lose him."

"That won't happen. He'll get along fine with Mario, just like he's done all right with the rest of the new crew."

Anna leaned forward and lowered her voice. "If Mario's staying around for a bit, maybe he'll be able to afford an apartment for his family and they'll all be together."

"Let's see how it goes."

"Admit it," she said softly, watching his face, "you're just an old softie."

Tyler shot her a quick look. "It was a business decision," he said, apparently unwilling to admit to any such thing.

"Oh, I see what you mean—and the cats were a business decision too. After all, if you'd had to buy cats to keep the mice population down, it would have cost you a lot more money. Now I understand."

He lifted a brow. "I've never been called soft in my life."

Tongue-in-cheek, Anna nodded. "First time for everything." A smile pulled at her lips as she acknowledged Tyler hadn't changed that much after all, he was still a man with a heart and she'd been shortsighted to think otherwise. "I was mad when I thought you'd turned Mario away. I was wrong to jump to conclusions."

"You do that a lot with me. Why?"

"I get impatient. I guess I want everything to be my idea of perfect."

Tyler's mouth curved. "Nothing's perfect, Annie."

Anna suddenly smiled and lifted a brow. "I can think of one morning that felt darned near perfect."

Tyler watched Annie's mouth move into a secret little smile and desire curled like a tight fist inside him. He thought of the morning they'd made love. He had the strongest need to enter the ring and kiss her until her eyes got serious and intent the way he knew they could. When she gave her attention to something, it was a singularly incredible experience and Tyler liked it when Annie focused on him.

However, knowing how things could get out of hand and mindful that he had a load of steers due at any time, he suppressed the urge and hung around a few minutes to watch her put Dealer through his paces. Despite being seven years old, the gelding was still relatively green so

Annie had been working with him on the basics; using leg aids and weight shifts to achieve smooth, tight turns as she walked and trotted the horse around barrels and poles. When the horse arrived, he'd videotaped Annie's first riding session with him. It was just a quirk of his, but he liked to have visible proof of their training successes in bringing horses along. He'd found in the past it was a valuable selling tool to show potential customers and they'd both agreed Dealer would be more suited as a pleasure horse than trained for any type of competition.

As they warmed up with more trotting and bending, Tyler's cell phone began to ring. He waved at her and moved away to answer the call. "Hello."

"Hi. This is Harris Stevens. I'd like to speak with Tyler Stanton."

"Speaking."

"Mr. Stanton, I read an article about the Double B in the Northeast Horse News and wanted to talk to you regarding two of my geldings. There's been a lot of talk about your place. The word around is you're one of the best."

"Thanks," Tyler said, turning to watch Annie in the ring. "Between myself and my trainers, we have quite a few years of experience."

"Well, I've got a coming four-year-old that was started last year, but his owner had to sell him. Long story short, I'm in the market for a trainer. I've seen some of the horses you've worked with out west but today was the first I'd heard you were in this area. I'm not familiar with the Double B's history. You mentioned other trainers?"

"I'm the man in charge, but I also have Anna Barlow working with me. Her specialty is barrels."

"I'd like to set up a meeting. My wife and I will arrive in New York tonight and we'll be staying for a few days. Do you think you can see us?"

Tyler quickly went over his schedule in his head. "I can meet with you tomorrow. Why don't we make it lunch? If that's agreeable I'll get back to you tonight with definite plans."

They agreed and ended the call. Tyler made a mental note to himself to make reservations in town for lunch tomorrow. The call from Harris was the fourth call he'd received in as many days from a possible client. Tyler re-hooked the phone on his belt and noted Annie had dismounted so he strode back to her.

"How's he feel?" he asked, opening the gate.

Annie's eyes sparkled and her skin glowed as she pulled a pink handkerchief from her back pocket and wiped it over her neck and cheeks. "Whew, it's warm. That was a good workout for both of us. He's willing and catches on fast." She stuffed the handkerchief back in her pocket. "Did you see him bend into those corners? I'm impressed with his progress. I'd like to take him on the trails tomorrow. What do you think, Tyler?"

Tyler liked seeing the joy in her face, her utter happiness in the moment. He kept getting glimpses of Annie the way she used to be, the girl he'd loved since he was sixteen. His thoughts drifted back to that time, and he swallowed hard. "You're the one riding him. I'll go along with your judgment."

Her initial surprise quickly changed to satisfaction. "Okay, good. I'm going to work with him a little longer."

Tyler put out a hand and caught the gelding's reins. "Annie, just thought I'd let you know we've picked up two clients this week for training, and there's the possibility of two more."

"Tyler, that's fantastic. I knew things would snowball once the word got out." She looked beyond him and shaded her eyes with one hand. "It looks like a stock trailer's coming up the drive."

He shot a quick glance over his shoulder. "Yeah, which means I probably won't see you until later." He reached over and cupped her shoulder. No longer wanting to hold back, he leaned forward and kissed her, leisurely tracing her lips, feeling her sudden, indrawn breath. He smiled against her mouth and pulled back just a fraction, enough so he could look down into her startled eyes. "Sorry, I've been wanting to do that for the last hour," he murmured. "Knowing it might break our agreement I think we should renegotiate the terms."

Her deep brown eyes got a soft look, but then she laughed out loud. "We'll just call it a minor lapse. Otherwise, I must applaud your self-control. . .and mine."

With the rattle of the stock trailer in his ears, Tyler moved to drop another kiss on her pertinent mouth. She looped her arm around his neck and he decided he definitely liked the feel of her fingers rifling through his hair. She placed a kiss square on his mouth, then her tongue darted out and swiped across his bottom lip. "There, now we're both even as far as minor lapses go," she said, softly mocking.

Tyler wanted more than that little flick of her tongue, but he contented himself with smoothing his palms down the side of her arms.

"I'm setting up a business lunch with a client tomorrow. Do you think you'll be available?"

Her eyes darkened and she suddenly looked very serious and remote. "Lunch?" She bit her lip. "I'll have to let you know."

"We can talk tonight. I have to go and unload those steers. Hopefully they're not as ornery as the last bunch. God knows it'll be hell chasing them in this heat."

Anna shivered. "Keep Tony out of the pen. He was almost gored when that steer broke from the herd last week." She turned and led the horse into the barn.

Tyler watched the gentle swing of her hips beneath faded denim jeans. He loved her unexpected moments of humor and the way she rose to a challenge. There wasn't another woman who'd ever tempted him to unpeel the layers. . .or another woman who made his heart beat so hard in anticipation of being with her. Annie sometimes hid behind an air of reserve, moody one moment, and vulnerable in the next. What worried him was the way she kept herself hidden on this ranch. He wondered if she'd ever be able to overcome her self-consciousness and enjoy the life she'd once embraced so ardently.

Ω

Danny watched Miz Anna ride the bay gelding out in the corral, and his mood settled a bit. He had a funny, anxious feeling in his stomach, kind of like when he was younger and the kids in school laughed at what they said were his strange ways. He liked watching Miz Anna ride. She had such a way about her that she seemed to be part of the horse. He smiled when the bay tried to pull her into a corner but she firmly urged him into finishing his circle.

Danny turned in his squatting position beside the door and stared back into the barn at the new guy, Mario, cleaning the stalls. Danny hunched his shoulders and pressed up against the wood. He looked outside but didn't see Miz Anna anymore. There was a lot of new people at the ranch now that Tyler was in charge. Danny wasn't sure how he felt about that. Most days he didn't like it. He liked to take care of stuff all by himself and there just seemed to be too many people around.

Today Tyler brought Mario up to him and said he was new and could Danny show him the barn. So Danny did what Tyler asked, but all the time he wondered if he was gonna get fired and Mario was going to do his job.

Mario knew his way around a barn, Danny could see that right off. It made him think of other people who had worked at the ranch. Some of them liked it here, the isolation, and some of them worked only for the summer and left. He could never figure out why they wanted to leave.

Tyler kept wanting to know about the bad time. When Mr. Martin died and the police were all over, Danny remembered hiding in the hay loft. It had felt safe that way, but he felt scared thinking about that now. He trusted Miz Anna, but if she wasn't the boss, he could get fired and he didn't have nowhere else to go. Mama always said just do a good job and nothing bad would happen, but Danny knew that wasn't true.

Sometimes bad things did happen and you couldn't tell anybody. Danny pushed his palms against the pain in his stomach, and that's when he noticed the pitchfork leaning against the wall behind him. He reached out and gripped the wooden handle, holding it so hard he felt a wood splinter dig into his palm. He came to his feet, still gripping the pitchfork. Mario had finished the first horse stall and was pulling the wheelbarrow out, his back to Danny.

Danny walked toward him, the pitchfork gripped tightly in his hand. The sweat rolled off his forehead and down the sides of his cheeks. He wiped at it with his sleeve, keeping his glance on Mario. Mario didn't turn around, but reached forward to close the stall door. Danny came right up behind him and raised the pitchfork.

"I'm through with my chores," Danny said abruptly.

Mario turned.

"I can help you finish." Danny added, then swallowed hard, ashamed that his hands were shaking.

"Thanks," Mario said. "It's Danny, isn't it? I'm glad

you're here. Tyler had told me to ask you what I should do next."

On familiar ground, the remainder of the tension eased inside Danny. "Don't worry, I can show you what needs to be done when we finish here."

Ω

Evening arrived softly, darkening the sky to a dusky orange, the clouds glowing as they held the last bit of light. For Anna, the quiet surrounding her and Tyler was in sharp contrast to the hectic day they'd passed. After a quick dinner of hamburgers and fries which she'd elected to cook, they'd walked to the barn for a last check on the grounds for the night.

As they turned back toward the house, Anna couldn't help but feel the companionship they'd shared all week had a somewhat unreal quality about it, leaving her swinging between varying degrees of hope and tense anticipation. Charting a new course could be frightening, especially when she acknowledged she'd been a bystander in her own life the last two years. That was changing. She was taking charge and she liked the newly emerging Anna.

Tyler clasped her hand. She traced the calluses on his broad palm with the pad of her thumb, recalling that morning they'd made love on the hillside and the feel of those rough hands so gentle on her skin. She squeezed his hand tightly, overcome by an excess of emotion. She wanted to make love with him again. She almost felt starved for his touch.

"Look Tyler." She pointed to the old swing beside the path. "Remember how you'd push me on that swing?" She left his side and sat down on the weathered wooden seat, her back to him as she gripped the chains. "After the fire, I spent countless hours on this swing, feeling sorry for myself. I'd just sit here some nights and stare at the moon."

She lifted her head to look at the stars. "Danny knew. He used to wait for me to go up to the house."

"Did he sit with you?"

Anna smiled. "No. The first couple times I caught him waiting I told him to go away, but he'd just wait in the shadows. I wasn't supposed to know he was out there, but we both knew the other knew."

Tyler gave her a gentle push. Keeping her eyes closed, Anna pumped her legs back and forth as she gathered momentum. Leaning back against the force of gravity, she relaxed her shoulders and dropped her head until her hair streamed out behind her. She could see Tyler standing just beyond the swing's arc.

She laughed. "It's glorious slicing through the air." Tyler stood so still behind her, and Anna trailed her toes in the grass, slowing her momentum.

"Annie." Tyler's hands, firm and sure, cupped her waist, bringing her to a total standstill. She closed her eyes as a shiver of reaction coursed through her. His touch had such power to move her, make her forget about anything else. She clenched her jaw at the pleasure of it, her body reacting to the slide of his hands up her ribs, across her shoulders, where they massaged a moment and then slid down the outside of her arms.

She grew tense with anticipation, wanting him to continue. This was no game they played. All week, the stakes had risen. Anna knew that soon, the stakes would be so high that neither one of them would step back, and then they'd make love again. It was a natural outcome, action and reaction, not merely hormones or a result of the moonlight. When she and Tyler made love, it would be because they knew and respected each other's skills and opinions. She cared very deeply about him and she wanted to demonstrate that feeling to him.

Tyler's hands hovered at her waist, then clasped her lightly as he pulled her back against him, the swing tipping forward. She tilted her head back and looked at him upside down. He bent forward and his mouth covered hers. It wasn't enough. Pulling away, Anna stood and stepped around the swing, right into his arms. She latched her arms around his waist, relishing the strength in him as he pulled her hard into him, loving the taste of his lips on hers. She thought hazily, how easy it would be to become addicted to his touch, to crave it every day. Each time they kissed, the same heated feeling washed over her. She wanted to push the world and her concerns back and just concentrate on him.

She took his face in her hands, gently running her fingernails over his stubbled chin. Tyler was a complex man. Despite a troubled childhood, he'd turned out to be an honorable, successful businessman. She thought of her insider's view of him all week. He competently directed crews of workers, took the time to rescue abandoned kittens and hired a man who was down on his luck. All these impressions of Tyler swam in her head as she wound her arms around his neck.

Tyler now held her in a vulnerable position, physically and emotionally, but from all indications he was in no hurry to take advantage. Part of her appreciated his consideration, but Anna decided that tonight she would take the initiative. She intended to propel their relationship forward to the next level.

Tyler cupped her shoulders with his hands and she felt their fine tremor. "You know this isn't enough," he said.

She nodded in agreement, wetting her lips. "I want more," she said, hardly recognizing the rawness of her voice. She gave a short laugh. "I don't want to wait one-hundred and eighty days."

She lifted up on her toes, bringing her weight against him, aware of the corded muscles in his arms as he held her close. His head dipped and she felt the warm brush of his breath on her cheek. Emotion pooled inside and she clung to him, her body trembling, undeniably excited by his strength, his closeness. With exploring hands, she traced the muscles along his back, letting her hands roam freely up to his neck. She held herself tightly, tensely against him, and felt an answering tension within him that told her he was as affected as she was.

Anna let out a faint gasp of wonder when his mouth dipped into her neck, trailing a sensory path along her shoulder. His breath was hot through her T-shirt as he moved lower, his mouth lingering, and she felt caught up in a sensual haze of need.

"Let's go back to the house," he said hoarsely.

"I'll be disappointed if it's just to say goodnight and go our separate ways," she said boldly, leaning back to stare into his eyes.

His hands pressed into her hips. "I'd hate to ever disappoint you."

Anna gripped his fingers as they walked toward the house. Never had she remembered the path being so long. She felt impatient and had the notion to tug him along so they could run.

Tyler pulled on her hand as the house came in sight and she spun lightly on the balls of her feet. He dropped a kiss on her mouth, and then another. Anna felt certain she'd burn up if she didn't have Tyler. At the edge of the lawn, she laughed and then half-ran, half-jogged across the grass, her feet so light she swore she was flying. Tyler raced beside her and they climbed the stairs to the verandah like a couple of kids, their feet thumping noisily across the wooden deck. Her hand touched the door handle first and she pulled open the outer storm door, but before she could open the main door, he sandwiched her between him and the wood. Laughing, breathless, she looked up at him in the glow thrown by the porch light, seeing the happiness on his face. For a moment, the world seemed very still, and Anna realized that the utter happiness she saw in his eyes scared her. If she messed up, that emotion could be turned around and extinguished in less than a blink of an eye. Thinking of her own responsibility in the actions she was about to take, sobered her quickly.

"Let's go inside," he murmured.

Watching his eyes, his mouth, the longing intensified. She cared so much about him. "Yes."

Tyler nuzzled her cheek and the hair rose on her neck and arms. Shuddering, her lids fluttered closed as he wound one hand into her hair, moving it ever so gently to her neck, down her shoulders, his touch light as it wove a sensual spell around her. His scent, leather and the subtle fresh scent of cologne, seduced her with its familiarity. One large palm settled flat and warm between her shoulder blades. His other hand cupped the base of her skull as he drew her slowly, ever so slowly, closer, pulled her up on tiptoes to meet his mouth; roughly, sweetly, deliciously.

"Last opportunity to run for safety," he muttered.

With a shiver Anna fumbled for the doorknob and the door opened behind her. She gave a gurgle of laughter but Tyler kept her close so she didn't fall backwards. His strength delighted her. It had been so long since a man had held her with such care.

Overloading on sensory stimulation, Anna welcomed the heat of lips hard and soft. She squirmed against him. His mouth on her cheeks and neck fanned a curl of fire to a hungry ache, clenching her stomach muscles into a painful knot. Vulnerable to his touch, unable to help herself, Anna squeezed her arms tightly around him, feeling as if she had been starved. Craving more, she wanted the ultimate union.

His hands were under her shirt, touching the sensitive skin of her stomach, the callused palms gentle and sure, remembering her pleasure points. Passion consumed her.

Anna was aware of harsh breathing but had no idea if it was his or her own. She allowed her entire being to become flooded with Tyler, his scent, his touch, the feel of him. . . rational thought clouded and faded away.

Somehow they had reached the second floor. Tyler's bedroom door stood open. She hadn't been inside the room since he'd moved in. She barely had time to notice the deep gray carpeting underfoot before they reached the bed. She twined her arms around his neck as she followed him down to the wide bed with its quilted top.

"Annie." His voice had turned low and husky. There was a flush high on his cheekbones and his eyes met hers levelly. She lifted her shirt and pulled it over her head.

For a moment, her hair fell all around her face, and before she could push it out of the way, Tyler's hand was there. He had discarded his shirt also, and she looked at his chest, the clearly defined ridge of muscle along his ribs, the deep breaths she could see he was taking. His uncontrolled breathing told her she was not alone in this feeling of excitement. She reached out a hand and boldly traced his ribs, then the firm muscles along his chest, the rigid bone of his collar. She felt such joy in touching him. His fingers traced the lacy edge of her brassiere, then found the hook and soon it was gone, leaving her naked from the waist up. Together they shucked their jeans.

Sitting on the edge of the bed, Tyler took her foot in his hands, spread his fingers up her ankle and pulled off her cotton sock, the pads of his fingers lightly scraping her instep. For the second foot, he did the same, then he cupped her ankle and brought it to his mouth, his gaze holding hers as he pressed a kiss on the inside of each ankle. His palms moved up her legs and Anna clenched her teeth, trying to hold back a ragged groan. The air left her in a whoosh as his hands cupped her hips, lifted her up from the bed and pulled down her wispy briefs, tossing them to the floor. He moved to stand beside the bed. Anna leaned forward, hooked her finger in the wide band of his boxer shorts and pulled the corner down off his slim hips.

Driven by an uncontrollable eruption of emotion, she was almost unable to absorb all the sensations. Now, as Tyler stood before her she wondered again for a vulnerable moment what this handsome, talented man saw in her.

Tyler placed his knee on the bed and came down to her level. The slide of his body along hers was an unbelievable pleasure. They fit so well, lying side by side. Marveling, she reached a hand out to bury it in the rich darkness of his hair, running her fingers along the back of his head where the hair was short. His neck was strong, yet she could feel the tremble in him as she delicately traced the whorls of chest hair and felt wonder at her affect on this man.

She leaned down to taste his skin, then absorbed his shuddering reaction.

Anna brought her breasts to Tyler's chest, enjoying the soft hair her sensitive skin encountered. He hauled her closer yet, so there was no doubt in her mind as to his desire as his leg captured hers.

Tyler rolled on top of her and reached over to the bedside table. She heard the drawer open, saw the condom packet in his fingers. Tyler pulled her back to him and she wound her legs around him, enjoying the hardness of his body while his lips and teeth branded her.

Anna covered his big hands with her own and looked into his eyes, and he made a low, guttural sound in his throat as, in perfect attunement, they came together. Sensation rocketed to her toes and up her body to the back of her ears. She held Tyler tightly and she knew in an instant of blinding truth that she had truly and absolutely fallen in love with this man once again and there was no going back.

Ω

Tyler pushed the tumble of reddish-brown hair from Annie's forehead, trying to find his way back through the lingering aftershocks from their lovemaking. Annie moved against him with a soft sigh and he stroked the long curve of her back, untangling the thoughts inside his head. The desire that had been riding him hard all week was only momentarily appeased, he could already feel himself wanting more. Was this only a physical release? No, he rejected that idea. They had discarded the past and had to look ahead.

He looked down at her face as her head rested against his chest, her eyes green and very serious. He cupped her jaw and she kissed him, and Tyler wondered about the years they'd missed together. He had to ask her, but he also knew the cold facts might dispel the euphoria. "I need you to tell me what happened that day."

At her puzzled look, he said, "That last day Martin caught us in the cottage. The sheriff deputies took me into town where my dad was being questioned. What happened after I left you and Martin?"

Looking troubled, Annie rubbed her hands up and down her arms. "What does it matter, Tyler?"

"I don't know. I have this feeling there's a key element I'm missing. Why did Martin come looking for us in the cottage? I was supposed to be away. How did he even know we were there?"

With a sigh, Annie sat up, pulling the sheet around her as she left the bed and sat on the rug. She rubbed her fingers over her forehead. "It was so long ago. . . I don't know. I returned early and found you in the barn. You'd had two flat tires on the truck and it had to be towed to town. You hitched a ride back to the ranch."

"So how did he know we were there?" Tyler rubbed his forehead. "Someone saw us." Tyler thought about that night when Martin opened the door so forcefully, heard again the sound of the dishes shattering on the floor. He'd deliberately put that night out of his thoughts for so long it felt almost like he'd watched it in a movie. He snapped his fingers. "Danny. Do you remember Martin said Danny told him he'd find us there but he didn't believe him."

She looked at him doubtfully. "I don't recall seeing Danny that night."

"He must have seen us." Tyler leaned forward. "Even back then he was always protective of you. He might have said something to Martin or told him where we were."

"Danny wouldn't try to cause trouble."

"It doesn't matter. Once Martin knew we were together, he probably saw red."

"What's the difference?" she cried. "Danny had nothing to do with what happened afterward."

"I'm not so sure. Tell me about that night," he said again.

Annie dipped her head. "When the deputies came in behind Martin and escorted you away, I was devastated and scared. Martin told me I could have my pick of any man. We argued and I turned to leave. I started to tell him I didn't care about other men, but there was such a frightened look on his face that I didn't get the words out. He stumbled forward and I tried to catch him, but he was heavy and we fell to the floor."

Tyler dropped to the rug beside Annie. "Why did you stay with him?" he asked hoarsely. "When you had the choice, why did you choose him?" Her rejection had haunted him for six years. After the initial disbelief, he'd been angry, hurt, disillusioned.

Annie lifted eyes brimming with moisture. "I couldn't leave him. He had been diagnosed that week with brain cancer. It wasn't my secret to tell. I thought we had time, that I would be able to explain to you—"

Tyler stood. "Dammit Annie! You should have trusted me."

She poked him in the chest. "Where was your trust?" She swung away from him, the sheet slipping off one shoulder. "But it doesn't matter now, does it? Maybe if Martin hadn't been sick, I still wouldn't have been able to leave. I felt dependent on him." She gave him an angry glare. "I was nineteen and I should have stood on my feet as you'd told me many times, but I didn't. I let him take care of me. When it came down to the crunch, I was scared. I didn't want to go back to the way it was when my mother died and I was in one foster place after another. I needed Martin's influence, the wall he put around me to keep me safe."

"Annie."

"You're a man, Tyler. You're the type that will always fend for yourself. When my mother died they put me in foster care. They didn't keep me very long and I was moved around. Some of those homes. . ." she let her voice trail off and he wanted to reach out to her, but she'd pulled away from him, emotionally, physically. "I didn't know I had anyone else. I was just a timid kid when Martin brought me here. I was glad to find someone who understood me the way I thought you did. I didn't feel so frightened. Those last weeks when our relationship changed from an easy friendship, it was so new, I didn't know where it was going. Everything happened so fast that night." She turned back to him. "But I never abandoned you, I never ran you and Grant out of town. How could you think I would do that?"

"I was running on fury. You choose Martin, then Dad and I were held in the lockup for a week and a half and then railroaded out of town. We heard Martin had died and the investigation went nowhere. At the bus station they made sure we left. It's a long ride from the east coast to the west. I had a lot of time to think about what they did to us. If it wasn't for my dad, I'd have stayed put. But he looked shattered. He wouldn't even talk about it for weeks afterward. That night they took me in you never showed up, what else would I think but that you'd told the sheriff to take care of us?"

"Tyler, after the funeral, legal fees and the mess of paying back the money for that breeding, I tried to get my head straight. The sheriff told me to wait a few more days. They were still trying to unravel what had happened. I demanded that you and Grant be released but I could see he was humoring me. When I went with my lawyer early the next morning, the sheriff wasn't there and they told me you'd already left, without a word or even a note."

"They hustled us to the bus station the night before." He looked at her. "I didn't know you'd come."

"And you never asked." The sadness in her voice ripped him in two because it was the truth. He hadn't asked. "So in a way we're both responsible for what happened," she said. "You let pride and temper get in the way and I didn't have the confidence to stand up to Martin. Neither one of us gets off scot-free." She lifted her chin. "Who should we blame? Where does this leave us now?"

"Nothing has changed."

"I'm not so sure. I understand your need to know the truth, but if we peck away at each other, we'll kill any chance at building a relationship on trust. We have to pull together on this."

"And we will—I will." He reached out to cup her shoulder, then pulled her against him, needing to believe they'd both acted with the best intentions.

Annie pressed against him and he wrapped his arms around her.

"It's such a mess," she said. "If it was a cover up, how can we ever straighten it out?"

"Someone knows the truth."

Anna rested her head back against Tyler's chest, and suddenly noticed the picture on his dresser. She disengaged herself from his arms and moved closer. "Where did you get that picture of me?" Feeling vulnerable, she held the sheet defensively against her breasts. How had she missed seeing a framed, close-up picture of her own face? "It's one you took down by the barn that day." She swung around to face him.

Tyler reached for his jeans and pulled them up his legs. Walking to the dresser, he lifted the framed picture to stare at it. Anna ached inside, not wanting to argue, but instead wanting to move up behind him and press against his muscled back.

He faced her. "I love this picture. It's captured the Annie I used to know."

Anna didn't want to look at it. A quick glance had been enough. It reminded her of the havoc that had been wreaked on her life, the mess that was her face in the bright sunlight. "I want you to take it out of the frame or I'll tear it out myself."

"Annie, be reasonable."

"Take it out. The light is so bright, that's all you can see."

"It's your blind spot—it's all you see," he said in a hard voice, nothing like the lover of a short while ago. "Just like you can't see that Martin or Danny may be responsible for where we are now."

Anna wanted to cry out that it wasn't fair, and that he'd never understand, but she stood quickly and hurried from the room. She clutched the sheet as she made her way down the hallway and then the stairs.

When she reached the foyer, she felt a hand on her shoulder and was pulled to an abrupt halt.

"Annie!"

She spun around. "My name is Anna."

"What the hell is going on?"

She looked at him incredulously. "We've just made love, the most wonderful, tender experience and now it's all ruined."

"Why?" he demanded. "Because of a picture—because of reality?" He shoved the picture in front of her face. "This picture shows a woman happy and healthy and alive. If you want to destroy it, if you think that'll make you feel better, I'll give it to you, but I need you to take a good look at it."

Anna didn't want to. Seeing that close up picture of her own face after they'd made such sweet love would bring back all her uncertainties. She shivered in the hall and hunched her shoulders. How could he possibly look at that and not remember how she used to be?

"Annie."

Reluctantly she looked at the picture, drawing in deep breaths, willing the tenseness and anger to slowly melt away. Tyler had caught her mostly from the unblemished side of her face. She wore a half smile and Spirit's head was just over her shoulder. With a deeply drawn breath, Anna realized the picture was reminiscent of numerous publicity shots taken before the fire. It was her face, her smile, with only a shadowy hint of the scarring and the slight pull at the corner of her mouth. Nevertheless, she was still caught up in a certain hopelessness. "I can't compete with the way I used to look."

Tyler's brows came together. "Who asked you to?"

"I can't help it. I remember what I used to look like. Now that picture shows parts of how I am today, the scarred part of my face."

Tyler let out an impatient breath. "Annie, this is the real you. The scarring has nothing to do with who you are. It's only on the outside, another facet of the whole you." He put his hand out. "This is how I see you. If I'd taken a picture of you full frontal view there would still be the same eyes, the same wistful expression on your face. The same person I care about. How can I make you understand the rest doesn't matter?"

The sincerity in his eyes made her feel like a fool. "Oh God." Her attempt at a laugh was pathetic. In reality, she wanted to cry over what this man was saying. His tender, kind words touched her deeply. "I'm reacting to my own insecurities."

She had to get out before she gave way to the pressure inside and started bawling like a baby.

"So were you exaggerating when you said it was the most wonderful, tender experience?"

Anna froze with her hand on the door handle, then slowly turned and looked into those deadly serious blue eyes. She took a shaky breath. "It was more than that."

"How much more?"

Carefully, she said, "If I haven't blown all my chances with my insecurities, I'd like to think there'll be more wonderful, tender, mind-blowing experiences."

Tyler pulled her to him, his knuckles against her breasts as he gripped the sheet. Anna unclenched her hands as Tyler cupped her hips and urged her closer, his jeans brushing against the linen.

Heart racing, she laced her fingers through his. "These scars have played a big part in my life, it's hard to believe there's someone who doesn't shy away from that part of me."

"Sara isn't bothered by your scarring, why think I'm less supportive than she is?"

Anna suddenly realized how unfair she'd been to him. "But I'm not involved with her. Our relationship is moving everything to a deeper, more sensitive level."

Tyler placed his warm palms on each side of her cheeks and his fingertips traced circles on the sensitive skin at the back of her neck.

Anna pressed her mouth to his and wound her arms around Tyler as he backed her up against the wall.

❧ Chapter Nine ❧

LATE THE FOLLOWING MORNING Anna stared into the mirror, then met Sara's glance as her friend stood behind her. "What do you think?" she asked, moving her face closer to the glass. Carefully, she used a fingertip to gently smooth the special makeup over her cheek.

"Perfect. The scarring is concealed and the makeup is light enough it looks very natural." Sara stepped back. "More to the point, how do you feel about this business luncheon today?"

Anna twisted around once more to look in the mirror, then faced Sara with a tentative smile. "Okay. . .I think." She grimaced. "I finally told Tyler I'd go, but I've tried not to think about it, which hasn't been hard, given my schedule the last few days. Carol, the girl I'm going to be giving lessons, will be starting in a few days. Her horse arrived first thing this morning and I've been getting her settled in, then some of the cows broke through the new fence and we had to round them up. To top that off one of the new stable hands got his finger jammed in a stall door and I ran back up here to get ice." She blew a wisp of hair out of her eyes. "Tyler's having an open house soon, and he asked me to consider doing a riding demo. So you can guess right now I'm running on adrenalin."

Sara smiled and stood back. "Well, sounds to me like you're having one hell of a time—you're absolutely glowing." She lifted a brow. "Being around Tyler definitely agrees with you."

Anna looked at her in surprise and then burst out laughing. "You're right, you know. I've never felt so alive, so—so—"

"Needed?" Sara supplied.

"Yes. I haven't felt this needed in a long time. I'm loving this. For the first time in two years I don't have the ranch weighing me down. I have money for the taxes and if something needs fixing, I know Tyler's crew will take care of it."

"He's seems to rely on you quite a bit," Sara remarked, smoothing the material along her shoulder. "From what you've said you're working with his horses, helping clients a bit here and there."

"It's amazing the way everything is working out," Anna said.

"And look at you."

Anna twirled on her high heels, feeling giddy as she almost lost her balance and laughed aloud when Sara steadied her. "I guess I'm more at home in a pair of riding boots than heels, but I'm ready!" she exclaimed, reaching forward to hug her friend. "Sara, thanks for making this possible. I couldn't have pulled off this shopping thing without you."

"That's where you're wrong," Sara said dismissively. "I only took you around town, the rest was up to you. You're like a whirlwind when you get going."

Anna gave her friend a quick hug. "You must have

released all that repressed shopping energy. I haven't shopped in years."

"Well, it's worth it. You look great and this emerald two-piece looks better on you than it ever did on that store dummy." She plucked at the narrow waistline. "Fits like a glove in all the right places. Sexy but business-like."

"Uh-huh."

"Honestly." Sara looked at her watch. "I have to get back, it's getting late. Listen, give me a call tonight to let me know how things went." She lifted a brow. "And tell Tyler I said hello, will you?"

There was a knock on the door and Anna turned from the hallway mirror to see Tyler standing outside. "Tell him yourself," she said over her shoulder. "Come in!" she called.

Tyler stepped inside. "Ready?" he asked, stopping just inside the threshold.

Anna moved toward him, wondering what he would think of her suit and her temporary new look. She felt very feminine. "What do you think?" she asked anxiously, stopping in front of him and holding her arms out.

"You're beautiful," he said, his voice husky. His blue eyes sent an electric current straight to her heart.

"Tyler—" she began, then stopped, deciding to take him at his word. "Thank you," she murmured softly, looking down at her dress.

"Well, I'm outta here," Sara said cheerfully. "Nothing like being odd man out. Have fun, you two."

"Wait Sara," Tyler said. He walked over to her. "I wanted to thank you for sending Mario around."

Sara looked pleased. "When I found out he's worked with horses his entire life, I thought of you. I'm glad to hear it's working out, but now I have to go." Sara threw Anna a kiss and closed the door behind her.

Anna looked up at Tyler in his dark pressed slacks

and suit jacket. "You look very nice yourself," she said breathlessly. He looked incredibly handsome. She touched her skirt. "I hope this is okay."

"Perfect." He touched her wrist and Anna turned her hand and gripped his fingers. "Don't be nervous, you'll be great."

"I'm not nervous," she said defensively, clenching her empty hand in the hope it would stop shaking.

Tyler dropped a slow, hot kiss on her mouth. Anna followed him with a murmur of protest when he pulled back.

"If you're ready, we'll leave," he said softly. "Unless you want me to cancel lunch."

Anna looked at him quickly. All she had to do was say the word and they could go into her room.

She groaned aloud. "Let's go before all this getting ready is a waste of time."

As they walked out of the guesthouse and toward the driveway where his car was parked, Anna held Tyler's hand tightly. "Just be yourself, Annie." He opened her door. When she was settled in the car he leaned down and kissed her. "You'll do fine. This meeting is not a live-or-die situation."

The words helped to put a bit of perspective on the luncheon. "Now you've smudged my lipstick," she complained. "I'll have to reapply it."

He merely grinned and went around to the driver's side.

When he was settled in the car Anna motioned him closer. "Since it's already smudged, you might as well kiss me properly before I reapply it."

"Always glad to help a lady in need," he murmured, his strong arms enfolding her.

Ω

The restaurant Tyler had chosen was the same one they'd eaten at once before. Anna hesitated just a moment, and then entered the imposing entrance. Realizing she held Tyler's arm in a death grip and had probably creased his jacket sleeve, she released him.

A tall, dark-haired man approached them in the foyer. "Tyler Stanton?" he asked.

Tyler reached out a hand to the man who appeared to be in his early thirties. "Yes, and you must be Harris. Call me Tyler please, and this is Anna Barlow." Tyler looked behind him. "Did you bring your wife?"

The other man nodded. "Of course. She's waiting at our table."

"Let's go sit down, then." Tyler indicated she should precede him so she followed Harris into the nearly full dining room. Anna saw Martin, the headwaiter she'd met on her previous visit.

"Hello, Ms. Barlow, nice to see you again," he said with a smile.

Anna returned his greeting, hardly able to believe she was pulling this off. She suddenly felt so free, suffering from barely any self-consciousness.

They moved from the main dining room to the outside balcony. Anna looked with surprise at Tyler and when his eyes met hers, she knew instinctively he had deliberately chosen the balcony, which afforded more privacy. Harris stopped beside the same table where she and Tyler had sat the last time, and she saw a woman was already seated there.

Harris bent over the woman and lifted her hand from the table. Petite in stature with jet black hair and big brown eyes, the woman radiated beauty, yet there was a definite sulk to her mouth which took away from her looks.

"Regina," Harris said, "this is Tyler Stanton and Anna

Barlow." He pulled a chair out from beside the table. "This is my wife Regina." Anna wondered at the intent glance he gave his wife. Regina, however, did not glance at her husband. Her smile seemed a bit strained, but she said hello pleasantly enough as they all moved to take seats. Anna sat on Regina's left, and that's when she noticed her chair was a wheelchair. Her startled gaze met the other woman's and at that moment Regina's hand knocked against her wine glass, toppling it over.

In a flurry of activity, a waiter removed the shattered glass, another replaced the wet tablecloth and a third appeared with new utensils and glasses. Regina sat miserably silent and suddenly Anna felt her own heart pounding in her throat.

Feeling paralyzed, Anna stared at Tyler, then at Harris, whose attention was centered on his wife. She swallowed several times, ran her tongue over her dry lips, painfully conscious of Regina's obvious distress. Although Regina's lips remained tightly closed, she looked on the verge of tears.

Impulsively, Anna leaned forward and covered Regina's clenched fists where they rested in her lap. "I'm glad to see I'm not the only one who knocks things over," she said lightly. Slowly, the other woman looked up and Anna saw the sheen of moisture in Regina's brown eyes.

"My dress will probably be ruined!" she blurted.

"Would you like to go to the ladies room? Perhaps they have something to take the stains out."

"I can help you, darling," Harris said quickly, rising to his feet.

"You two can talk business," Anna said to the men. "I'd be happy to help you, Regina." She moved to stand beside Regina. "That is, if you want my help."

The other woman looked disconcerted by the offer, but then suddenly she nodded. "Yes, I would appreciate your help, Anna." She looked up at her husband. "I'll be fine. We'll clean this up as best we can."

Anna tucked her purse under her arm and wheeled Regina through the main dining room and then to the ladies room. She smiled at several people she recognized, but did not stop. Opening the door to the ladies room, she pushed Regina's chair inside.

"I'll bet they have something in this basket for stains." She sorted through an assortment of items located on the outer room's counter. "Here's a stain stick. Let's put this on and see what happens." Regina remained silent while Anna rubbed at the wine spots near the hem of the long skirt. "Luckily, you only got hit by splatters."

"I appreciate your help, Anna." The sulk had returned to Regina's mouth. "I never used to be clumsy. Not until I was in this thing," she confessed, slapping the arm of the wheelchair. "I hate it—hate it!" she said passionately, then put her hands to her cheeks. "Forgive me, you don't want to hear this."

"Sometimes strangers are the best sounding boards." Anna hesitated a moment, then she pressed on, her words deliberate. "When I was in the hospital two years ago, if it hadn't been for the kindness of strangers, I'd have gone stir crazy." She straightened. "That seems to have taken care of most of the stains. You might want to soak it when you get home."

Regina didn't even look down at the material. "Why were you in the hospital?"

"I was badly burned."

Regina looked at her with bewilderment. "You were lucky. I see no scarring."

"My hands were burned, but they healed remarkably well. Luckily for me, it never affected my riding." Hesitating only for a moment, Anna turned toward the sink. Pulling a paper towel from the dispenser, she ran it under warm water, then slowly wiped the camouflage makeup from her cheek. She turned to face Regina.

The other woman's eyes widened as she looked at the scarring. "Oh Anna, I had no idea. That must have hurt terribly and here I am complaining of this wheelchair."

Anna smiled. "I think we're both allowed some whining. I did it for two years, but I'm finally taking my life back."

Regina's eyes held an incredible sadness. "My horse fell with me six months ago. The doctors don't know if I'll ever walk. Some days I can't stand to be alive. I'm afraid I'll lose Harris, but I can't bear to have him touch me," she ended in a tortured whisper. "I'm not the same woman he married."

"Did he tell you that?"

"No, of course not. He's been understanding, putting up with my rotten moods. I used to be so full of life, but now I feel as if all the life has been sucked out of me. My Harris swears he still loves me."

"Maybe you should believe him."

Regina regarded her uncertainly.

"I care a great deal about Tyler," Anna confessed, "but because of my scarring, I didn't think any man could really care for me in turn. What makes it doubly hard is that he's so—so—"

"Good looking?" Regina supplied.

"Yes. But what I discovered is, a good man doesn't care what you look like or how well your legs work." Anna shook her head, and could feel the silly grin splitting her face. She felt like she'd just learned a momentous truth. "I sound like a Sunday school lesson, but I saw the way Harris looked at you. That man loves you. Don't push him away because of your own fears."

Regina clasped her hands together. "I can't believe I've been so selfish," she wailed.

"Regina."

Anna looked up and saw Harris standing in the doorway.

"Are you okay?" he asked with obvious concern.

Regina smiled radiantly at her husband and Harris returned her smile, but Anna could see he was clearly puzzled by her transition from tears to smiles.

"Harris, I'm fine," Regina called out. "We'll be along in a minute."

After Anna reapplied her makeup, she and Regina returned to their table, Tyler lifted a brow in surprise as she took her seat. Anna placed her napkin in her lap and calmly met his gaze. "I'm ready to order."

Regina nodded vigorously as she threw an all-encompassing smile around the table. "I'll second that. I'm famished."

Ω

Several hours later Anna relaxed in the car seat and opened her side window to let the breeze rush past her face. She looked over at Tyler, admiring his dark good looks, studying the sturdy hands on the wheel as he guided the car onto the main street.

She put her head back against the seat with a sigh. "This afternoon was really enjoyable," she said. "What do you think?"

He tossed her a grin. "Since Harris's promised three horses next month for training and full board, I'll say it was pretty successful. I'll have to put the construction of the new stalls on high priority. Whatever you said to Regina really turned everything around. After you came back, things took off like wildfire."

Anna pushed her hair away from her face. "She was feeling a bit down so we talked. I have to admit I was comfortable all during the luncheon. I even stopped and said hello to a few people I haven't seen in years. All this time I've been worrying about my face, people's reactions," she murmured, half to herself. "It feels anticlimactic that nothing terrible happened."

"You almost sound disappointed," he said, his voice teasing. "You're quite a woman, Annie. I'll bet you can achieve anything you set your mind to."

Anna laughed softly. "When you say it like that, with such confidence, I'm ready to believe you. Thank you for today."

"Thank you. I know how hard it was to go in there, but no one would know you were nervous." He stopped, one brow lifted. "Maybe I'm assuming too much. Maybe you weren't nervous after all."

"Oh, I was nervous. My stomach was doing flips and turns."

"You handled everything well."

She gave him a big smile and settled deeper into her seat. "Yes, I did, didn't I?" However small, it still felt like a victory.

Ω

Early the next morning Anna cross-tied Carol's horse Lady in the barn's center aisle, speaking to her softly as she brushed her down. She'd lunged her in the ring earlier on a short line so she could see how she moved and responded to basic commands. She had a nice, easy gait and seemed willing. The next step would be to ride her so she could get a feel for her manners and skill level under saddle.

Anna had been keeping on the lookout for Danny and it wasn't long before she saw him step from the edge of the woods. She glanced at her watch. Eight o'clock, right on time as always, and no doubt he'd walked from town as he'd done countless times through the years. She hadn't been able to stop thinking that he might know something about what had happened six years ago. She knew she'd have to tread carefully. Danny got skittish if he felt he might be in trouble about something. She'd seen it a few times through the years when Martin had taken him to task for something.

"Good morning, Danny," she said now as he entered the barn.

He stopped just inside the entrance, his red brows drawn up in surprise. "Miz Anna, I didn't see you. You scared me out of a day's growth."

Anna pulled the mane comb through Lady's tail as she smiled at Danny, genuinely pleased to see him. "At six-foot-two, I think you can spare a few inches. I've already taken care of the horse's hay, but I need you to look at the watering system. There's no pressure and Tyler won't be back until later today. He went to look at some mares."

He nodded quickly and moved down the barn aisle. Anna finished brushing Lady and led her outside. Returning to the barn she found Danny systematically checking the line for leaks.

"I think it might be real easy to fix," he declared, turning to look at her. "Shouldn't only take me a short while." He gathered tools from the toolbox and began to work a wrench onto the pipefitting. "I need a light," he muttered, starting to rise.

"Let me get a flashlight."

Anna returned from the tack room with a light and knelt beside Danny. As she shone the light down, she noticed white lines and a puckering of the skin on the back of his hands. Without thinking, she reached out and touched his hand. "Danny, what happened to your hands?"

He jerked away, dropping the wrench and thrusting

his hands behind his back. "Nothing."

"You have scars."

He stood and his bulk towered over her.

"Danny, please let me see."

He shook his head.

Anna felt an urgency to know what had caused the scarring. "Why haven't I noticed those scars before? I won't hurt you Danny, but I need to see what happened." When he remained motionless, she stepped back, her hands trembling. "It happened that night, didn't it—when you pulled me from the fire?" It was a stab in the dark, but she saw a glimmer of emotion in his eyes and anguish touched her deeply. "You were burned and I never knew," she whispered. Anna stumbled back, her breath coming so fast it hurt her chest. "How come I never knew?"

He blinked quickly and shifted his feet. "Miz Anna, it's okay. They don't hurt me the way you were hurt. People don't care about them."

Emotion choked Anna, hot tears filming her eyes. "Just because they're not easy to see doesn't make them less important. You should have told me. I thought it was a miracle you got me out without getting burned." A sudden thought occurred. "Where else were you burned?" She reached forward and gripped his arm, felt the hard muscle through his flannel shirt. "You always wear long sleeve shirts, no matter what the weather." She looked at him, her eyes wide with shock. "Oh God. Danny, your chest and your arms were burned too."

Danny didn't answer, but Anna suddenly knew she was right. She slumped back against a wooden post while Danny patted her shoulder awkwardly.

"Did you see a doctor?" she finally asked. "Did anyone take care of you?"

"Mama's real good at that stuff. She put on special

cream and it was okay. I had to work."

Anna closed her eyes, her fingertips against her cheek. "I feel so selfish. It's my fault you're scarred. You pulled me out of that fire." Vaguely, she recalled fighting him, not wanting to leave her horses if there was the least chance they were still alive. "I can never make it up to you."

"It's okay." He gave her a happy smile and knelt, intent on returning to work as he retrieved his pipe wrench. Anna watched him for several moments, then realized he was waiting for her to direct the flashlight.

She pointed the light at the pipe again, but it kept wavering so Anna gripped the flashlight tighter. "Danny, there's something else I need to ask you."

He looked up at her expectantly.

"Do you remember the time before Martin died, when we boarded Rafferty's spotted stallion here at the ranch?"

He frowned. "Sure. He'd bite you if he got the chance and cow-kick you at the same time."

She nodded in agreement. "That's right. I remember being afraid of him after the time he cornered me in the stall. If you hadn't been around, I could have been hurt. Nobody wanted to work around him, so Martin had you take care of him. You always had a gentle hand and you weren't afraid." She paused, then said carefully, "Did anything bad happen while that horse was here?"

Danny worked the wrench back and forth while Anna held her breath.

"Danny? Do you recall?" She tried to see his face but he'd turned away from her. Anna had the feeling he was deliberately avoiding looking at her.

"No."

Anna bit at her bottom lip. "No, you don't remember or no—nothing happened?"

He stood abruptly. "Just no. I don't like to remember the bad stuff." He indicated the pipe. "I have to fix this so Tyler likes my work. If he gets mad at me I won't be able to come back. There's lots of people here now. He might like somebody better than me."

"You'll always have a job Danny, as long as I'm here." Anna studied his set expression. "Did Martin know about the bad stuff?" Apprehension filled her. It couldn't be her grandfather behind all this mess. Lives had been ruined, all their lives touched by what had happened. She didn't think she could handle it if Martin had caused all the trouble and let Tyler and his father take the blame.

He pressed his lips tightly together, then finally said, "Miz Anna, you gotta promise you won't tell." He looked up and down the barn aisle, then sat cross-legged on the floor at her feet. "Mr. Martin yelled at me and told me to be quiet or he'd fire me. He was the boss, he was right." He shook his head with a worried frown. "I didn't say anything. I shut up so there wasn't any trouble."

No, her mind shouted. No. What had Martin done? She wet her lips. "What did you shut up about, Danny? I know it was a while ago, but it's really important that you tell me exactly like it happened."

He rubbed his knees, fists clenching and unclenching. "Please don't ask me. I promised I'd shut up. I don't tell nobody anything."

Anna felt dizzy. Tyler was right. Danny knew and he didn't. . . or couldn't tell.

She wanted to scream with frustration, but it wouldn't do either of them any good. "Okay, Danny, go ahead and get back to work." She took a calming breath. "But you know we're going to have to talk about it again. Sometimes a secret can hurt innocent people."

Slowly, he nodded, his eyes never leaving her face. She smiled at him, not wanting him to guess how desperately she wanted the truth, not only for Tyler, but for herself. What had Martin made him promise? Was the secret Danny had kept all these years so devastating that it had shielded Martin and the ranch but in turn ruined Grant's life?

Danny went back to working on the pipe, but as Anna watched him, her mind raced. There had to be an explanation of why Martin had told Danny to keep quiet. The truth had to be brought to light, but right now Anna felt only heaviness in her heart. For the first time she knew real apprehension over what the truth might reveal. Tyler could be right, the truth might drive them apart forever.

$$\Omega$$

For several hours after her talk with Danny Anna concentrated on her stained glass. Working with the bright glass soothed her, pulling her concentration away from troubling thoughts of what Danny might know, disturbing questions of why Martin had told him to keep quiet.

She stepped back from her worktable, kneading with her fingers the ache in her hip from bending over for so long, pleasure filling her as she looked at the glass panel she'd just completed. It was the first of a pair she'd planned for the house entryway.

With her finger she followed the wisps of green as they twined their way over the glass and her thoughts slipped to earlier that morning when she'd awakened beside Tyler. How wonderful it had been to wake beside him. At five a.m., she'd been drowsy, but her senses had responded immediately to the site of his long, muscled back as he'd reached for his jeans. She had touched that warm skin and he'd turned to her, pulling her from the warm cocoon of the sheets and up against his chest. She remembered seeing her splayed fingers in the dusting of hair on his chest, and then the rest of memory had blurred into pleasure. Their lovemaking had been slow and yet searing. Even after he'd left with a brush of his mouth across hers and a murmured word, she hadn't wanted to leave the bed. Was she truly in love with this man? How could she tell him what she'd learned from Danny? She'd agreed to go forward to discover what had occurred six years ago, but what if it split them apart? She didn't want to lose him again.

Anna pushed her fingers through her hair, leaning against the table, looking up to see Tyler striding across the lawn toward her now. Long and lean, his body muscled and hard, she thought about how strong he was when he held her. When Tyler reached her, she kissed him, loving the sizzle burning up her insides.

"Hey," he said, his eyes deep blue and intent, the same intensity when they made love. A shiver worked its way across her shoulders and up the back of her neck. With a sweeping gesture she indicated the glass. "What do you think about this as a sidelight for the door?"

He ran a finger over the panel. "If there's even a hint of sun, this glass will draw it. I like it. You've done a great job, Annie." Tyler gently touched the pink scar on her arm. "How's the arm, does it still bother you?"

"Sometimes it itches, but that's about it. Nothing compared to the way my face itched after it began to heal," she added.

"You're lucky it wasn't worse," he said. "I still think about it, when I saw that glass cutting into your arm."

She squeezed him arm reassuringly. "It turned out okay." She smiled and pointed out the pots of flowers she'd planted. "Come and look at my flowers."

They walked the narrow path lined with flame red blossoms in stone pots.

"They look great. You've done a good job."

"Martin always liked the southerly side of the house since it gets sun most of the day." Anna bent down and snapped off some dead buds. Taking a deep breath, she looked up at Tyler. "The renovations really make the place look classy. If people see a place that's well-tended, it makes a good impression."

"This ranch will always draw people. There's a certain old world elegance here."

Standing once more, she looked beyond the house at the newly mowed lawn and painted fence along the front yard. "You're right, but I remember when Martin brought me here, I felt intimidated and out of place. I didn't know anything about animals or living on a ranch." She gave a sigh, recalling the fear and uncertainty of that time. "After being in foster care, shuffled from place to place, I thought the only thing I had going for me was my looks. People—men, took notice of me. It was flattering, but frightening. When Martin appeared, he seemed to care about me. I let him mold and protect me and I was happy to let his money cover my insecurities about fitting in."

"You made your own mark on this ranch, Annie. No matter how you started out, you've created your own style."

She smiled ruefully. "Which I more or less abandoned."

"You just need to decide if you want to reclaim that person."

"It sounds simple but I still need my camouflage makeup as a safety net." She stared up at the scaffolding beside the house where the men had been painting. "I'm making progress. At least it's not tearing me apart like it used to." She pressed her hands together. "There's something you should know. I've been wrangling with this all afternoon and I almost don't want to tell you, but

I spoke to Danny and I think you're right. He knows something."

Tyler gripped her shoulder. "What does he know?"

"He gets upset so I wasn't able to find out. I almost didn't tell you. . .I didn't want to."

Tyler stared at her grimly. "You weren't going to tell me?"

Anna chewed her lip. "I know I said I wanted to know the truth for both our sakes, but I'm scared. If we leave it, we can go on the way we are, growing closer. If we pursue it, it could be a can of worms." She looked up at him. "Deadly worms."

"We have to know," he insisted, his voice hard. "Tell me what Danny said."

Her heart beat so hard it hurt her chest. "You have to remember Danny has limited recall, and sometimes his recall seems to be skewed." She told him what Danny had said. "When I pressed him about the secret, he wouldn't talk anymore. It's like talking about it really scared him."

"I'll find out."

Anna recognized his hard urgency. "That's not a good idea right now. He looked pretty uneasy when I questioned him. Let it rest for a day or two."

Tyler set his jaw. "He's going to have to talk. I'm not coming this close to the truth and just let it go."

"I'm not saying let it go." Anna grabbed his arm. "Not today, not right now."

He pulled his arm away, his glance hard and accusing. "You don't get it. My dad was ruined. If there's something Danny knows, I want it out in the open. Right now this minute. We're talking six years too late."

Anna stood back, anger making the hair on the back of her neck stand up. "Why? So you can yell it all over town that it wasn't Grant, it was Martin or Danny. . .or me? Will that suddenly make you feel better after six years of being angry? You'll blow everything we've worked at here just for a few minutes of satisfaction?"

"Annie, you know I'm right about discovering the truth," he said harshly. "And I never once said it was you."

Her mouth twisted. "Oh, that's right. You only said I had you run out of town."

"How many times can I apologize? I messed up."

Anna put her arms around herself. "If you go down there like a bull you'll scare Danny off and we might never find out what happened, if he even remembers everything."

Tyler hesitated a moment and Anna hoped that he'd see reason, but he shook his head. "Let me do it my way." He strode back down the path toward the front of the house.

"Tyler."

Anna quickly covered all her tools, then turned and followed Tyler to the barn. When she reached the paddock area, she didn't see Tyler or Danny. With uneasiness gripping her, she hoped that Danny had already left and Tyler hadn't found him.

Running into the barn, she found Tony cleaning tack. "Tony, have you seen Danny or Tyler?"

Tony, his eyes wide with concern, put aside the bridle he was cleaning. "They're both out back. Is something wrong?"

"I hope not." Anna turned to leave.

"Maybe I'd better come with you."

Anna stepped around the side of the barn and drew in a startled breath when a horse and rider trotted past her.

"I'm sorry—sorry!" Danny yelled.

Anna saw the flash of his red hair as he rode past her on horseback, toward the woods, his words hanging in the air. She looked away from him toward the back of the barn and suddenly she saw Tyler on one knee in the dirt as he rubbed the back of his head.

"Tyler!" She ran to him, knelt by his side and gently probed the back of his skull. He jerked his head back from her touch.

"You've got a bump as big as an egg." Worried about possible concussion, she looked at his eyes. "Are you dizzy? Do you feel nauseous?"

"No." He gripped the wooden post beside him and that's when Anna saw the wildflowers that had been trampled in the dirt.

Anna put her hands on his arms and helped him stand. "Did Danny hit you?" she asked, puzzled. Even as she said the words she didn't think it could be possible.

"No."

"Boss, are you okay?" Tony asked, coming up behind them.

"I'm fine." Tyler brushed the dirt off his knees. He looked at her. "You were right," he said harshly. "I went about this all wrong. Danny panicked when I insisted on answers and like you saw he rode out of here like a bat out of hell. He'd picked you flowers," he added, "but they got trampled when he took off."

"If it wasn't Danny, how'd you get hurt?"

"I thought I latched the gate but it swung out and whacked me on the back of the head. I think Danny saw me on the ground and thought he was responsible, but it was my own fault. I tried to calm him down but it was too late."

Anna was relieved he wasn't seriously hurt. "You scared him," she said accusingly.

"I should have backed off but I could see he knew something and I couldn't let it go." He hit the flat of his hand against the fence rail.

"I'll saddle up a horse and go after him," Tony said. "I'll bring back the mare he took."

"Don't bother." Tyler rubbed his head. "If Danny doesn't want to be found, you can search 'til hell freezes over and you won't find him. He knows these woods too well. It was more my fault."

"All right, Boss," Tony said. "I'll be in the barn if you need me."

When Tony left, Tyler said abruptly, "Maybe I'll stop by Danny's mother's house and explain what happened."

She put a restraining hand on his arm. "No, let me handle this. If Danny sees you there he might really take off. I'll give her a call later to make sure he gets home okay." Danny might be the size of an adult, but sometimes he reminded her of a nine-year-old boy.

Tyler looked grim. "I should have left it alone."

"Yes, you should have." Anna wondered if Danny was okay.

"Maybe you can talk to him."

"I understand your urgency for the truth, Tyler, but I have to protect Danny too."

He snapped his head around. "Like you protected Martin?"

Anna narrowed her eyes. "Am I supposed to abandon the people I care about when things don't go your way?" Angrily, she added, "When Danny's ready he'll come back. He's never let me down. I trust him."

"I have to wonder what else Danny knows? I get the idea he's protecting you but he cares about you too much to say anything." He stared at her hard. "Is there anything else I should know?"

"What do you mean?" she asked stiffly.

"You never told me why Danny had to take you to the hospital that week Martin died. Did Martin beat you up or something when he found out about us?"

"No! He never touched me."

"Tell me," he demanded.

Suddenly, Anna wanted to be done with the secrets. "I was pregnant! I'd fainted and Danny took me to the hospital. He thought I was dead."

Tyler stepped back as if she'd slapped him. "A child?" His voice came out strangled. "You were pregnant and you didn't tell me?"

"No." She'd been so afraid, insecure.

"Jesus, I can't believe you never told me."

"Dammit, Tyler, you were gone!"

"You found out after I left?"

Anna looked away. "I knew before." She pressed her lips together. "I had a miscarriage."

Tyler swung away from her, as if it was all too much. Anna understood his pain, his confusion, she'd gone through the same thing years before and the sense of loss still lingered today. "I'm sorry, Tyler."

"Me too."

Anna winced at his swift departure, then looked back toward the woods where Danny had fled, but the area was empty and she knew Danny wouldn't return today. Regret ate at her for the mistakes they'd both made. . .the mistakes they were still making.

Tyler would never willingly hurt anyone, yet he'd frightened Danny with his intensity. Again, it was brought home to her how important finding out the truth was to him. The past wouldn't let go, it haunted them all.

Ω

Tyler jumped in his truck and backed out of the driveway. He could see Annie in the mirror as he drove away. They'd conceived a child and she'd never bothered to tell him. Anger rode him all the way to town and he wondered how he could believe a word she said when she'd kept something so important from him.

As for scaring Danny off, Tyler felt pretty disgusted with himself. He'd never gotten anywhere letting his temper guide him, and he'd certainly proven that point again. It was like he'd reverted to that hot-tempered kid again, ramming his way through life with no real control.

Tyler drove into town and by the time he pulled into the rutted parking lot at O'Kelly's bar he'd pretty much cooled off. As he watched the flow of people in and out, he thought back to when he was thirteen. How many times had Mike O'Kelly snuck beers out the side door to him and other thirteen year-olds? Now, Mike O'Kelly was in the state penitentiary doing two years for burglary. As Tyler entered the bar, he thought that maybe he hadn't done so bad after all. He could have ended up like Mike.

As he breathed in the smoky air and stale beer smell, Tyler conceded that O'Kelly's hadn't changed in the time he'd been gone. He spotted Starla O'Kelly at the end of the bar at the same time she saw him.

"Tyler!" Starla rushed toward him, hands outstretched. Tyler pulled her close and gave her a hug, smoothing back her dark hair as it swung into his face.

"Starla, it's good to see you."

She pulled back, a big smile on her face. "Tyler, I was wondering how long it would take you to come around. I was just telling Bob that I heard you were back."

"I've been busy," he said quietly, noticing several heads turning his way. The place seemed to be nearly full.

"Everybody's talking about the work you've been doing out there at the Barlow place."

Tyler gave her a half smile and made no attempt to lower his voice. "Small town gossip never changes, does it?"

She swiped a dishtowel at him. "You know the answer to that, and you also know it blows away when the next bit of news comes along."

"You'll be able to see for yourself how the ranch is shaping up," he remarked idly. "We've got a big open house coming up. Public invited."

"Well, that sounds like fun." She moved back behind the bar. "So what brings you into town?"

He shrugged, glancing around as he dropped onto a barstool. "Just riding around. Came by the corner and thought I'd drop in to see if anything changed."

"In this place?" She laughed and placed a draft beer in front of him.

Tyler stared at the thin line of foam topping his beer. "How's your brother?"

"Mike? Still doing time." Starla leaned over the bar toward him and lowered her voice. "I was surprised when I heard you were back. You're lucky you got away from here when you did. Some of us aren't so lucky."

"Are you thinking maybe I should have stayed away?" He met the curious stares around him one-by-one. "Nobody really knows what happened six years ago. I for one want to know what happened."

"If people are willing to let it go," Starla said, "maybe you should too. Sometimes you have to compromise. If you stir things and blacken the Barlow name, you might get the short end of the stick."

He stood and took a deep swallow of his beer. "I'm well acquainted with that stick. So you're saying people don't care about the truth?"

She shook her head and smiled at him sadly. "I'm not saying that at all, but I guess you'll do what you need to do, Tyler."

"I usually do." Tyler walked away from the bar and stopped in front of the jukebox, staring blindly at the music selection.

"Tyler Stanton," said a gravelly voice behind him.

Tyler turned. A man somewhere in his sixties stood behind him, topping him easily by six inches. He wore a heavy black mustache and was dressed in jeans, T-shirt and a dusty denim jacket.

"Hi, I'm Cole Benton. I've heard talk that you're taking on horses for training at the Double B." Cole took a deep swallow of his beer and eyed Tyler over the glass rim. "Just like old times, eh?"

Tyler straightened his back. "Not exactly. I'm leasing the ranch from Anna Barlow."

Cole indicated the pool table behind them. "Care to play a game?"

Tyler shrugged. "Sure." He put down two quarters. "Let's rack them up."

"I might have some work for you. Are you as good as Grant?" Cole asked conversationally as he racked the balls and chose his stick.

Tyler leaned his hip against the side of the pool table. He'd never claim such an honor. "My dad taught me all I know."

Cole nodded with satisfaction and Tyler saw a trace of a smile under that bushy mustache. "Good. Then you should do well." He took the first shot and managed to drop two balls into pockets, then missed on the third shot. Cole turned to Tyler. "I've got the small ones. Your turn."

Three games later Tyler had won five dollars but lost ten. After sinking the eight ball on the third game, he conceded defeat. "I'll have to get myself a table so I can practice. I'm rusty."

Starla came to stand beside Cole and she laughed. "Tyler Stanton, I remember a time you'd hustle pool for beer shots."

Tyler grimaced. "Yeah, well, those days are over. I don't hustle anything anymore."

"Just as well," she said, "You were never very good at it."

Tyler felt as if there was a sudden hush in the barroom. "Thanks," he said dryly. Finishing his beer, Tyler handed Cole a business card. "Give me a call when you're ready to talk. It's been nice meeting you Cole." He saluted Starla and gave her a grin. "Starla, see you the next time around." As he walked out the door Tyler nodded at people sitting at the bar and at the tables, wondering idly if the talk would now center around him, raising new speculation about his family and what had happened six years ago. What the hell, he told himself. He wasn't hiding. People might as well know he was going to be right out there, dragging in business if he had to, and if he tweaked a couple sensitive hairs by digging into the past, so be it. In that moment, he had an insight as to how Annie felt when conversations stopped around her and people stared.

Tyler drove through the quiet streets, all the way to the other end of Marsh Plains. He parked outside the cemetery gates, wondering if he'd have to climb the fence to get inside, but the gate was still unlocked.

He found his father's plot easily enough, and stood in the cooling night air, staring at the stone in the meager light. The wreath he'd placed there a few short weeks ago had already begun to wilt, but he noticed someone had planted flowers beside the stone. Even in the failing light he could tell they were a flaming red, like the flowers Annie had put in stone planters all over the ranch.

He knelt down to touch the flowers. Who else but Annie would take the time to care? She had always been a caring person, but why hadn't she told him she was pregnant?

Tyler looked up at the stars, wondering what his father thought about being back home and he hoped he was finally happy. Tyler thought if he could get his dad's name cleared, maybe then he'd find his own brand of peace. He didn't want to hurt anyone by digging around in the past, but he had to get to the truth and he couldn't let it go, no matter what truth turned up.

❧ Chapter Ten ❧

THREE DAYS LATER ON a hot, sunny day, Anna walked toward the back pasture lots where she knew Tyler would be baling hay. She passed the barns and the field where the horses grazed and tilted her head back to let the late morning sun fall on her face. She and Tyler hadn't spoken much since the day Danny ran off and she'd told him about the miscarriage. Today she intended to bring him lunch so they could talk. Someone had to make the first overture and she knew it had to be her.

Since the fire she'd stayed away from the fields when the hay was cut, there was just too much pain, but today, courage seemed to be holding her hand.

Now she heard the tractor running and the distinctive clatter of the ancient hay baler. Tyler had worked magic and somehow managed to get the baler running. It was a familiar sound, one she'd heard every summer since arriving here. As she walked between lots, she came to a double row of short, gnarled apple trees and wove her way between them, the sound growing louder all the while.

As Anna skirted a short hedgerow she saw Tyler on the tractor with the long green baler hitched behind. As she watched, the baler kicked out two bales, and the second one fell apart as it hit the ground. She started to jog across the field but the scent of newly cut, sun-warmed hay met her squarely. She stopped as a wave of nausea hit her.

She'd thought, mistakenly, that she could handle being out here. It was humiliating to see how easily she was brought to her knees. Vaguely, she heard the clatter of the baler and tractor, and looked up and realized Tyler had seen her. With renewed strength Anna made her legs move forward. Dammit, she could do this. She clenched her jaw and gritted her teeth. She'd always loved the smell of fresh hay in the field. She would learn to enjoy it again and maybe release the pain from the past.

Tyler set the brake and jumped down, his long strides bringing him to her as she took three steps in his direction. He wore a hat but no shirt, and the sweat glistened in his hair and on his chest, tiny fragments of hay clinging to his skin. Anna thought how good he looked, his skin already a golden tan.

"Annie?" He placed his hand on her shoulder and Anna welcomed that slight touch. They hadn't touched each other in three long days.

Hoping he didn't notice how her hands shook, Anna brushed the chaff from his chest. Breathing deeply, beginning to feel a bit more like herself, she forced her glance away from that muscled torso with its dusting of dark hair.

"I brought your lunch." She held up the small knapsack. "Did you notice the baler's not tying?"

With a muttered curse, Tyler looked at the last several bales that lay on the ground. Some had tied on one side, the others hadn't tied at all. "The needles keep getting out of line." He moved back to the baler and bent over it, his fingers deftly adjusting the path of the twine.

The baler continued to rock and as Anna watched Tyler she felt a lump form in her throat. She remembered watching Martin perform the same ritual. The baler had been old back then, spitting out bales that wouldn't tie, and he'd patiently set everything right, just as Tyler was doing. Martin had always acted as if he had all the time in the world to see to such mundane matters. Anna found it curious, though, that Tyler, who liked everything modern and up-to-date, had elected to use the old baler.

Determined to resume some type of normalcy, if only for her own satisfaction, Anna placed Tyler's lunch on the tractor seat and then walked back to where the untied bales lay. Reaching down, she picked up the flakes and dropped the loosened hay into the wide slot where it would be caught in the baler's long teeth.

Tyler came up beside her. "Thanks."

Anna couldn't tell much by his expression or tone of voice. She picked up the pieces of baling twine on the ground and fastened them with a half-hitch knot to a handle on the back of the baler.

Her arm brushed Tyler's shoulder and she stared at the definition of muscle, then followed the long smooth length of his back, noticing how the muscles bulged and moved under his skin. She looked up and knew he'd caught her staring.

She looked instead out over the field. "I always loved the smell of green hay, but now it just reminds me of what happened to my horses. It's like a punch in the stomach. . .but I'm really trying to put it in the past." Anna dropped another sheaf of grass into the baler and faced Tyler squarely. "We need to talk about Danny."

A frown shadowed his face and his jaw clenched.

"Any word on him?"

"Yes. His mom called me. He's been in the tree house he and his father built when he was a kid. She can't get him to come out."

Tyler closed his eyes briefly. "That's a relief. I was getting worried when nobody knew where he was."

She pressed his arm then quickly moved her hand away. "I know. But I took it as a good sign he returned the horse, even though it was in the dead of night."

Tyler stared a moment at the tractor, then shifted his glance to her. "Must be he's afraid to come back. He's afraid of me. This has really gotten out of control. I've given this a lot of thought, Annie." He pushed his hand through is hair. "It's all I've thought about. I'm letting this go."

"I'm not sure what you mean."

Tyler kicked at a windrow and hay went sailing from the end of his work boot. "Maybe we'll never know the truth of what happened six years ago. It could be there isn't anyone who knows. I have to let it go. If Danny is our only lead, and I've somehow hurt him by trying to get at whatever he might know, I can't do this. I have to let it go once and for all." He clenched his jaw a moment. "All of it."

Anna knew he was referring to her pregnancy also. That was something they really hadn't talked about. "What about your dad?" she asked quietly, unable to imagine him giving up what had become a mission for him; discovering the truth.

"I think he'd understand. He certainly wouldn't appreciate me scaring Danny away from here."

Instead of the relief she expected, Anna felt even more unsettled. "But now it seems we're so close."

"We don't know that. Will Danny come back?" he asked abruptly. "What did his mother think?"

She shrugged. "I don't know. I told his mom that he's not in trouble. If she can get him to come out of the tree house, she might convince him to come back. I'll give it to the end of the week, then I'll go see him. At this point, we have nothing to lose."

Tyler lightly touched her waist. "Thanks. I've got to get back to work."

The brush of his fingers felt good against her. Anna had a sudden, wanton thought that she'd like to drop to the grass and make love to him in the warm air of the open field, make him forget about the baler and its worn mechanisms. As Tyler walked back to the tractor she tried to ignore the way his jeans rode low on his hips, reminding herself he had work to do. She ran up behind him.

"You have to eat lunch!" she said loudly, leaning across the seat and snatching it before he sat down. For a moment they were very close and she saw the skin stretched taut over his ribs. As she clutched the bag in her hand, she thought of how this man had changed her life. He'd made her want and care about him and long for a future together.

She held out the bag.

He shook his head. "I wasn't planning on stopping."

Anna looked across the pasture at the grass that lay in neat windrows. "You've got most of it baled and the rest has to dry anyway. You have to eat," she insisted.

He put a hand to his ear. "What?"

"You didn't have breakfast!" She shouted so he could hear her, but at the same time he cut the tractor motor.

"No need to shout," he said, his eyes suddenly beginning to twinkle with some of the old mischief. Tyler climbed down, then he killed the engine on the baler and walked back to her. She caught her breath as his hands, warm and sure, cupped her face. She closed her eyes, not fighting the sensations that rose to the surface. Three days ago she hadn't known if he'd ever touch her again. Long, supple fingers splayed across her shoulders, the callused palms kneading and caressing as they worked over her skin.

A tremble began deep within Anna. Without conscious thought, her body leaned into him, craved his attention, the ministrations which felt so good. Hunger gripped her and she looked up at him, caught off guard by his slight smile.

"I'm full of hay," he muttered, resting his chin on the top of her head.

"Somehow, I don't care."

A hush hung in the air. Her breathing seemed overly loud. He tilted his head, his nose brushing against hers, wide lips grazing with tantalizing slowness the contour of her cheek.

Anna's gaze collided with his, eyes intensely blue and changing. Tentatively, she ran her hand along his arm, watching the dark hair rise under her touch.

He groaned. "If I'm going to get anything done today, we'd better have lunch right now."

Anna's heartbeat eased just a bit, but her reaction to this man continued to frighten and fascinate her. He made her tremble with need and ache with desire. Right now lunch was the furthest thing from her mind. All she thought about was they hadn't made love all week. She felt as if she'd lost an essential part of herself.

"Lunch. Great." She stepped back and looked around. "How about in the shade of those apple trees?"

Tyler nodded, grabbed his shirt and pulled it over his shoulders as they walked toward the shade.

"I didn't bring a blanket or anything to sit on, I guess I didn't think that far ahead. But I know you like roast beef, and I went into town to get some fresh rolls and deli pickles from Grossners—"

"You went into town to get this stuff?" he asked with a frown.

"Well, yes. I know you prefer the rolls for sandwiches."

He looked at her with a serious expression, almost a frown on his face. "Annie, I don't expect you to be doing this kind of stuff."

"What stuff?" she asked, puzzled.

"I know you don't like going into town unless you have to, and to go in for some rolls just so I can have them with my lunch, I don't expect that."

She looked around the shaded area under the tree and then dropped down gracefully to the grass. She held out a plastic-wrapped sandwich. "I wanted to do it for you," she said simply. She'd only had a moment's hesitation before she'd walked into the busy delicatessen, but she'd done it and it had felt like a major step.

He stared down at his sandwich. "You put your makeup on?"

"Of course, although I almost forgot, if you can imagine that," she said lightly.

He didn't say anything, and Anna wondered why it bothered him that she'd done that for him. Didn't he want her to care about him? This was just a small measure of caring. Anna looked down at her own sandwich. She swallowed quickly, feeling momentarily panicked. What if he just wanted the physical side of their relationship without any of the feelings that went with it? Without any of the love? What did Tyler want from their relationship?

"I appreciate it, Annie."

"It was no big deal."

He smiled at her. "I think it was."

She nodded, some of the tension inside uncoiling.

"You're right. I'll confess when I first went in there I was shaking, but nobody stared at me, in fact the few people I knew I spoke to and they seemed real glad to see me. It was hard at first, but it was okay."

"You've been working really hard, with the horses, and the house looks great inside and out. You should be proud of the job you're doing. You've dealt well with the extra press we're getting. It's got to be tough for you, dealing with people coming around."

"That's the whole idea," she said carefully. "Making people take notice. Isn't it?"

Tyler put his sandwich down and shifted so that he faced her directly. "Yes."

Anna felt a moment's disappointment that he didn't elaborate or give her more words. She knew he wasn't a man who put his feelings easily into words but she wished for once he'd be more open with her. Watching him eat his sandwich, she knew that countless times he'd showed he cared, but caring didn't necessarily mean love.

Anna gathered up the remnants of their lunch and placed it in paper bags, then stowed them in the knapsack. Taking the bull by the horns, knowing she had to try to somehow dispel the tension between them, she said, "If you want to talk about that last week six years ago, we can do that, you know."

He stared hard at her a moment, then merely nodded. Plucking a blade of grass, he stretched, reaching his hands up toward the sky. "How is Carol's horse coming along?"

"No big problems. I'm working with her on the right way to discipline Lady, when to reward her, when to be firm. She's a good rider, just a bit timid, but she's working hard."

"I remember when I didn't know one end of the horse from the other," Tyler mused. "I had a lot to learn too."

Anna looked out over the field, the Double B land stretching as far as she could see. She'd loved this ranch for as long as she could recall. "It's kind of interesting that we both started off the same." She swung her hair back. "But now you're a success and people look up to you."

For once he didn't dispute her words. Instead, he rolled over on his back, his face not far from hers. "I know you're not thrilled about the idea of an open house," he said, "but I think we've got a good chance at making it a success. Have you thought anymore about riding?"

She studied him for several moments. "You really want me to do this, don't you?" She still felt some resistance to the idea. "I'm thinking about it," she conceded. "That's all I can promise."

He laughed and squeezed her hand. "That's a start. We're creating so much from scratch. Can't you just feel that old excitement?"

Anna nodded and knew in her heart she wanted it to be like old times.

He tugged her to her feet. "Come on, we'll go for a ride."

She looked at the field. "I thought you wanted to finish baling."

Tyler's fingers pushed through her hair to the back of her scalp. "I have a few minor adjustments to make on the baler, then it'll only take me about another half-hour to finish tying what's dry. I can have some of the boys bring the truck and hay wagon out here to load them up. What do you say? Would you like to go for a ride?"

"I'd love that." She'd never say no to spending time with Tyler. "I'll saddle two horses. Do you want me to meet you back here or at the barn?"

He dropped a slow kiss on her mouth and turned

toward the baler. "Why don't you meet me back here?"

His cell phone began to ring. With his hands busy on the baler, Tyler said, "Can you get that? It's in the tool box."

Anna stepped up to the tractor and pulled the phone out of the metal toolbox. "Hello."

"Tyler Stanton, please," a female voice said.

"He's busy, could I take a message?"

"This is Samantha from the Rollaway Center. I'd like to talk with Mr. Stanton about setting up his job interview."

Numbly, Anna stared at Tyler. He straightened from the baler and glanced at her as he pulled a rag from his back pocket and wiped his hands. He went still, then glanced at the phone gripped in her hand. "Annie, what's wrong?"

"There's a call for you from Rollaway Center. It's about your job interview." She dropped the phone in his hand. "You could have mentioned it." She walked quickly away, distressed at the implications of him seeking a job. How could he consider leaving? Anyone in the horse business knew of the Rollaway Center. It was one of the biggest horse training facilities in the United States. There was no competition between the Rollaway Centre and the Double B Ranch.

Tyler took the phone, spoke into it briefly. He shoved the phone back in his pocket.

"Annie!" She ignored him and walked as hard as she could, but he caught up with her a few moments later and pulled her around to face him. Breathing heavily, Anna stared at him with resentment. "Why didn't you tell me?" Angry, she lifted her chin. "We were just talking about the open house. You've said you wanted to make a success out of the ranch. That's hard to do if you're not here. What's going on?" She shook her head and backed away from his outstretched hand, denying the hurt as it twisted inside. "I thought all this was for you, your sense of pride in bringing it back and building your reputation. I was naive to think you'd settle here." With me, but she didn't say the words. "I can't believe you're being so short-sighted."

She didn't understand how he could even consider leaving. Anna felt overwhelmed by a sense of inevitability. "Look at this place—the land! Your horses are grazing in the pasture. Doesn't that mean anything to you?" She felt cold. She wouldn't beg. If he didn't want a life here with her, she couldn't make him stay. He hadn't stayed before. "I had hoped you'd grow to love this land as much as I do, that maybe you came back because you couldn't stay away." The despair she felt was in her voice, she knew it, but right now she couldn't control her emotions.

"I'm not disputing this is a great place." He reached out to her but Anna stepped back. "Annie, this interview isn't what you think."

"And what is it that I think? You're ambitious, you can go anywhere you want, but you want more than this place." The pain of heartache gripped her. "I guess neither one of us wants to change. I won't leave," she said fiercely, "and you can't stay."

Tyler put his head back and his expression grew hard. "That's what it always comes down to, this ranch. Annie, it's stone and dirt and wood. There are plenty more beautiful places. What difference does it make where we are if we're together?" He pulled her close but she stood stiffly in front of him. "The Rollaway Centre came to me, I didn't go looking for this. They've been bugging the hell out of me to agree to an interview. It was professional courtesy, that's all, and I told them I'd think about it. It got them temporarily off my back. This doesn't change anything."

Carefully, she pulled back from him. "Tyler, you could have told them to go away, right from the start. Admit it, you could happily go on the rest of your life never settled, one place after the other. To tell you the truth I can't understand that. I don't want to search for something else. Everything I need is right here."

He swore. "I'm not searching for anything. I'm a businessman and talking with the Rollaway Centre is business! I admit this position is a once in a lifetime opportunity but I haven't even scheduled the interview."

"I can't believe I was so wrong about you."

He seemed to go very still. "What are you saying?"

Annie loved him but she couldn't push the words past her lips.

"I care about you a great deal, Annie. Doesn't the fact that I'm letting go of the past tell you that?"

"You say you're letting go but everything's still there between us, the questions, who is right and who is to blame." She watched him. "Isn't that true?"

"It's always been between us," he said harshly, "but I'm telling you I'll let it go." He drew in a deep breath and looked away from her.

Anna blinked quickly against the tears smarting her eyes. She looked at the face of the man she loved, the deep blue eyes, the lean planes of his cheeks with its strong jaw and chin. Why couldn't they understand each other's needs? "Why does the past have to ruin everything?"

"Don't throw away what we have," he said urgently.

"I'm very careful about what I throw away." She put her head up and flicked her hand quickly over her eyes. "I'll help you with the open house, and you'll see what a great success it is and you'll see everything you could ever want is right here."

Anna didn't know what else to say. Briefly, she touched his shoulder, knowing in her heart everything she needed was standing right in front of her. Walking away from Tyler was the most difficult thing she'd ever done.

Seeing again that blank look in his eyes, she felt like she'd wounded him.

Anna stared angrily at the mountains all around her. As she walked toward the barn and past the clearing where the new shed stood on the old foundation, she saw the flowering bushes. The landscape was coming alive with color and the ranch was off to great beginnings, but she knew in her heart without Tyler it all wouldn't be worth a damn. The ranch was all she had left. Why couldn't she have everything she'd ever wanted and still have Tyler?

❀ Chapter Eleven ❀

"THE DOUBLE B RANCH'S First Annual Open House. The Double B, currently under the management of three-time reining champion Tyler Stanton and barrel racing veteran Annie Barlow—" Anna grimaced, thinking their wording made her sound old and retired "-- will host a day of fun-filled excitement. Look no further for quality reining horses and professional training. Live demonstrations include reining and barrel racing, chainsaw carving, blacksmith techniques, petting zoo and balloon sculpting for the kids, and a daylong barbecue and pig roast. A treat for the entire family."

Anna peered at Tyler over the top of the newspaper. "There's more on the history of the ranch, but this is the fourth paper that's given us a headline. We've been lucky to get such good coverage. You must have really pulled some strings."

He shrugged. "It doesn't hurt to talk to people and I did know a few people who knew a few people." He lifted his hat from the peg by the kitchen door. "I'm going down to the barns. I need to check any last minute arrangements."

When he didn't leave right away Anna held her breath, wondering if he'd say something to ease the tension that had been between them all week, ever since their confrontation in the hay lot. Many times she'd wanted to go to him, but stubborn pride had held her back.

"Any word on Danny coming back?" he asked.

Hiding her disappointment, she shook her head. "I've talked to his mother several times but all she knows is he's still really upset." Danny had never missed a day of work and she didn't understand it, but his mother had asked her to have patience. "All I can do is keep trying. I told her I'm going to come by on Monday."

Tyler didn't answer but merely nodded before turning to leave. Anna sat down with a thump in the kitchen chair, wishing they could turn back the clock. Things had deteriorated all week. They hadn't talked again about the Rollaway Centre, but she knew they'd called again only last night. She'd been there when the call came in but he'd gone into his office and he hadn't discussed it with her.

They'd worked on the open house, but their personal life had taken a back seat to everything and they hadn't spent any time together unless it involved the ranch. Anna worried about the future of the ranch if Tyler took the job, but she couldn't bring herself to break the silence. They had a contract and Tyler wouldn't break that, but the thought of him leaving just made her miserable. She knew everything was coming to a head, there was no avoiding it, but for today she had to concentrate on the open house. Today, the ranch was her first priority.

Ω

Forty minutes later Anna rechecked her list as she walked through the barn area, glancing at her wristwatch for the hundredth time to make sure she was on schedule. She loved the excitement of organizing events, pulling all the pieces together so everything meshed in an orderly fashion. So far, everyone was on task and things were moving along smoothly.

"Anna?" Carol's mother entered the barn. "I've got some bad news," the older woman said. "I'm not sure Carol is well enough to ride her mare today. She's sick to her stomach."

"Oh, poor kid," Anna said sympathetically. "I know how much she was looking forward to this."

Angela bit her lip. "It's not that she's deliberately ducking out of this, but I think she's made herself sick with nerves. Her dad called this morning to say he was coming, and I think she's afraid she won't measure up. She doesn't have a lot of confidence."

Anna glanced at her watch. "Would you like me to talk to her?"

Angela looked hopeful. "Would you? I know how much she respects you. Riding has helped her confidence tremendously." She grimaced. "Only not where her father is involved."

"Is he critical of her?" Anna asked carefully. Carol had barely mentioned her father, only that he and her mother had separated last year.

"He has been in the past, that's one of the reasons we split up. But he's been getting help and his being here really means a lot to her. I thought she'd be okay with this, but last night she started snapping at us, so now I'm wondering if it's been bothering her all along."

"Carol's a good kid. If we can get past this I know she'll do fine," Anna said confidently. "It's basically a canter through the barrel pattern and a trot around the barrels. She's been practicing that all week and I know she's got it down pat."

"She's in the tack room."

Anna went directly to the barn. Inside the tack room she found Carol huddled on one of the couches, her legs drawn up and her arms hugging her knees. She looked pale and her eyes were enormous, and filmed over with tears as soon as she saw Anna.

"I'm sorry," she blurted. "I know you're gonna be mad, but I can't do it."

Anna sat down beside her and put her clipboard on the floor. "Have you ever seen me mad? So let's talk about it. Why won't you be able to ride?"

Carol looked down. "I don't feel good."

"Nerves?" she asked with sympathy, gently touching Carol's ponytail. "I know how it is when you're afraid of not measuring up. Your hands get cold, you start to sweat, and that little voice in your head assures you you'll fall on your face."

Carol shot her a quick look, then wiped her nose with a tissue and nodded.

"So, are you afraid of trying and failing or are you afraid of being in front of everybody?"

"I'm not afraid of any of them," Carol scoffed, then she dipped her head. "But my dad will be here. If I mess up, he'll think I haven't learned anything. I don't see him that much," she continued, her voice muffled. "I want him to be proud of me."

Anna put her arm around Carol's slender shoulders. "I bet your dad will be proud no matter how you do." She hoped she was right. "How about I make you a deal? If you decide you can do this, and that decision is entirely yours, I'll ride my mare after you do your demo."

Carol's head shot up. "You'd do that, even though—you know, you don't like being in front of people?"

Anna hugged her again. "I'd do it for you and maybe I have to do it for myself. What do you think? Is it a deal?"

They shook hands.

"Deal," Carol said. "If you can go out there, so can I."

Ω

Anna entered the paddock area where most of the demonstrations were to take place. One of the girls she'd hired to help out was having a difficult time winding decorative gold ribbon around the paddock posts as a slight breeze played havoc with the lightweight trimming.

Anna tucked her clipboard under her arm and stepped forward to grab one end of the wayward ribbon. "Maggie, I'll tie the beginning knots and you can wind it around the rails, then we'll leave about ten inches of ribbon dangling."

Anna moved on from there. The temporary bleachers had been set up, the picnic and barbecue area was all set. She checked off items on her list as she walked around the barn and ran smack into something. . . someone. Tipping her head back, Anna stared into familiar deep blue eyes. Her stomach did an immediate, unsettling churn as desire arced through her. She had a yearning to be in Tyler's arms. It had been a long week, and she'd missed him so much. Anna looked up into his face shaded by his hat. She could just see his dark hair on the back of his neck. He'd gone into town for a haircut yesterday and he'd had it cut really short on the sides. She found the close cut incredibly attractive.

"Sorry," she murmured, not sorry at all.

"Keep looking at me like that and I'll have to pull you behind the barn for a private talking-to," he said, surprising her as he traced his finger lightly down her nose. "You look pretty busy," he added more seriously, as if suddenly remembering they'd been cool to each other all week. "Is there anything you need me to take in hand?"

Anna gathered her thoughts, still affected by his nearness and the intimacy of his words. "Um, let's see—as long as you've got the sale horses all tagged and people on hand to answers any inquiries, I think we're all set."

"Tony's overseeing the sale barn and since Danny isn't here, I put Mario in to help him."

"Okay. The only change might be Carol. She's not feeling well and may have to pull out."

"I saw her mother. Who's going to fill in if she doesn't ride?"

Anna looked up from her papers, tapping her pencil against the clipboard. "I thought I'd move up the chainsaw carving demonstration. Wade told me he brought extra wood just in case."

"Mmm." Tyler rubbed his chin thoughtfully. "You could do that, of course." His eyes zeroed in on hers. "Angela said you're going to ride."

"I made a deal with Carol," she said quietly. "If she's up to riding, I'll do a short stint also. By the way, congratulations, everything seems to be running smoothly and you've done a great job organizing."

"Thanks, but I couldn't have done it without you."

"Yeah, well—" she let her voice trail off as she stared hard at the men in the picnic area. They had an area roped off where they were basting the roasting pig on a barbecue spit. The aroma caused her empty stomach to growl and she remembered she'd only eaten a couple pieces of dry toast this morning in her rush to get down here.

"You'll be riding Spirit?" he asked.

She looked up at him. "Of course, but I don't want to

think about it too much or I'll really get nervous. I thought we'd demonstrate Carol and Lady in the early stages of training compared to Spirit, who's ready to compete. So I'm presuming you're happy it's turned out this way? I'm getting before a crowd again."

"Only if it feels right to you," he said. "I hope you don't think I planned this," he said, his mouth curled mockingly. "But if you think about it, you'll admit you have the skills to go out there and fill in at a moment's notice. You're top notch, all you have to do is step back into that slot."

"Thank you." Anna stared into Tyler's face and some of her protective shell cracked. They'd both worked hard all week and she really wanted him to do well today. Unable to resist the temptation, she stood up on her toes and pressed her mouth to his.

Tyler put a hand behind her neck and held her still for several moments while he proceeded to kiss her slowly and thoroughly. It had been so long. His fingers relaxed, slid down to her shoulder, squeezed and were gone.

"I'll make sure Spirit is ready and saddled for you," he said, his voice husky.

Anna reminded herself that she used to be considered one of the top riders. Nothing had changed, just her confidence. Maybe she and Carol had more in common than she realized.

"Make sure you put out Spirit's best silver bridle!" she called out as Tyler walked away. Anna's heart felt like a freight train in her chest as she acknowledged she couldn't back out now.

Tyler lifted his hand in acknowledgment and Anna wiped the moisture from her forehead, suddenly determined that she would be up for the challenge and she wouldn't let anyone down, least of all herself.

Ω

Outside in a small area he'd penned off, Tyler finished saddling Frisco. It was early yet, but quite a few people had already wandered down to the barns and the pasture where some of the demonstrations were to be held. Whistling, Tyler turned, brushes in hand, and came face-to-face with Tara Dakins. The whistle died on his lips, but, remembering his manners, he said good morning and removed his hat.

"Annie is around here somewhere," he said pleasantly, knowing there was no way she'd come looking for him. "You might want to try the picnic area."

"I've seen Anna and congratulated her on the turnout today. I came to see you, Tyler."

Surprise didn't describe the way he felt. He contemplated the pasture beyond her shoulder, then settled his gaze on her. "What can I do for you?"

She looked uncomfortable, but she said, "First of all, let me congratulate you on the fine job you've done with this ranch. I hardly recognized the place. In bringing this place back, you've helped Anna a great deal, perhaps even more than I know. I haven't been around here much for her lately, which I regret, but I intend to rectify that." She drew a deep breath. "Second, I must apologize for my rudeness during our initial meeting. I was shocked—you look very much like your father when he was younger. I wasn't expecting it."

Not sure he even wanted to have this conversation, Tyler let out a deep breath. "You knew my dad well?"

Tara gripped her leather purse, but she nodded. "It was a long time ago. Grant and I used to see quite a lot of each other."

"I didn't know."

"It was over long before you came along. We were

both young and hotheaded. We each wanted our own way. One night we had a big fight and neither one of us would admit we were wrong. Several weeks later it broke my heart when I saw Grant with your mother. I knew I'd made a big mistake. I went to see him one night."

She brushed her hair back, her eyes carrying a heavy sadness. "I was ready to beg his forgiveness, ask him if we could start over. He met me at the door of the place he and your mother lived. There was sadness in his face, but resolution too. He told me they were getting married. I later found out your mother was pregnant with you." Tara pressed her lips together. "I held bitterness in my heart for a long time. When I saw you that day in the restaurant—you look so much like him—" her voice trailed off and she cleared her throat. "All that old hurt came to the surface. I was reminded of Grant and what I'd thrown away. It was wrong to let it out on you."

"I'm sorry for what happened." He took no responsibility for his father's actions, but he felt sympathy for Tara's apparent upset. He'd never known about his father and her. It shed some light on why his mother and father never really got along.

She searched his face, and hers softened. "I'm not asking you to be sorry. I met Gill and I'm happy. All week Gill has spoken of nothing else except the expected success of the Double B with you and Anna combining forces. I imagine you've worked hard to become a successful businessman and accomplished rider."

Surprisingly, she lifted his rough, calloused hand in her much softer one. "I wish you the best of luck Tyler, as do a lot of the people hereabouts. Gill really believes in you and Anna, and I do trust his judgment. Even without that, we can see what you've done for Anna. She's finally coming back to the lovely, happy girl I once knew, and that alone is worth more to me than anything in the past."

"Annie's pretty strong." Tyler cleared his throat. He had to admire her courage in seeking him out. "She considers you and Gill the best of friends, I'd like to think some day I can claim the same honor."

"As long as you treat Anna well, we'll be friends," she said simply.

When Tara left, Tyler stared into empty space, replaying their conversation. A small knot eased inside. Wryly, he wondered why he should be gullible and begin to feel differently about the place where he'd grown up, but that's just what was happening. It wasn't just Tara, but a whole combination of events since he'd returned to the place of his birth. He began to wonder how he could have been so shortsighted about so many things.

Ω

Anna made her way through the crowd, excited by the number of people who had shown up for the open house. Some were strangers, many were local people she recognized. In sheer numbers alone, the day was already a success.

She stepped into the small holding corral where her horse waited patiently, saddled and ready to go as Tyler had promised. Spirit gave her a friendly whicker in greeting, and Anna rubbed her velvety muzzle while blowing softly into one nostril. With a grin, she noted the decorative silver ribbon threaded through Spirit's ash-colored mane.

What surprised and delighted her the most, was the tied bunch of deep purple Irises that had been tucked into the stirrup fender. Anna looked all around the area, knowing it had to have been Danny who placed the flowers there, but she didn't see him. Anna smiled to herself, taking this as a good sign, but knowing she wouldn't see Danny unless he intended it.

Touched, Anna carefully retrieved the flowers, breathed their sweet perfume and placed them with her clipboard outside the ring. Returning to her mare, she untied her from the hitching post and made her way to the area above the paddock. From here she'd have a bird's eye view of the riding ring where Tyler would demonstrate reining techniques. She had no intention of missing his ride. The only regret she had was that she didn't know where Danny was, but the Irises were a good sign.

She'd seen Tyler work his animals numerous times, but she still found it exhilarating to watch him put his horses through their paces. Today, he'd elected to ride Frisco. The announcer explained in brief detail the purpose of the demonstration, then introduced Tyler and his horse.

Mounted and ready, Tyler stood in the middle of the arena and signaled for the gate to be opened. A dozen or so steer were herded into the arena and then the gate closed behind them to prevent their exit.

With a fluid economy of movement, Tyler rode Frisco toward the herd, causing them to mill and turn away almost as one body. With lowered head and his ears flat, Frisco moved forward and after a series of short passes to the left and right, he cut a steer out of the herd. Each time the steer attempted to return to the herd, Frisco kept him back, counter-acting each move the steer made with one of his own, his movements so pure and fluid it was an incredible demonstration to witness.

Sitting straight in the saddle, his hand steady, Tyler used his weight and legs to aid Frisco, but anyone could see it was all the horse. When the steer made a quick lunge to the side, Frisco rolled back on his haunches and once again blocked the steer, then turned the animal to the opposite end of the corral in record time. Anna knew a horse's instinct played a part in the making of a top notch reining horse, but Tyler and Frisco made the entire demonstration appear effortless. She applauded their efforts as enthusiastically as the other spectators.

Next, the work crew set up the three barrels in the arena for the cloverleaf pattern. Anna moved closer to the arena so Carol would be able to see her if any problems cropped up. As Carol entered the arena, she gave her a reassuring smile and noticed that the younger girl looked much better than when she'd talked to her earlier.

Keeping in mind her promise to Carol, she watched the teen take Lady through the pattern, heart in her throat the entire time. She wanted this to be a good ride for Carol. They rode well and Anna's heart filled with awe for this young girl who'd confessed her fear and uncertainty and yet had had the courage to go out there anyway. Anna whistled for Carol's performance and she clapped as Carol exited the ring, a huge grin spreading across her face. She saw a dark-haired man waiting for Carol outside the ring, and there was no mistaking him for Carol's father. Even from this distance Anna could see his proud smile as he congratulated his daughter.

As Anna and Spirit entered the arena, she passed Tyler and he tipped his hat, giving her the thumbs-up sign. Anna dipped her head slightly and smiled as she ran a soothing hand over Spirit's withers. Looking out over the expectant faces in the crowd, Anna suddenly caught sight of a tall man standing next to the fence rail, the distinctive Rollaway Center logo emblazoned on his white shirt. For a split second her concentration broke and she was brought back to that fact that the ranch's future was at stake. Her heart skipped a beat but she knew she needed to regain her concentration.

Anna breathed deeply and tightened her fingers around the reins until she could just feel Spirit's mouth. Her mare tensed, her anticipation evident as she pranced in place, dipping her head forward, pulling against the bit, testing her. The muscle and power beneath her legs, the control and yet cooperation of her mare, filled Anna with a sense of familiarity and serenity. Leaning forward, she dropped her hand to Spirit's withers, allowing the mare to leap ahead. They wound tight to the right on the first barrel. Anna knew the barrels, knew how close she could get without knocking them over, how much she could ask of her mare. They pulled around the barrel in a cloud of dust, then raced to the inside of the second barrel. Anna stared hard at the barrel as they came into it, pulled Spirit back slightly and to the left and then they raced for the third and last barrel, Spirit executing a flying change of lead as smooth as butter. Around the barrel and then they raced in a beeline for home.

The arena rail drew near. . .Spirit tucked her haunches, her front legs almost straight in a walking motion as she came to a sliding stop. Sitting deeply, tears filmed Anna's eyes over the pure poetry of her mare's strength of movement. The dust settled and Anna felt enclosed in an almost surreal hush. Chest heaving, adrenaline high, she threw her arms around Spirit's neck. "We did it, girl."

Only when she straightened did the applause impinge upon Anna's awareness. Startled, she looked out over the crowd. She saw Carol's beaming face and Tyler stared at her with a knowing grin, as if he'd never doubted that she could pull it off.

Anna laughed with sheer enjoyment, her heart bursting as the earlier uncertainty fell to dust. She was a horsewoman, she had the skill to be a competitor, and embracing that truth empowered her.

Ω

Tyler skimmed his glance over the now empty paddocks. The extra help he'd hired to help set up for the open house had long since left. He hadn't seen Annie since her remarkable riding demonstration. She and Carol had banded together and they'd been surrounded by people offering congratulations and asking questions, and he knew that was right. Anna had ridden like the pro she was and deserved the recognition. Already, a lot of interest was being generated, a sure indication that the next several months would see an increase in business.

Tyler sat on the rail outside the barn, enjoying the fading sun as it began its regal slide behind the mountain. The day had been a success, there was no doubt in his mind, but he still found himself surprised by the enormity of the turnout. He'd seen people he hadn't been in contact with in years, and he sat here still blown away by their well wishes.

Annie had been right all along. He had been welcomed here. He'd always known who he was, until he came back to this town, then he'd let doubt settle in. People came, liked what they saw and it didn't matter that he was a man with a past. He was Tyler Stanton, a man in his own right and maybe people were realizing he dealt an honest hand in all his negotiations.

"Hello Tyler." Her voice swept over him like a caress, firing his blood. Twisting around, he gripped the fence post and watched Annie walk toward him, the last bit of sun silhouetted behind her shoulders, outlining her hair in a blaze of red.

His heart began to pound. When had he begun to love her?

"Hello, Annie." Did she hear the longing in his voice? He needed to touch her. Tyler jumped to the ground.

"It's been an incredible day. It turned out well."

"Yes." She turned from him to watch the sun disappear.

"You'll never guess who stopped by to offer congratulations—your friend Tara."

"She knows a good man when she sees one."

He sighed. "Maybe. She used to love my dad. She didn't say too much about what happened, but they hurt each other really bad and he didn't stay with her. Maybe he should have. I don't ever remember him being happy with my mother. I have mixed feelings about their past history, but in a way it makes me understand my dad a little more. I realize I'm a lot like him."

"Tara never said anything. It's awful to know the one you love is out of reach."

Tyler slid a hand across her stomach from behind, felt her indrawn breath, then she leaned against him and he closed his eyes briefly, wanting her so badly. "Feel sad for me. I've missed you." He heard the roughness in his own voice and he ducked down to kiss the side of her neck, breathing in her unique scent.

She looked up at him solemnly. "How could you miss me? I've been right here."

"I've missed you all week."

The urgency inside made him want to devour her. He turned her to him, cupped her face and put his mouth on hers, feeling her intake of breath. He wanted that breath, he wanted all of her, but he made his hands go still on her face and he dropped his forehead to hers.

Slowly, Annie reached up and traced her fingertips along his cheeks.

"I need to shave again," he said gruffly, gripping her hand.

She smiled. "I don't care." Standing on tiptoe, she leaned against him. "I missed you all week," she said, giving him back his own words, then she placed her mouth against his and Tyler was lost. He put his arm around her waist and pulled her hard up against him and he couldn't get close enough. "Come with me."

They were in the barn and Tyler looked around, realizing somehow they'd made it to the tack room. The new horse blankets were still piled on the desk. Tyler pulled one out, opened the blanket and placed it on the old leather couch. When he turned his heart dropped to his toes, then raced back up into his throat. Annie locked the door and then stood there with just her T-shirt and jeans. She'd already pulled off her boots and vaguely he noticed them in the corner of the room.

"Good thing you thought about a lock on that door," she said softly, meaningfully.

"It doesn't matter," he said hoarsely. "I sent everybody home." Tyler stood stock still, and she came to him, her fingers deft as she unbuttoned his shirt. She pulled the shirttail from his jeans and spread the shirt away from his chest. When she moved in closer and put her mouth to his skin, he closed his eyes and his body began to shake. He lost control. Tyler yanked his shirt off his arms and dropped it on the floor.

He reached down with one hand and pulled a boot off. Still holding Annie to him with one arm, he reached down on the other side and pulled the other boot off. All the while she drove him crazy, kissing her way up and down his chest and neck.

The soft sounds she made almost put him over the edge. Pulling her into him with a hand at her waist, he felt her slimness, then dropped his hands to her hips and brought her hard up against him. She looked up at him then, her eyes bright with desire, lips parted. He took her mouth, tracing her lips with his tongue, hardly able to get enough of her. She pushed against him, so he stepped back, dazed, then realized she was nudging him toward the couch. He felt the edge against his knees and dropped down on the couch, spread his legs and pulled her between them. He pushed her T-shirt up and put his mouth to her stomach, traced his way with his tongue along her warm flesh. She gave a small squeal, then a murmur as he moved closer, her body straining against him.

With shaking fingers Tyler unbuttoned the snap on her jeans and slowly eased them down past her hips, her legs, and she shifted her weight, lifted one foot and then the other. He threw her jeans in the corner and pulled her down on top of him, but it wasn't close enough. Trying not to scratch her soft skin with his rough, calloused hands, Tyler put his hands under her shirt alongside her breasts and pushed the shirt up and off her head. He grabbed her hair as it filled his hands like silk. Tyler stood and quickly shucked his jeans.

Annie lay on the couch, her arms lifted to him and he dropped down to her slowly, sliding his body along hers, feeling her bare toes and as she moved them up the back of his legs and then down. Her hands pushed at his boxers and then the material was gone, but still they weren't close enough. Tyler gritted his teeth as her hands moved all over him, exploring, caressing, molding his body to her needs, which became his need.

He pressed her down into the couch and her legs came up around him and she pushed up against him. When she shifted back once more and discarded her briefs, Tyler took advantage when her breasts moved within inches of his face. He kissed them, loving their feel, the softness, her generosity in offering them.

Anna was sure she had gone to heaven. Never had she experienced such an unbelievable storm of desire. When Tyler's mouth closed on her breast, she felt as if all the breath in her body let go. She felt his desire for her, yet he held back, even though his hands shook. She brought his hand to her waist, felt it move to her hip and lower. Joy filled her, joy in knowing how much this man meant to her, how much she loved him.

She squirmed out from under him, then moved to straddle him, dropping her head to plant kisses on his face, his passion darkened cheeks. She stared a moment into his eyes, dark and intent, his concentration so completely focused on her.

She dropped her body to his, felt his instant reaction, yet he let her be the aggressor. Slowly, she sank down upon his body, threading her fingers with his, aware of his strength and the fact that he could take over at any moment, but chose to let her lead him in this dance. She played upon his body, taking him inside and retreating, clenching her teeth in an agony of feeling, wanting to go fast, to speed up the sensation, yet prolonging it, tormenting them both.

Tyler suddenly pushed up against her, and they rode the sensation, taking and giving until all energy was spent and they lay in each other's arms, silent and unmoving.

Anna's thoughts whirled in her head as she stared at the saddles and bridles hanging neatly side by side along the wall, the cleaning hook where she'd wiped down countless bridles after riding. She stared at Martin's old pine desk with the pigeonholes, remembering how she'd stuffed little notes in the holes for Martin to find, notes with pictures she'd drawn.

"I want you in my life," he said, his voice husky as he drew circles on her arm with a fingertip. "I love you."

Anna looped her arms around his neck and squeezed him as emotion threatened to spill over. "I love you too," she admitted, resting her palms flat against his cheeks.

"I want a future together."

"Here at the ranch," she said, excitement filling her totally. It was all she'd ever dreamed. Tyler, the ranch, the two of them together. She suddenly went still, and she dropped her head forward. "How could I forget?" She put her head back. "The Rollaway Centre has already made you an offer, haven't they, one that's too good to turn down. I saw the guy from the Centre here today."

Tyler's expression suddenly became guarded. "There were a lot of horse industry people here today, I'm sure they knew about the open house."

He was right but Anna felt choked, unable to speak. The warmth from their lovemaking dissolved and she bit her lip as she stared at the wall behind his shoulder. Why couldn't she be happy that he loved her and wanted her with him? Why wasn't it enough?

"I want to marry you," he said.

"Tyler, I love you more than anything, but I can't leave."

"Let's get it straight, you won't leave." His eyes darkened and his mouth straightened. "Apparently, that love doesn't extend further than the ranch." He sat up abruptly. "But then, that's old news, isn't it?"

Before she could protest the unfairness of that statement, he rose to his feet. His features looked cold, imposing, and a chill touched her. Quickly, she picked up her clothes, devastated that this was a scene from long ago replaying itself out. Would they always leave each other?

"Come on, that's not fair! Their offer could be a great opportunity—but what about the Double B and the lease you signed?" Everything was spinning out of control.

She yanked her shirt down over her head and quickly dressed. "You've just asked me to marry you, knowing what this ranch means to me, knowing—knowing how I feel about being anywhere but here. But you're talking to others about a high profile position." She threw up her hands, feeling wounded and betrayed. But why should she feel that way, she reminded herself, she'd always known how ambitious Tyler was. He'd never made it a secret. Maybe she'd naively hoped things would turn out differently, that he'd love her so much he'd stay here, because this is where she belonged, where she felt whole. "I know you can't turn it down, I'm sure it's too good an offer."

"Annie—"

"Tyler, I won't be the one standing in the way of something you want. In your heart you want it so bad, I know that, so don't deny it." She shook his hand off her arm. "Do what you have to do," she said, not knowing how they'd make it through this. All she knew was she had to get away because the anguish inside was too much to bear. "I've got to go."

Ω

Tyler strode back into the barn, feeling like he had a hole in his gut eight inches wide.

From out of nowhere, a ball of gray fur shot across the small room, executing a series of hops and jumps before it stopped by his feet and wound its small body around his boots. With a shake of his head, he leaned down and scratched the kitten's head, momentarily taken back by the animal's loud purring. He picked up the kitten and continued to stroke her, willing his emotions to calm. He wouldn't lose Annie, he vowed fiercely. He carried the purring animal with him and deposited her in her blanket-lined crate with her brothers.

Tyler turned off the lights and closed the barn door. The thoughts in his head told him he was on the verge of losing everything he wanted. Annie.

❀ Chapter Twelve ❀

ANNA LIFTED HER FACE to the morning sky, grateful for the gentle breeze. After a night of restless tossing, she'd come to the barn early for a ride and she and Spirit had ridden for hours.

Rain showers during the night had brought new life to the landscape. As she rode now along an old logging road, Anna enjoyed the earthy scent of leaves and dirt churned by her horse's hooves. It was as if everything was fresh and clean and life felt full of new possibilities. But how could that be when her chest felt tight and heavy with fear? Fear that she'd pushed Tyler away.

Anna nudged Spirit toward home. A sprinkling of light gave chase through the trees, but they eluded the sun's rays with feet as swift as the wind. Spirit's hooves ate up the track, the sound like a heartbeat in the late morning hush.

As they entered the barnyard she saw Tyler immediately. Joy filled her, but she stopped herself from calling out to him, suddenly afraid of why he waited for her, bareheaded, the slight breeze lifting his hair. She slowed Spirit to a walk, noticing how the sun glinted off Tyler's dark glasses, hiding his eyes from her. The time had come where neither one of them could hide any longer. If they were to have a future, their feelings and needs had to be brought out in the open.

Tyler pulled off the glasses. Now she could see the warmth and caring he made no attempt to hide. She caught her breath, feeling as if the air around them sparked and a little of the heaviness lifted inside.

He lifted his arms and without hesitation Anna slid down against him, her glance scanning the hard angles of his face, loving him so much.

"I'll help you get Spirit squared away," was all he said, and he led her horse inside the barn. Anna followed, pushing damp tendrils from her forehead.

"Actually," she said, "I'm glad you're here, I have something to tell you." His smile started a flutter deep in her stomach.

Tyler slid Spirit's saddle and blanket off and carried them toward the tack room.

Anna led Spirit to the outside paddock and once inside the gate removed her bridle. She ran her fingers lovingly through her horse's forelock, then shooed her away.

Tyler came up behind her as she hooked the bridle over the fence post. "It's good to be home."

Simple, heartfelt words but they stopped her heart and then made it beat furiously fast. "I've never heard you call the ranch home," she said softly, wondering.

"Annie," he said in a low voice, "There's something you should know. I've been obsessed for years over what happened, what I was certain Martin had done to my father and what I felt the town had done to us with their censure." He drew in a deep breath while she faced him fully. "Or what I thought was their censure. I've been thinking about this a lot, and when I think back, I realize you might have been right. Maybe it was one shortsighted sheriff who thought he was doing what was right by getting us out of town. I'll never know. I had it in my mind when I returned here that I'd buy the place from you. I didn't think you could hold on much longer. But gradually that changed, and I knew I had to help you make it work.

"What amazed me is I found acceptance where I expected none. I was ready to fight for my right to be here, but you opened your arms and let me back in. I can't forget that. It speaks of the generosity of your heart, and the heart of the town is the same. Without knowing all the facts they were willing to give me a chance."

"So many people turned out for the open house."

"That's what brought home to me that I have a place here. I feel like I've come full circle." He looked at her with wonder on his face. "Do you remember when you asked me about how things come full circle? I was wrong when I said you couldn't go back to where you were. We've revisited that place and made it better. I was wrong to deny my love for you. Can you forgive me that, Annie?"

"I understand that I won't let anything come between us," she said fiercely. "There's something you should know." Anna frowned and pressed her fingers to her forehead. "When Martin was diagnosed with brain cancer, his finances were so bad he was on the brink of bankruptcy and that's why I sold off most of the horses. Martin had a lot of pride. Can you imagine how he'd have felt if people knew? Even I didn't know the extent of the problem until after he died."

"It seems like there was so much against us."

She touched his arm. "But not anymore. I've made no

secret of the way I feel about the Double B, but I'll sell the ranch. I love you and you're more important to me than this land. I won't give up what we have." She gripped both his hands. There, she had said it and with everything that was in her, she knew she had to be with Tyler, wherever he was, but she needed his answer.

Anna laughed at Tyler's amazed expression, then beyond his shoulder she suddenly saw a blue station wagon pull into the parking area. "There's someone here. Why now?" she cried softly. "We need to talk." She stared at the woman exiting the driver's side. "It's Danny and his mother." She kept hold of one of Tyler's hand and together they moved toward the vehicle.

Marie, Danny's mother, was a small woman with short hair as brilliantly red as her son's. Danny sat in the passenger's seat, unmoving, staring straight ahead through the windshield. Anna turned to Tyler as Marie approached them. "Tyler, this is Marie, Danny's mom."

Tyler could see worry in the woman's pale blue eyes as she nodded at him.

"Hello Tyler," Marie said hesitantly. "I hope you don't mind me calling you by your first name. Danny has spoken so much this week of you and Anna."

"Of course not," he said. "It's nice to meet you, Marie, after all this time."

Marie seemed to draw a trembling breath. "There's something Danny needs to tell you both. I didn't know any of this until one night Danny broke down and just started talking. It's like he couldn't stop. He's had it stored inside of him all these years and he's been scared." She looked at Anna. "Anna, Danny would do anything in this world for you. There is no excuse for not telling the truth, but I think he was so afraid you would make him leave. It's taken me most of the week to convince him to come here." She looked at Tyler. "I'm sorry for the pain your family has suffered, and I swear Danny didn't mean to harm anyone."

Anna tried to breathe normally, but the fear escalated inside. She knew the moment had finally arrived. After all this time they would learn what had really happened six years ago. Two good men had died, and the survivors from each side of this controversy had had their lives ripped apart because of a secret kept. Anna was anxious but determined to know the truth once and for all. From the look on Tyler's face, she could tell it was all he could do to keep himself from barking at Marie to just get on with it.

"Please tell us what you know, Marie," Anna said quickly.

"It has to come from Danny." Marie turned and motioned toward Danny where he sat in the car.

Danny opened the door and climbed out to stand beside the vehicle.

"It's time to tell the truth about what happened six years ago," Anna said quietly, moving closer to put her hand on his arm. "Danny, do you remember the last time we talked, I told you secrets can sometimes hurt innocent people?"

He dipped his head. "Yes Miz Anna."

She smiled at him, not wanting him to be frightened. "You've always called me Miz Anna," she said. "It's all right if you'd like to just call me Anna."

"Mr. Martin said I should call you that."

"And you always did what Martin said, didn't you, Danny?"

"He was the boss." It was a simple, definite answer.

"You told me that Martin told you to shut up. What did he tell you to shut up about, Danny? I need you to remember."

Danny backed up against the car, his big hands

gripping the metal behind him. "He didn't want me to tell anyone about you. Keep my mouth shut and do my work." Danny visibly swallowed. "I did what he said." He dropped his head. "I didn't want to be fired."

"What did you talk too much about?"

"I told those people where to find you."

Confused, Anna looked at his mother.

"Danny, start at the beginning," Marie said gently.

He nodded quickly. "We were at the rodeo in Ohio, you know, the one where you won that fancy buckle with the pretty stones in it. When you were riding, two bull riders came by our pen and asked me for your number and where you were staying. I didn't know I wasn't supposed to say nothing. Martin run them off and told me to tend the horses. He got in my face and said if I didn't keep my mouth shut from now on, I was fired. He was the boss, he was right. He'd make it so nobody would want me to work."

Anna was disturbed by Danny's words, and the sheen of tears in his eyes. She took a deep breath and looked over at Tyler, trying to figure out the simplest way to get the truth about the breeding mix-up. Then again, maybe this was just another dead end.

"Danny," Tyler said quietly, "we don't want to fire you and we don't want to send you away. We need you here at the ranch. All we want is the truth. Can you understand that?"

Danny nodded.

"Six years ago they accused my dad of breeding McMyer's mare to the wrong stallion and there was a lot of money involved so my dad got in a lot of trouble. Do you remember?"

Danny nodded and looked down at his feet. "I liked Grant."

"Do you know how did that mare end up with a

spotted foal?"

"Rafferty's Appaloosa stallion," he said promptly.

Every muscle in Anna's body tensed.

"Who bred Rafferty's stallion to that mare?" Tyler asked.

Danny clenched his hands by his side and Anna swung her gaze to Tyler, saw the intensity in him, the need to know that his father was innocent. Who did that leave as the guilty party? Martin. She bit her lip, almost wishing now that Danny wouldn't speak, knowing it wasn't right, but so afraid of what the truth would be.

"Who made that mistake, Danny?" she asked.

"I did," he whispered, hunching his shoulders.

Anna heard the small sound of distress Marie made.

"Explain." Tyler's voice hadn't risen, but Anna knew he had to be feeling outraged and angry.

Tears slipped down Danny's cheeks as he looked at each of them. "Somehow that App got out of his stall in the night. When I went to the barn the next morning, he was loose in the barn. McMyer's mare was outside in a paddock but nobody was hurt, so I thought everything was okay. I put the App back in the stall and didn't tell nobody."

"Nobody knew," Tyler muttered. "Did he jump the fence where McMyer's mare was pastured?"

"I guess so but I didn't know. If I told, I knew I was gonna be fired. I couldn't be fired. I didn't do it on purpose. One more mistake and I was fired. That horse was gone the next day because he was so much trouble. At that rodeo I told Mr. Martin there'd be no more problems. I didn't want to be fired."

Tyler stuffed his hands in his pockets. "Why didn't you say something after my dad was in trouble?"

Danny's chest heaved, his agitation clear. "I was scared. I tried to tell Mr. Martin but he was so mad, his face so red I couldn't talk. Later I went to see the sheriff, but he ran me off." He looked at Anna, his eyes wide. "I didn't mean to do it. Mr. Martin died and everybody was very, very quiet. I went to tell you one night, Miz Anna, and you were so hurt and crying and you had to go to the hospital. It was a bad time and I couldn't tell you, Miz Anna. I know you hate me. I tried to make up for being stupid. I came everyday for my job. I brought you flowers to make you smile. I don't make any more mistakes."

His agitation wrenched at Anna's heart. "Danny! You've always been a good friend, and you pulled me from the fire. I could never hate you and you're not stupid!" Anna said fiercely. "You know more about horses than I ever will."

"Thank you for telling us the truth," Tyler said. "Finally, we know what happened. That's all I wanted. I can't believe how simple it all was."

"What will happen now?" Marie asked, her fear obvious.

Tyler looked at her. "Nothing," he said, "it's over."

Marie began to cry and Anna looked at Tyler, her heart swelling incredibly with love and admiration for this man, but she also ached, because he had to be hurting anew over the ruin of his father's life. . . over all their losses.

Marie reached out and gripped both their hands. "Thank you for your understanding. I wish there was a way to erase the pain you've had to bear."

"It's a relief to have it all out in the open," Anna said. "Danny has been carrying this, but it was really no one's fault." She pressed her lips together. "Maybe if Martin had lived, it would have turned out differently."

"Danny!" Tyler called as Danny ducked to get into the vehicle.

Danny straightened once more, his shoulders

slumped with resignation.

"Will you be back to work on Monday?"

Danny looked confused for a moment, and then his eyes widened and he gripped the door handle. "Monday? I surely will." He nodded several times. "Yes, I'll be here Monday at eight in the morning." He looked at Anna, his pale blue eyes wide and then he looked at Tyler. "I promise."

As the car pulled away Anna hugged her arms around herself and met Tyler's troubled glance.

"That night Danny got you to the hospital, that's when you lost the baby, wasn't it?" Tyler moved away, his shoulders stiff. "When I left I never called or told you where I was going and you were rushed one night to the hospital. Dammit, what kind of monster does that make me?"

"I should have told you before you left."

Tyler clenched his fists, an incredible anger filling him. "Intentionally or not, I abandoned you. When the bus left I turned my back on you and this place." Whose fault was it now, he thought? Annie, at nineteen, alone, scared, dealing with everything on her own. His pride never let him call her, even just to hear her voice.

"It was an ectopic pregnancy." Tyler heard the tears in her voice and the pain squeezed inside him. "There was no chance of survival."

Annie grabbed his arm and he faced her. The tears ran down her cheeks, ruining her makeup, her beautiful greenish-hazel eyes awash in tears.

"We should have talked to each other," she said. "We both acted badly."

Tyler felt the burn of his own eyes. "Christ, Annie, I'm sorry for being so angry with you. As an apology that's damned inadequate."

"Tyler, we've already lost six years, do we want to lose

even more? No more beating ourselves up over the past."

Tyler closed his eyes and reached out to hold her tightly. "I want to believe it can be left in the past."

Annie's smile was gentle. "It might not be easy, but we need to forgive each other."

Ω

They sat outside for a long time. Tyler stared off across the fields. "It's strange, but after wanting the truth all this time, having it feels almost anticlimactic."

"Now people will know the truth," Anna said.

Tyler shook his head. "No."

She looked at him, not understanding.

"I meant it when I said it was over," he said. "The people that matter will always know my dad was innocent. The rest don't matter."

Tears came to her eyes. "You'd do that for Danny?"

"I'm not letting anyone else be hurt by this. It's done."

Anna put her arm over his shoulders. "How did you learn such generosity?"

"From you," he said, squeezing her. Tyler pulled away from her. "Before we were interrupted you said you'd sell the ranch?"

She lifted her chin, feeling very certain of herself. "Yes. Don't doubt for one minute your importance in my life. I've already contacted Gill Dakins. He wants to buy it."

He grinned, and then he began to laugh. "You are full of surprises. When I think that I didn't want to come back here . .." He let his voice trail off. "But that was before," he added softly.

Looking into his eyes, her heart beat so loudly she could hear it in her ears. "Before?"

"Before I was honest and admitted how much I loved

you," he said, his voice intense. "Before I got smart and realized I'm not letting anything come between us. I have to tell you I never seriously considered the offer with the Rollaway Center. I told you the truth. They pursued me relentlessly until I gave them an interview."

She looked at him, bewildered. "But you let me think it was done."

"No. You believed what you were certain I'd done. I got angry that you jumped to conclusions, thinking I'd abandon the ranch. That I would walk away from you."

Anna tried to remain calm. "Tyler, don't say this because you think it's what I want to hear. We have to be honest with each other. I know this offer meant everything to you."

"No, Annie," he said gravely, "not everything. Only you mean everything. You make me a better man. You make me whole. How could I come here and put all this time and effort into the ranch unless I was doing it for us? Not that I knew that in the beginning, but it slowly grew on me."

"You came back to avenge your family."

"I admit that's what I thought, but I also came back to see you. I couldn't let us go. I tried to avoid the truth for six years, but not having you in my life has been eating me up inside."

It was everything she had ever wanted to hear from him. Anna pushed her shaking hand into her jacket pocket and pulled out a slightly crumpled envelope. "I had Randal France draw up this release." She handed him the envelope. "It frees you from the lease." He slid the envelope open and pulled out a legal-size, double-folded paper. "When I was faced with losing you, I woke up." Tightness gripped her throat. "I had all night to think of what I was throwing away. I could not let you walk away from me."

He took the paper and slowly tore it in half, then in half again.

"Tyler!" Shocked, Annie looked at the pieces of paper dangling from his fingers. With a flick of his wrist they scattered to the ground.

"I'll reimburse you the lawyer's fee," he said as she continued to stare at the paper.

Annie leapt forward and pressed her mouth to his, but pulled back after several moments when his arms began to tighten. "About the job offer," she gasped. "I think you should take it. Maybe you can work something out where you work seasonally."

"It's not necessary. We'll work this place together."

"I think it is necessary," she stated. "If we're going to be married, we should talk about it."

Tyler shook his head in amazement. "You can be pretty pushy when you get an idea in your head."

"You haven't seen anything yet." Annie gave him a secret smile.

"You realize people might say I married you to get my hands on the Double B, since it's such a prime piece of real estate."

Annie wound her arms around his neck. "When people see how happy we are they wouldn't dare think our marriage is anything other than a love match. But then, we know it's not about what others think. . .don't we?"

✿ Epilogue ✿

SPRING HAD COME TO the mountains once again and with the green grass and budding of trees, a new life had also enriched their lives. Gracie Stanton, with eyes as deeply blue as her father's, rode happily in the baby carrier on Tyler's chest.

Anna and Tyler finally reached the summit of the hill overlooking the Double B, and they paused to look down at the house and barns below, which were in tip-top shape after a long winter. Anna breathed deeply of the cool, crisp air. "There's nothing like a spring morning at the ranch. I admit to liking our place down south, but I'm so happy to be back. Do you suppose we'll ever get tired of looking at it?" she asked now, smiling at Tyler.

"Nope." Tyler carefully unsnapped the baby's protective harness from his chest and turned her so she faced the ranch below. Anna leaned forward and pressed a soft kiss on silky dark curls.

Together Anna, Tyler and the baby faced the ranch. Tyler held his daughter aloft while she gurgled, her tiny hands waving in the air.

"Is this a new tradition we're starting?" Anna asked, tossing her husband a big smile.

"Yes. Each spring we hike to this summit so we're reminded of all we have." Tyler clasped Gracie protectively to his chest and dug in his jeans pocket with his free hand. "There's another tradition I'd like to start." He held out a small, tissue-wrapped object.

Anna took it and slowly peeled the tissue paper away. Inside she found an emerald ring flanked by diamonds. Breathlessly, she touched the emerald with her fingertip. She blinked quickly and looked at her husband. "It's so beautiful, Tyler, thank you."

"This is the beginning of a Stanton tradition," he promised solemnly. "I wanted to get you something special for our second anniversary."

"You mean more special than a new show saddle or a state-of-the-art glass band saw?" she teased.

"You need the saw so you can cut your glass quicker and have more time with me," he said reasonably. "And I couldn't resist the saddle."

Anna stared at her husband, her glance taking in the faint shadowing of beard along lean cheeks and the dark hair spilling over his forehead, a tough man who held their daughter as tenderly and securely as he held her heart. She marveled that she'd once been afraid to love this man who now filled her life with joy. "Oh, Tyler, you've already given me more than I'd ever dreamed possible."

He reached out an arm and pulled her close. "More great things are ahead, Mrs. Stanton," he promised solemnly. "I can feel it."

∞ *THE END* ∞

Excerpt Wishing on a Rodeo Moon

Someday, that bull would kill someone. Tye Jenkins just knew it. She straddled the top rail of the bull chute as old Hit Man moved restlessly from side to side.

Tye let her gaze roam the rodeo yard. Her heart jumped like a young colt on a brisk morning as she stared, transfixed, at a dark-haired man. Jake Miller. He stood close by, a cocky look of assurance on his lean face. He was a head taller than most of the men around him, a stranger in business clothes among mud-spattered cowboys. His suit looked expensive, not the most common attire down by the pens. She had never before seen him dressed like that, yet he carried it off with nonchalance and elegance. He stood, feet planted on ground churned up by countless boots and three days of rain, his dark head bare to the falling mist. Tye didn't try to stop the smile spreading across her face. Only Jake could pull off a suit at a rodeo in the drizzling rain.

She hadn't seen or heard from Jake in ten years, not since that terrible night she'd left. He'd showed up now, the night she planned to remember for the rest of her life -- the night she'd make the rodeo finals. With the bittersweet knowledge of the past firmly in her mind, Tye sensed it was fitting Jake should be here to see her triumph.

Even knowing she was short on time before her ride, she continued to stare at Jake. Why was he here? What was that expression in his face -- a mixture of pain and want? Tye wiped the mist from her eyes, knowing she was wrong. She drew a deep breath.

He had changed, matured, yet something in his eyes remained the same. How long had she loved that strong face with its wide cheekbones, no-nonsense jaw touched by the faintest shadow of beard and deep-set eyes of the lightest blue? Her seventeenth summer she had loved him with a young woman's vibrancy. They'd spent endless time together, planning, talking, dreaming. Back then, Tye had thought Jake could do no wrong.

She drew a deep breath and looked around. Why was he here? It wasn't to see her! He was already drawing attention: she could see some of the girls nudging each other. Her throat dry, Tye drew a deep breath and then pressed her lips together. There were a lot of handsome faces like Jake's, but he had a presence. He always had. Jake was special, that's why she had loved him so much, until she had walked away.

"Tye Jenkins!"

Hearing her call, Tye stood up against the metal bars, gripping the top rail tightly. As she did so the bull in the chute hopped sideways, rattling the metal gates.

Adrenaline pumping, Tye jerked her gloves on, her gaze sweeping the yard, oblivious to everything until her glance lit once more on Jake. He was still there. Seeing him broke her concentration, brought in a flood of memory. Live, intense heat struck Tye and she closed her eyes tightly for a brief moment in exasperation. She had gotten over him. Anyone with a lick of sense knew ten years was a long time to pine over any man.

Deliberately, she looked away. Rubbing rosin on her gloves and rope, Tye centered her attention one hundred percent on what she knew of the bull, Hit Man. True to form, he was bouncing in the chute like a young kid throwing a temper tantrum. Hit Man shot her a glance now and then, probably to see if his head games were rattling her. He was one of the oldest bulls on the circuit, but anyone in rodeo knew he'd give you the ride of your life.

Excerpt Heartstealer

Jacie's stomach churned as she stared at the ground two thousand feet below. What insanity made her put herself through this punishment—just to prove she wasn't washed up as a stunt woman?

"Just do it," she muttered. "You've done it thousands of times before. Get your foot out the door and jump."

Automatically, she ran her fingers over her knee support and then the pull ring on her parachute harness. Lastly, she braced the toes of her boots against the door lip.

She had to jump. Skydiving was her life. It had always defined who she was; a member of her family's business, Aerial Antics. Her brother Con would pull her off this job if he thought she wasn't ready. She couldn't go home with her tail between her legs. Her family would try to put her back in cotton wool. Again.

How long did she have to pay for one dumb mistake—two—if she counted the one she'd made thinking Brad loved her.

With a low growl of impatience, she stepped out and an updraft pulled her up and away from the plane. As she plunged downward, a flashback to her parachuting accident thirteen months ago at Angel Falls came dangerously close. She could see again that mountainous ledge of rock, nothing but water and uninhabited jungle below her, the glorious release as she began her freefall, and then her parachute failure. . . .

Her chute opened. Years of training took over and the tightness eased inside her chest. Of course she could do this, she'd been jumping far too long to stop now.

As her feet touched solid earth a gust of wind lifted and pulled her forward, past the camera crews, past the gathered crowd. She caught a glimpse of surprised faces and then she came to a dead stop as her body lightly impacted with another. She had a fleeting impression of a hat flying through the air and they both fell to the ground in a tangle of arms, legs and billowing parachute.

Echoes From the Past

A woman, a man and a child with nothing in common but their respective troubled pasts. Three wounded souls determined to survive alone until they realize all they need to heal is each other.

On the verge of a nervous breakdown, Christie reacts by running away, emotionally and physically. Down to her last twenty dollars, she's determined to fulfill her dead sister's last wish—to locate their sister Judith who left home twenty years before. Her quest brings her into the lives of Garrett, Judith's husband, and the emotionally fragile Hannah, Judith's daughter. Christie is devastated to learn Judith died two years before. When Christie insists on getting to know her niece, Garrett agrees on the condition she doesn't reveal her identity. He hires her to work at his horse farm but what he doesn't count on is the turmoil and hope Christie brings into their lives.

Christie's own emotional journey forces her to come to terms with her family's alcoholism and her perception of herself.

¤ ¤ ¤

Women of Strength Time Travel

Once Upon a Remembrance: Book 1. Photographer Isabeau Remington travels to 1894 Virginia and falls in love with a man she must ultimately leave behind when she returns to her own time...but things are not always as they seem.

Modern day photographer Isabeau is pulled from the present time and thrust back into the year 1894 in Virginia. She must help save Hawk Morgan, a man threatened by a killer, a man endangered by his own erased memories. Hawk must survive in 1894 so his present day ancestor Pierce Morgan, will be alive in Isabeau's future.

Isabeau begins to fall in love with Hawk Morgan but with both their future's uncertain and a killer on the loose, neither one of them may have a tomorrow to look forward to.

Soulmates Through Time: Book 2. Thrust from her own time in 1822, Elise has been separated from the man she loves for 24 years. She has adjusted to modern times, raised a daughter, and become successful in her own right. When she stumbles upon the way back, she must make the decision to step back into that time.

Will Darien still love her and will Elise be able to turn back the clock and regain the love they once shared? Does she want to turn back time?

Treasure So Rare: Book 3. Captain Erik Remington has been haunted for three years by a black haired sea witch. They spent seven glorious days and nights before she vanished as mysteriously as she appeared.

In 1850, when his ship is pulled into a strange vortex, he ends up in middle ages England. Forced to assume another's identity, Weinroof of Camdork, he travels to the home of the man's affianced, the Lady Iliana. This world is nothing like the England of history books. Danger lurks everywhere, even the skies. As Camdork, he meets the Lady Iliana and instantly recognizes her as the woman who's haunted him.

Iliana wants nothing to do with Camdork and will defy her Queen to not marry him. All she sees is the man known as a murderer, whose attack four years before on an innocent maiden haunts her memories.

Iliana has her own secrets, but her unwavering mission is to find the perfect green gem and restore it to her people. Camdork stands in her way, so she must kill him if she ever wants to see the return of her old life.

Romantic Short Stories

Two Babies, a Cowboy and Sara: Short, sweet romance, 24,000 words. When Sara is appointed co-guardian of her deceased cousin's infant girls, their father Lucas is glad to accept Sara's help in caring for the twins. For Sara it's a labor of love and also a dream come true since she can't have babies of her own.

For Lucas, having Sara on his ranch is a reminder of how his life could have turned out so very differently, if only he'd met Sara first.

Deception

Short, sweet romance with a hint of suspense. Trey's boss is old, sick and his days are numbered; and he wants to see his missing granddaughter Katharine before he dies. Trey will do almost anything for the old man, even if it means having artist Sacha Fortune pretend to be Katharine.

Sacha is forced to assume the other woman's identity, because if she doesn't comply, Trey will expose her criminal past to the art world which has so recently embraced her art.

But Sacha has more to lose than Trey could ever guess.

Thanks for reading!

Faeries Lost Series Coming soon!

Visit my author page at www.GraceBrannigan.com to read all my contemporary, time travel, faerie stories and short romantic stories.

Grace Brannigan